THAT I WERE AN ANGEL

A Novel of Alma the Younger

Robert H. Moss

Other Books by Robert H. Moss:

Valiant Witness, A Novel of Moroni
I, Nephi, A Novel of Nephi
The Covenant Coat, A Novel of Joseph
The Waters of Mormon, A Novel of Alma The Elder

Copyright © 1987 by Robert H. Moss.

All rights reserved. Reproduction in whole or any parts thereof in any form or by any media without written permission is prohibited.

ISBN: 1-55517-032-3

Printed and distributed in the United States of America by:

ACME PUBLISHERS
1795 Ann Dell Lane
Salt Lake City, UT 84121

Cover painting is the property of The Church of Jesus Christ of Latter-day Saints. Used with permission.

Contents

Preface		ii
Prologue		iii
Chapter 1	Seeds of Rebellion	1
Chapter 2	Ruth	11
Chapter 3	Escape from Helam	18
Chapter 4	Nephite Warrior in Zarahemla	26
Chapter 5	Gods of Flesh	34
Chapter 6	Angel of God	42
Chapter 7	Missionaries	50
Chapter 8	Letter from Ammon	57
Chapter 9	Letter from Aaron	68
Chapter 10	Chief Judge of Zarahemla	74
Chapter 11	War with the Amlicites	84
Chapter 12	High Priest	96
Chapter 13	Amulek and Ammonihah	107
Chapter 14	Prison, Fire, and Repentance	121
Chapter 15	Anti-Nephi-Lehies	135
Chapter 16	That I Were an Angel	148
Chapter 17	A Blessing for Helaman	162
Chapter 18	Blessings for Shiblon and Corianton	168
Chapter 19	My Last Days	176
Epilogue		182

Preface

Alma the younger has often been characterized as a new-world Saul: he zealously persecuted the Christian Church; through a miracle—the visitation of an angel—he was converted to the Church; he then became zealous in building the Church.

Alma's father, Alma, heard the Prophet Abinadi preach. Abinadi's words brought to Alma's mind the teachings of his father, Abimolam. Alma the Elder secretly taught his friends and relatives the words of Abinadi and the earlier prophets, then led his people from the city of Nephi to the Waters of Mormon where he baptized them. Threatened by the army of wicked king Noah, he then led the people into the wilderness, establishing the Land of Helam.

Helam was a choice land with a beautiful climate and fertile soil. Alma and his people prospered there and lived in peace for thirty years. The younger Alma was born in the Land of Helam. While he was still very young, the Lamanites stumbled upon the Land of Helam and made Alma's people their slaves. Amulon, the leader of the Lamanites in Helam, had been one of King Noah's wicked priests.

After escaping from Helam to Zarahemla, Alma organized the Church in its fullness. For fifty-one years Alma's father, Alma, governed the Church.

The younger Alma rebelled against father and Church. His conversion was miraculous. Though visited by an angel he still had to go through the purging fire of repentance. He served as a missionary to the people he had previously led away. Then, after a short training period serving with his father, he became the leader of the Church.

This is the younger Alma's story. Through his own eyes, Alma tells of his turbulent childhood, his loss of his childhood sweetheart, his rebellion against his father, his conversion, and his later life. His is a story of repentance and forgiveness, of rebellion and conformity, of great sorrow and greater joy, of hatred and love. It is also the story of a family's love for a wayward son, and of his struggle to return to that family's embrace.

This book is dedicated to all who have gone astray and have had the courage to return to the fold.

Prologue

Alma glanced out through the open doorway, then sipped some sweetened chocolate from the cup he held in his hand. He looked at his father. Alma senior was aged and gray-haired. At forty, himself, Alma knew his own hair had grayed at the temples.

"Father, I feel I need to tell you about myself."

The older Alma leaned forward in his chair, "Speak up, son."

As I look now at my own young sons, I have attempted to analyze just what happened in my youth; why I rebelled against you."

His father's sunken eyes were almost hidden beneath beetling gray eyebrows. He sat there listening intently.

Alma spoke quietly, "I watched you as you helped our people. You won them to the church not by your eloquence, but by your sincere conviction. I watched and listened and was deeply impressed. I learned even before my teens that sermons did not come from your mental discipline and scripture reading alone—however essential these may be—but from your life."

He was thankful his father did not interrupt him. He had much to say.

"I knew you loved me and wanted me to be a part of your life. But your life seemed to be wrapped up totally in the Church, and rather than being happy about that, I tried desperately to escape. I had hang-ups about freedom. I didn't want to be restricted. I didn't want to be fenced in like one of the goats I tended. I didn't want to be inhibited but wanted to make up my own rules. As the high priest's son I was watched and I didn't like being watched."

A look of wonder was on his father's face.

"Always gnawing away at my mind was the faint suggestion that someday, I, too, would be called to the ministry. I tried to stifle such thoughts. No matter how good my home background was, no matter how insistent the call of God to my young heart, I determined to silence that inner voice and discover life for myself."

The older Alma cleared his throat, then settled back in his chair, still looking intently at his son.

"I decided to make sure I wouldn't be called to the priesthood by entering warrior training. The training was good for me, but I'm convinced now that I didn't want to be a warrior. I just didn't want to be a priest. All this time, however, I had a lurking suspicion that the thing I was really fighting was the very thing I wanted. I was all mixed up and unwilling to admit it—to myself or anyone else."

Alma leaned forward in his chair, intent upon every word.

"I am so thankful to be where I am, and to know how narrow was my escape."

Finally the older Alma spoke. "Did the fact that an angel appeared to you make your conversion easier?"

"Perhaps. But I think conversion was easier for me because of my knowledge of the awfulness of my sins. I knew where I stood. There was no guesswork. I knew the depth of my sins and my need for God. I was lost to the Church. Oh, I would go and listen to your sermons and would sometimes eavesdrop as you counseled other people who were troubled, but when I tried to tackle my own weaknesses, I seemed helpless."

Alma looked puzzled. "I am still not sure why you rebelled in the first place?"

"I think that I felt religion—at least my experience with religion—was a weakness. 'What use,' I would ask, 'is a religion that does not seem to satisfy.' So I rebelled. I took up with every symbol of rebellion. I became so weary of boredom and defeat that I even tried to run away from my conscience. But thank the Lord, I learned that conscience—unless you kill it—will never let you go."

"You mean that you had feelings of doubt, even while you were rebelling?"

"Yes. God did not leave me alone, though I wanted to be left alone. I often remembered sermons you had taught. While I walked between cities, I attempted stubbornly to put out of my mind the things you had said to me, but God was always right there to remind me, and it made me uncomfortable. I didn't want Him to be that close. I felt as if the war between the Nephites and Lamanites was going on inside me."

Alma smiled, a look of understanding on his face. "What did you do?"

"With such turmoil inside me, I came back to Zarahemla and attended one of your meetings. You didn't even know I was there. I stood in the back of the temple plaza and listened. There you stood—my ideal of a man.

"Even though you were speaking to the congregation, every word cut through me like a knife. I finally walked away from the meeting and moved restlessly through the streets. I shall never forget those moments. In that still summer evening, looking up past the trees into God's own sky, I actually shook my fist at the heavens and cried aloud, 'God, leave me alone.'"

Alma could tell his father was shocked at his words. He continued, "I was shocked by my own defiant words. But I couldn't call them back. I felt cold inside. God's spirit had left me."

"Then what happened," Alma asked.

"Even though God had perhaps left my life, I did not seem to be alone. I still had my conscience. I struggled. I had a deep sense of guilt that would never go away. My guilty feelings haunted me night and day. My guilt persisted in making me completely miserable. The only way I could fight back against it was in trying hard to fight against you and the Church."

"Did that help?"

Alma smiled. "No, my conscience still demanded attention. It refused to be still. Like a small pebble in a sandal, it just irritated and cut."

The older Alma smiled as he asked, "And you didn't realize that at that time the only way to rid yourself of the irritating pebble was to take off the old shoe of rebellion?"

Nodding, Alma continued, "I suppose that it is human nature to fight against those things which we know to be right. Each of us dislikes to admit that we are wrong, or are doing wrong things. I guess I operated behind a mask, trying to coverup, to camouflage, but all of the time I was searching for peace of mind. Now I realize I was searching in the wrong places, with the wrong people.

"I had opted for freedom, but what I found was slavery. I tried to remove the fences and the rules, but found myself trapped behind fences of my own making."

"So rebellion led to sin?" Alma asked gently.

"I think sin is just an attitude of rebellion," the younger Alma responded quietly. "Sin caused a separation between me and God. That separation had to be healed." He smiled. "God just chose a dramatic way to do it."

His father leaned forward intently. "Could you have done it without the angel?"

"I don't honestly know," Alma replied. "Heaven only knows I tried many times. But no matter how I tried, I always failed. I didn't know how to break the power of wrongdoing. Each time I really tried hard to change I became discouraged and drifted further away from the truth."

His father pursued his previous question. "I am still curious to know. If you had not been visited by the angel, would you have changed."

The younger Alma thought of his response. He looked his father in the eye. "Yes, I think that the seeds of repentance were within me. I was still feeling pangs of guilt over what I was doing. I honestly believe that even without the angel, I was ready for the fire of repentance to burn away my sins. It was only a matter of time."

His father leaned back and breathed a sigh of relief. "I am glad." He paused, then added, "The reason for my persistence in questioning you is that there are many people in similar attitudes of rebellion. God will not send angels to each of them. It is up to them to bring their own lives around and return to God's way so he can forgive them."

"Father, after all this time it is still difficult for me to realize that I can be totally forgiven."

"One of the comforts of the scriptures to me is that God forgave David, even though David had sinned greatly."

"But you don't yet realize what a sinner I was. I know God forgave David but I feel that I was much worse than David. Is a debt of sin ever just too big to forgive?"

Gently, his father said, "Isaiah said, 'Though your sin be as scarlet, they shall be white as snow; though they be red like crimson, they shall be as wool.'"

Breathing a sigh of relief, the younger Alma said, "Thank you, father. That helps, even though the hurt of what I have done still troubles me."

His father nodded and closed his eyes, resting.

Alma leaned back, letting his thoughts travel back to his childhood.

Chapter 1

Seeds of Rebellion

Westward the high white volcanic cone of Tanza dominated the horizon. The mountain, bathed in afternoon sun, seemed to float in the sky. The evening breeze carried to us the scent of river, of acrid woodsmoke and pine, and an occasional nose-wrinkling whiff of skunk. Rain had drizzled down most of the day and the lake far below reflected the murky sky.

A single, colorful parrot flew up the side of the hill, dangling feet brushing the tips of grass in its flight. I watched as it slowed its wings and dropped to a branch high above our heads, preening its bright feathers and scolding us with raucous voice.

Nehor and I, bare torsos sweaty and burned by the hot jungle sun, followed the parrot's course up the hill. My dog, Noah, his tongue flopping pink in the side of his mouth, dripping saliva on the rocks he climbed over, led the way. By the time we reached the crest, Nehor and I were gasping for breath. Noah was off in the bushes, his busy tail signalling his location.

"Are we almost there?" Nehor groaned, plopping himself on a large boulder.

I glanced at him as I continued to climb. "It's just over the next ridge. We'll be there in a moment."

Though only eleven, I was bigger than any boy my age. Nehor, a year older, was three inches taller and twenty pounds heavier. I envied him his corn-colored hair and his blue eyes. My black hair and dark eyes made me look too much like a Lamanite. I smiled to myself. Nehor might be bigger but I was in better condition. We made a good pair. None of the boys in Helam dared challenge us; we could beat any of them in a fight so they showed us proper respect.

As we crossed the ridge I whistled to Noah. He came crashing back through the brush, his hair tangled with burrs. With no courtesy at all he stood on his back legs and licked my face with his sloppy tongue.

"Down, Noah."

Nehor growled at me. "Why do you put up with that animal?" he asked. "He's more trouble than he's worth." His dark eyes danced merrily, "What we should do is use him for archery practice."

I sat down, protectively cradling Noah's head in my arms. I knew Nehor was teasing, but his words still hurt. Noah was really all I had—my very best friend. He was the only one to whom I could really talk. My older brother, Zoram, had given him to me on my first birthday. Nehor stood above me, impatiently digging his toes into the dirt of the hillside. He was a good friend, but not like Noah.

"Where is this cave that you are so excited about?" he again asked.

Pushing Noah away, I stood up and pointed towards outcroppings of lava rock which split the hillside. "Up there."

I looked back the way we had come. The grassland cut a narrow swath through the heavy dark forest. Far below us, near the edge of the lake, was Helam. It was our home—or at least it had been. Smoke from cooking fires blued the air over the city. Sounds of swords banging against each other carried up the hill. Unconsciously my fists clenched.

The Lamanites had captured the city. It was still hard for me to believe. If only father...I shook my head in frustration. No, it was too late for father to do anything. I angrily kicked at a rock with my sandal, then grimaced with pain from my exposed toes. No, I thought to myself, even though father was Alma, the high priest, he wouldn't do anything against the Lamanites.

I started up the hill again. It was too pretty up here to stay angry for very long. Besides, we had some things we could do about the situation in Helam. I smiled as I contemplated what Nehor and I planned.

Grass, waist high, waved with the wind. Its fresh green color contrasted beautifully with the almost blackness of the forest on both sides of us. I stopped again to look back at the view, but Nehor was not very patient.

"Come on, I'll race you to the rocks!"

He was off running before I had moved. I sprinted up the hill after him. He seemed all arms and legs. Even though he ran in a loose-jointed disheveled sort of way he always beat me in footraces. Swimming was different; he was really quite awkward in the water. Now he slowed down at the rocks and I caught up. Noah had taken the short race as an excuse to go exploring again.

Nehor climbed onto a large rock and sat down. "You said you had come up here many times," he panted. "How did you find the cave?"

I shrugged. "I was hunting for rabbits when I just stumbled onto it. I don't think anyone else knows about it. The only tracks I found inside were those of a jaguar."

"Are we close to it?"

I smiled. "Practically on top of it."

Nehor looked around suspiciously. "I don't see anything that looks like a cave."

"If you could see it so easily, do you think it would be a good hideout for us?"

Nehor grinned sheepishly as he climbed down from the rock. I led the way around behind the rock he had been sitting on, and pushed aside some brush, revealing the dark opening.

Nehor whistled. "Wow! It is hidden."

"Didn't I tell you?"

Nehor pushed past me. He stood in the narrow opening for a moment adjusting his eyes to the dimness, then stepped inside. I was close on his heels.

From the narrow slit of the opening, the volcanic cave opened into a large room about the size of our tent. The floor was sandy, clearly showing our footprints. I looked carefully around, seeing that no footprints or animal tracks had disturbed the sand since my last visit. Something cool touched my hand and I reached down and scratched Noah's ears. Nehor continued exploring, looking around and feeling the walls until he returned to where I stood.

"It's perfect," he exclaimed, excitement in his voice.

I reached down and picked up the bow and arrows I had cached there on my last visit. "Amulon and his Lamanite warriors think they have taken all weapons from our people. One of these days they will wish they had!"

Nehor grinned a sly, crooked-mouth grin.

"Let me show you one other place where we can hide," I said as I stepped back outside.

Blinking rapidly as the glare of the afternoon sun hit me, I looked around. It would be dark in several hours and I knew we would have to hurry. Still, I stood there for a few moments while my eyes adjusted to the sunlight. I glanced up. The sky was an unblemished blue-white. Two hawks soared above, flat wingtips parallelled.

The panorama of the hillside we had climbed stretched before me. The hill's rocky face petered out some three of four hundred paces below us. Beyond that was the mixture of fissured and eroded rock and brown earth we had climbed through, and below was the belt of lush grass which led to Helam. We were out of sight of the city, even though I could see the slight greying of the sky from the city fires.

"Where to?"

Without answering Nehor, I started around the side of the hill.
A hundred paces and we were into pine forest. Interlocking branches formed an almost impenetrable canopy that effectively screened out the sky. I had been here at high noon and there was never more light than at twilight in the open flat. Now, the afternoon sun provided hardly more light than a starlit midnight.

From quiet of hillside, we were plunged into raucous forest noise. The volume of sound was terrific: unnamed stumbling thuds in the near underbrush; falling things; spider monkeys gibbering; the bleep of frogs;

the chatter and branch-shakings of parrots and other innumerable birds which crowed, cawed, and cried for attention. And now at evening, the trilling of cicadas: an endless unbroken chorus borne across the forest like an unrelenting wind.

Monkeys swung from the branches overhead to get a closer look at us.

I was glad I had been here before. Nehor walked cautiously behind me, his head swiveling and turning as he looked around and above him. I smiled to myself at his nervousness, but still kept a firm hand on my bow and arrows. Other times as I walked through the forest I had seen jaguar tracks and felt as if their eyes were watching me. Even now the hair on the back of my head tingled as I walked. The gloominess of the forest was catching. I reached down and scruffed the back of Noah's head.

"How far are we going?" Nehor's voice was shaky.

"Just a little way," I responded.

It made me feel good to be braver than Nehor. Feeling rather than seeing the swale in front of me, I stopped. Nehor stood next to me, his elbow touching mine. Noah sniffed at my feet. Before us lay a small natural amphitheater surrounded by dense forest. Looking straight up we could see the almost–purple sky. A spring gurgled nearby. The swale was carpeted with grass and ferns.

"This would be a perfect second hideout," I said. "I think the Lamanites are afraid of the deep forest and would never come anywhere near here. If by chance they find the cave we could always hide here."

Nehor nodded. "I prefer the cave, myself."

"The cave has no water. I wouldn't want to get trapped in it."

Nodding again, Nehor turned to go. I could understand his anxiety. I didn't want to be in the forest after dark myself. We passed through a thick, swirling nebulae of mosquitoes, so teeming that they obscured the trees in an opaque mist. Their concerted whine added another level of sound to the cacophony of jungle noise.

* * *

"Where have you been all day?"

My mind was distracted as I answered father. "Nehor and I fixed us a hideout where we can hide from the Lamanites."

I looked around the room. Father was still talking. Where had all the furniture gone? Our home was almost bare.

"I don't like you hanging around with Nehor. He is not a good influence on you."

"He's all right." I gestured at the room and changed the subject. "What's happening?"

Father shrugged. "Amulon has ordered us to move. We will live in our tent."

I couldn't believe it. Father was letting Amulon force us from our own home. "You just let him tell you to move out?" I shook my head in disbelief. "You didn't fight him or anything?"

"There was nothing I could do," Father responded. "As for you, since you were not home to help move our furniture and possessions, please hurry to Helam's house and help his family move."

"Helam's family? Are they moving, too?"

Father nodded. "The Lamanite guards will live in Helam's home."

I gritted my teeth as I looked at Father. Was he a coward? Why hadn't he stopped the Lamanites? Then I thought of Ruth, Helam's daughter. How would she be feeling to have to move from her house? She was younger than I but I really liked her.

As I turned to the door, I could tell that Father wanted to say something else to me but I didn't want to listen. I hurried out.

It was fun to help Helam's family move. Ruth seemed to like me as much as I liked her and I couldn't help showing off a little. As I carried furniture up the hill to where they had put up the tent, Ruth walked beside me carrying some of the smaller things. The sun had set behind Tanza by the time we finished. Fires burned brightly before each tent and mother was cooking supper.

Ruth's mother was also preparing the evening meal. I turned to Ruth, "Shall we go to the lake and wash?"

She nodded, her dark eyes shining big in the warm afterglow of sunset. I took her hand and we walked through the city to the lake, Noah following behind. We passed several Lamanite guards. Angry feelings rose within me but I didn't want to disturb Ruth so I just ignored them. But I hated all the Lamanites. Determination to make them pay for what they had done filled my very being. Noah, echoing my feelings, growled at each Lamanite we passed.

The lake was warm and pleasant, even though the air was cool. We splashed and swam and had a good time. Noah didn't like the water so he stood on the shore and barked.

On the way home I looked at Ruth. Her wet dress clung tightly to her body. My heart beat faster and I felt a stirring in my groin. She was my girl.

* * *

The night was perfect. Clouds prevented even the little starlight to reach the streets of Helam. Lances of lightning illuminated our surroundings for fleeting moments. My shirt, limp and sticky from sweat, was a hindrance. I slipped it over my head and threw it into the alley. In the darkness ahead I could hear soft scrape of Nehor's bare feet and behind me the more pronounced footfalls of Jacob and Aaron.

"Shhhhh."

Shsshing did no good, I thought. The brothers hadn't learned yet how to walk quietly.

With darkness, noisy boys behind me, intermittent lightning, and need to use great caution, it took us half an hour to reach the east gate of the city. And when we got there, pressed against the city wall within sight of the gate, I wasn't at all sure I was glad we had come.

Nehor had selected me as the one to go over the wall of the guardhouse and unlatch the door. But now I was afraid.

To make matters worse, we didn't even know if any weapons were in the guardhouse. Our entire effort could be a waste. I was about to suggest that we retreat to our homes and wait for another night.

I gave a short cough but didn't get a chance to say anything. A fork of lightning showed the wall straight ahead. Nehor was frozen tightly against it, his arms spread wide. Just to his right, briefly illuminated by the lightning, was the huge wooden door leading into the guardhouse.

"This is it," Nehor whispered as I slipped to his side. "Put your foot in my hands and I will boost you up."

Placing my hands on his shoulders, I raised a foot and put it into his cupped hands. I could feel him straining as he lifted me. He lifted as high as he could but I still had to stretch to reach the top of the wall.

"Up you go," he whispered. "Hang on to the wall. Crawl along it until you reach the door. Then drop down and open it for us."

I laid my elbows over the top of the wall and pulled myself up. After throwing a leg over, I grasped the wall with my knees, shinnying along it. The only sound was the scrape of leather pants against rocks. I prayed that lightning would hold off until I dropped inside. I sensed rather than saw the doorway. Reaching down, I felt the rough wood of the door. Swinging my leg over, I hung by my fingers for a moment, then let go. The drop was short, only about five feet. I flexed my knees as I landed, attempting to make no sound. Then I pressed myself against the wall. Was anyone in the guardhouse? My breathing was ragged. I sucked in and held my breath until I could hold it no longer. Not a sound. I exhaled slowly and turned to the door. I wasn't sure how it was secured, but I had to open it. If anyone was close around we would be caught, but that was the chance I had to take. I didn't want Nehor and the others to know I was afraid.

Unlatching the door from the inside was easy. I held it tightly and swung it open. Faint squeak of leather hinges grated loudly on my ears and I expected Lamanite guards would be running towards us. The night was still—no sounds of running feet.

Nehor and Jacob were just darker shadows as they slipped in beside me. Aaron stayed outside to watch and listen for the guards. I was so scared my heart throbbed like a captive bird's. Slowly, awkwardly, I followed Nehor through the blackness to the guardhouse armory. I still wasn't sure what we would find in there. He disappeared inside; I was close behind him—so close that when he stopped I bumped into him.

"Be careful," he whispered. "See if you can find the weapons."

I dropped to my knees on the hard dirt floor, sweeping my hands out in front of me as I advanced. They hit something solid. I felt the large lump of rough fabric. It was a tent. Beyond it my fingers felt the edges of swords, their points buried in a soft log.

"Sssst."

"What is it?"

"Swords."

I could hear Nehor's quick breathing as he dropped to the floor beside me.

"What's this?"

"A small tent."

"Do you think you can carry it?"

I reached down and girdled the tent with my arms. Still on my knees I hefted it. The tent was not that heavy.

"I can carry it if you can get the swords."

"We might have to make several trips," Nehor said.

"I think we ought to take what we can carry and get out of here fast."

"Okay. Take the tent. Jacob!"

Jacob's quavering voice answered from behind me.

"What?"

"Come over here and get some swords, but don't let them rattle."

I lifted the tent and started for the door. The bundle of it was awkward and obscured what little sense of sight I had.

"Alma." Nehor's whisper came from behind me.

"What."

"Wait at the door. Tell Aaron to come in."

At the door I rested the tent against the wall and whispered for Aaron. I couldn't see him, but felt him pass me in the dark. Before I knew he was close, Nehor nudged me from behind.

"Let's go."

I didn't need any urging. I moved through the door, almost stumbling as the ground dipped before me. Nehor passed me and led us back the way we had come. Our whole operation had only taken a few minutes, but I could still feel the sweat running in rivulets down my back.

As we turned down the alley, a shout came from behind us.

"Who left the guardhouse open?" It was the strident voice of a Lamanite guard.

I didn't dare turn and look but increased my pace. The slap of sandals on hard-packed earth reverberated in the still night.

More shouts as guards discovered the missing tent and swords. I glanced over my shoulder. Flickering light from several torches appeared at the corner far behind us.

Nehor led us around another corner and pulled us into a dark alley. I was grateful that he knew this part of the city so well. I was lost.

* * *

The retreat in the forest was perfect. The stolen tent was erected proudly beside the spring. Enough dried food was in the tent to last for days. Piled in one corner were skins and blankets for bedding, and there was even a supply of weapons: some swords, bows and arrows, and an axe.

From inside the tent I listened to the forest's muted sounds. I could hear bird cries and the soft swooshing of the breeze as it played in the crowns of the trees high overhead. The tent's interior was gloomy to the extreme. A rabbit, impaled on a stick, hung grotesquely over the fire. The only brightness in the tent was the occasional hiss and spurt of flame as rabbit fat dripped into the fire.

The atmosphere of gloom was significantly deepened by the behavior and expressions of the boys seated on the floor. Nehor and the other two boys ate in moody silence, heads lowered, not looking at one another. The events of the previous night had affected us all. Jacob's food was untouched.

"I'll bet Aunt Lea is getting nervous with me not coming home last night," Nehor said.

I looked at Nehor. He played with a short stick, chopping it into the grass in front of him.

"I've never stayed out all night before," he continued.

The other boys watched him. Aaron was my age and his brother, Jacob, was a year younger.

"Well, she'd better get used to it," I said. "We have to stay here at least one more night."

"Do you think the Lamanite guard saw any of us?" Aaron asked.

"Nah." Nehor looked up from his nervous chopping long enough to answer.

"It was too dark," I interjected. "Besides, they were looking for men. They would not have noticed four boys."

"I'm still scared," whispered Jacob. "What would the Lamanites do if they caught us stealing weapons?"

"Probably cut off our heads," Nehor grinned wickedly.

Jacob looked up quickly to see if Nehor was joking. "Seriously?"

Nehor didn't answer. Reaching over, he pulled the hind leg off the rabbit. He gnawed off a bite, the juice running down the sides of his mouth.

I felt the conversation had gone far enough. The two boys were already scared without Nehor giving them additional fears.

"Nothing is going to happen," I said. "Even if the guards saw us, they couldn't tell one boy from another. Besides, we got the tent and the swords didn't we?"

The boys nodded.

"Even if it took all night to carry them here," Nehor said. He was not finished. He spoke with his head lowered. "If our leaders had fought the Lamanites when they came into our valley, we wouldn't have to steal weapons now."

"What does that mean?"

He looked up into my eyes. "If your father and Helam had been brave enough to stand up against Amulon and his Lamanite friends, we wouldn't be slaves to them now."

I clenched and unclenched my fists but had no response. It was true, I thought. My father, Alma, had agreed to let the Lamanites take over the city without a fight. Now we were all slaves. Aaron and Jacob looked at me, waiting for my reaction. As tears came to my eyes, I turned and stumbled out of the tent without saying anything. It wasn't fitting for a twelve-year-old to cry.

Noah lay by the tent's entrance. He quietly fell into place behind me as I moved into the darkness of the night. I sat down on a log and he placed his head on my lap.

"Why, Noah? Why didn't father have his people take swords and drive away the Lamanites?" For a long time I talked to my dog about my feelings.

Later that night I lay in darkness and stared across the tent at the patch of gray where the door was. Some light filtered down into our little retreat from the thin slice of moon. I could not sleep thinking about my father.

I recalled the day when the Lamanites marched into the city. That day we moved from our house and set up our tent next to the forest. Thoughts of Amulon and his Lamanites living in our home made me seeth. The day's only fun had been helping Helam's family move, which meant being close to Ruth. I thought of Ruth and how much I liked her. I wonder what she would think of our stealing from the Lamanites?

My thoughts sleepily drifted back to my father. I had heard Zoram ask him why he hadn't fought the Lamanites. But father had never answered. Maybe he was a coward.

I thought of Nehor. He lived with his aunt because he didn't have a father. He didn't have to do the things I had to do, I thought enviously. He didn't have to attend the school of the scribes and spend hours each day practicing his writing; he didn't ever have to bathe. As I thought of him, my boy heart filled with envy. I had a father, but he had let us all down. It would be better to be like Nehor—without a father.

But regardless of what my father had or had not done, my way was clear. I and my friends were going to make life miserable for the Lamanites. With that thought I fell asleep.

Chapter 2

Ruth

"The tree is called a strangler fig," Father said, pointing to the lush tree. I glanced up from gathering wood and noticed that tendrils encased the tree all the way to the ground. I tried to keep busy and ignore his words. Father was a coward; he had let the Lamanites take over Helam without a fight. I gritted my teeth and again convinced myself that I could no longer respect him or his words. The Lamanites had tasked us with gathering wood and I continued picking up dry branches from the forest floor.

Father talked on to Zoram, something about host tree and Lamanites being the strangler fig. The next words caught my attention.

"If we let them dominate us long enough we will die and rot away."

Zoram hissed, "Then we must rid ourselves of Amulon and his priests and Lamanites before it is too late!"

Once again I was disappointed in Father's response. He said something about the Lord taking care of the whole thing. That was a bunch of goat droppings. I shook my head and continued gathering wood. No, God wouldn't take care of anything; I had prayed often to have the Lamanites destroyed and He had never answered my prayers. In fact, I had almost convinced myself that my father's god wasn't even real.

It was almost sundown when we arrived back in Helam. I ate supper quickly for I had important things to do after dark. Clouds above Tanza reflected the sun for many minutes, prolonging the twilight. I stepped outside to look at the sunset, then ducked quickly back inside.

"What's the matter?" Mother asked, noticing the disgusted look on my face.

"It's that Lamanite guard and his wife." I looked around for a way to escape. "The ones you have been so friendly to." I had no intention of remaining in the tent with Lamanites, even if they were friends of my parents.

Mother parted the door flap and looked out. "Oh, and they have their daughter, Abish, with them tonight." She turned reprovingly to me.

"Alma, Malkish and his family are thinking of joining the Church. It is time you acted like a gentleman instead of a scalawag. Stay here and be nice to them."

I didn't often disobey mother, but I did this time. While she was busy greeting the Lamanites, I sneaked under the flap into the gathering darkness. Glancing back, I could see the hurt look on the Lamanite girl's face—a girl about my age. I didn't care. I had no intention of being friendly to any of our enemies, girl or adult. A grin spread across my face. In fact, I thought, tonight will be a good joke on them all.

Nehor and Aaron were hiding outside the north wall, right where they had told me they would be.

"Where's Jacob?"

"He got scared," Nehor replied. "We don't need him anyway. The three of us can handle tonight's job."

"We need to be more careful," I said. "Last time when we threw the rotten eggs at Amulon's house, we almost got caught."

"This will be easy," Nehor said. "No one will expect anybody to be crazy enough to steal their flags." His body shook as he tried to keep from laughing out loud. "Will they ever be surprised!"

"You're sure we can do it?" Aaron asked timidly.

"No problem. Every night the flags are left outside Helam's house where the guards sleep. Only the night sentry could sound the alarm, and usually he is asleep."

Nehor and I had gone over the plans several times. Aaron and I were to sneak up to the front of the house from both directions. We would hide in the darkness in shadows cast by the flickering torch. Nehor, being the biggest, would approach the house right down the street. While he distracted the guards, Aaron and I would take the crossed flags before the door. It sounded like a good plan.

I was to take the far side of the house. Using darkness as cover, I trotted around the town, outside the wall, until I came to the East gate. Guards sat on both sides of the gate, their torches throwing flickering shadows. Nodding my head at them I went on through. I couldn't help but glance at the guardhouse where we had stolen the swords on our very first attack against the Lamanites. I smiled as I walked quickly down the dark street.

A few minutes put me near Helam's house. I darted from dark shadow to dark shadow until I stood by the south side of the house. By now Aaron should be in position on the north side. Where was Nehor? I could hear the hum of guard's voices from inside the house; the sound of my heart beat almost drowned out the voices. Would Nehor never come? I stepped on one foot then the other, trying to stay calm.

A dog barked across the street. Soon other dogs up and down the street joined in. Chickens started cackling in their coops. It was bedlam. Nehor was doing his job. Lamps were lighted in the building directly across from Helam's house, spilling light into the street. The guard moved off the steps and stood in the street, apparently wondering what was causing all the racket.

Now was the time while his attention was elsewhere. I peered around the corner. Aaron was looking back at me. I nodded. Three steps took me to the guidon. Grabbing the staff, I yanked it out of the dirt and was back into the darkness around the corner before the guard could have noticed. I hoped that Aaron had his flag. Barefooted I raced down the dark street.

Several times I almost tripped but I kept on running. I was breathless by the time I reached the alley behind Nehor's Aunt Lea's where we had agreed to meet. Before I could even catch my breath Aaron arrived. He had the flag! We patted each other on the back and laughed. We had done it! Stolen the flags from under their very noses! At the guardhouse!

A "shhh" came from the blackness. Nehor was back.

"Be quiet or we will yet be discovered," he said.

"What do we do now?" Aaron asked.

"We have to decide what to do with the flags, now that we have them," I said.

"What do you think would be most embarrassing to the Lamanites?" Nehor asked. I could tell from his voice he was laughing.

"Tear up the flags and dump them in the lake?"

"No," Nehor said. "I have a better idea. Alma?"

"Yes."

"You have been taking care of your father's goats. Where are the goats kept at night?"

"In the goat pens east of the city."

"If we dumped the flags in the goat pens, what would happen to them?"

I laughed as I realized what Nehor was suggesting. "The goats would eat up the feathers and mess all over them," I said.

We hurried over the wall to add to our night's mischief.

* * *

"Alma," Father said. "I would like to speak with you."

"Not now, Father. "I'm on my way to my scribe lesson."

I had no desire to talk to Father. He must have suspected I had helped desecrate the Lamanite flags and was apparently concerned about it. What does he know, anyway? I asked myself. If he is unable or unwilling to fight against the Lamanites, at least some of us are doing something.

After my scribe lesson, I started for Ruth's tent. I wanted to go for a walk with her.

"What are you doing here?"

The voice came from a dark-skinned Lamanite who stood spear in hand before Ruth's tent. Before I could answer, a scream came from the tent. Ruth! I tried to push my way into the tent but the guard barred me with his spear. I tried again and again was pushed back.

Two Lamanites, Ruth struggling vainly between them, emerged from the tent. They held her arms but she continued to kick and bite at them. The guard at the flap joined in the procession and they marched toward the city gate.

I stood there as if rooted to the ground. I wanted to go after them and wrest Ruth away but seemed unable to move. I was scared.

Tears of frustration hung on my cheeks as I ran to our own tent. Father sat at his table, papyrus and plates of bronze scattered before him.

"Father. Father," I cried. "Come quickly. The Lamanites have taken Ruth."

"What."

"Amulon and his Lamanites. They have taken Ruth."

"But, why?" Father shook his head, not seeming to comprehend. "Why would they take Ruth? She is but a girl."

I became more frustrated by the minute. Before I could answer, Helam lifted the flap of the tent and stumbled in. His clothing was mussed, his white hair in disarray, and he had a large bruise on his cheek.

"Alma just told me that Ruth was kidnapped by the Lamanites," Father replied. "Helam, what has happened?"

Helam bit his lip and breathed deeply, attempting to control his emotions. "Several Lamanite guards came to our tent. They forced their way inside and grabbed Ruth. I...I tried to stop them, but they just pushed me aside." He looked at Father, "Alma, what can we do? They have Ruth. I'm afraid of what they will do to her."

Father put his arm around Helam. "This shocks me. I don't know what happened but I intend to find out."

Tears scalded my eyes as I sat there. How could this have happened?

Helam sat down, his head in his hands. He muttered, "Oh, why did I let you talk me into not fighting the Lamanites. We should have resisted them the day they came into our valley."

I nodded my head in helpless agreement. That's right, I thought, then we wouldn't have had any of these problems.

I sat on my pallet, my mind so troubled I couldn't think about what I could do. What could I do? I glanced at mother. White-faced, she followed Father and Helam outside. Nehor! That was it. I would talk to Nehor. He would know what to do.

I slipped out of the tent and ran to the city, my bare feet making no noise in the meadow grass. I was out of breath by the time I arrived at Aunt Lea's. Nehor opened the door and let me in. I gasped out the story. He listened sympathetically, then shrugged.

"Alma," he said. "There is nothing we can do."

"But..."

He put his hands on my shoulders, pushing me to the floor. "We can't fight their whole army."

"We must do something."

Nehor smiled. "Yes, we can at least see where they have taken Ruth."

Without a word to his aunt we slipped out into the dark street. We didn't know where to start looking, so we went by the guardhouse first. No one there. Then to Helam's house where the guards lived. No one there, either. Flickering torch light from the church square caught our attention. We circled around through dark streets and alleys until we were opposite the church.

There they were. Under flickering light of the torches we could see several girls huddled before the church steps. They were surrounded by Lamanite guards. I couldn't tell if Ruth was there, but she must be. Amulon stood above the guards on the temple platform, apparently giving instructions.

I turned to Nehor. He always had a plan. "What can we do?" I whispered.

"There's too many Lamanites," he whispered back. "Let's go get Aaron and Jacob and wait for the Lamanites to put the girls somewhere for the night. Perhaps then we can find a way to free them."

We hurried away from the square, taking a circuitous route to Aaron's house.

When we got back to the square with the other boys, it was empty. Only one torch still burned at the front of the Church. Sadly, I and the boys worked our way back through the dark streets. A fiery resolve was burning within me. I had to get Ruth back, no matter what it took. The other boys were mere shadows in the dark but I sensed Nehor stop.

"Alma," he said.

"What?"

"Don't do something foolish."

"Like what?"

"Like trying to rescue the girls from the Lamanites by yourself."

My answer was somewhat sullen. "I'll do what I have to do."

I left the boys at Aunt Lea's house and continued to the gate. Once outside I walked for some time, trying to decide what to do. As I passed Helam's tent I could hear Annah's muffled crying. I became even more angry and determined.

At our tent I paused. Someone was talking loudly inside. I made out the voices of Helam and my father. They were discussing Ruth. I listened intently. Father told how Amulon had said the Lamanites were taking Ruth and the girls back to the land of the Lamanites, and that they had already started. Helam said something about going after them.

"I can't blame you for wanting to try," Father replied. "If I were in your place I would probably do the same thing. But I have tried to stop them already. They are heavily guarded."

I had heard enough. Father was being fainthearted again. Angrily, I slipped into the tent and faced Father, in my anger hardly noticing his bloodied face. "It is your fault Ruth was taken. You are the one who kept the people from fighting and protecting their families." I stepped close to him and rapped him on the chest with my clenched fists. "I hate you! I hate you!"

Turning, I ran sobbing from the tent. The night was dark with no moon, but I ran blindly on. Without consciously thinking about it, I headed around the wall toward the south gate—the gate the Lamanites would have used to take the girls towards the land of Nephi. I ran until I was exhausted and gasping for breath.

Stopping, I dropped to my knees, clasped my hands and looked up into the dark and starry heavens.

"God, if there is a God, hear me," I cried. "I vow before You this night that I will go to the land of Nephi and free Ruth and the other girls." I knelt there for a few moments, hoping against hope for an answer of some kind. All I heard were the chirps of birds and the call of monkeys and frogs from the nearby forest.

There was no time to go to our cave to get a sword. What could I do without a weapon? I didn't know, but I had to do something. Standing up, I started off in the direction I thought the Lamanites would follow. There was no trail but I knew that the way to the land of Nephi led south through the meadow and into the forest. It seemed like hours before I entered the deep darkness of the forest. Without a torch I couldn't even find the trail. Going on was hopeless. Vines and heavy undergrowth covered the forest floor. The Lamanites would be on the well-used trail which had been cut through. I didn't even have a sword or knife to cut away the underbrush. Discouraged and exhausted, I lay down under a huge tree and slept. My sleeping was fitful as I dreamed of rescuing Ruth from the Lamanites.

The light of morning filtered through the dense forest. I awakened with my face and body on fire. I burned all over. Stumbling to my feet, I looked down. My chest, arms, and legs were swollen and splotchy from hundreds of mosquito bites. When I stopped to drink from a stream, I noticed my face was even more swollen. I was a sorry sight outside, but my insides were in sorrier shape. I had failed in my quest. Now what would happen to Ruth? Reluctantly, I turned and headed back to the city, my head hanging in shame.

The sun was straight up before I reached my father's tent. I wasn't sure how Father would greet me, but shrugging, I stooped and entered the tent. I avoided Father's eyes, dropping to the floor to give Noah a hug.

Mother hurried to me and clasped me tightly to her. Then she held me at arm's length, looking at my splotchy face. "Oh, Alma, you must have a thousand bites." She left me to get some herbal salve.

Father knelt beside me, lifted my chin with his hand, and asked, "Son, I am glad you are home. We have worried about you. I know how you must feel. Ruth was very special to you."

Tears came to my eyes. Father had forgiven me my harsh words of last night. I was confused. Was I still angry at Father?

Mother fixed me turtle soup and I ate hungrily. Only after I had eaten my fill did I speak.

"Father, I hate Amulon."

"I hated him, too, for awhile," Father said.

"You don't hate him now?"

"No," Father said. "I don't hate Amulon. I hate what he has done and what he stands for."

What's the difference? I though bitterly. It's Amulon's fault that Ruth is gone. It's Amulon's fault that we are no longer in our home. Amulon was to blame for most of what had happened.

Father had continued talking, his arm on my shoulders. "Hate is a destroying emotion," he said. "Your hate cannot hurt Amulon. It can only hurt you."

"I still hate Amulon," I said angrily. "I'll make him pay for stealing Ruth."

"The Lord will punish him," Father said.

The Lord again. I pulled away from him. I couldn't wait on the Lord. "Father," I said, "instead of teaching me to write, teach me to use a sword like Zoram."

Father again placed his hand on my shoulder. This time I didn't shrug it off. He was saying something about retaliation.

"Knowledge is power," he said. "To be able to read and write our language will give you power greater than a sword. Your power will be preservation of the language of your fathers and writing of scriptures."

I shook my head in wonderment. Here we had lost Ruth and all Father could think of was the scriptures. "Would that power save Ruth?" I asked bitterly.

Father shook his head. "Perhaps not, but that power could save a people."

I could not understand what he was getting at. All I could think about was how to rescue Ruth and how to drive the Lamanites from our city. All Father could talk about was record-keeping. Couldn't he understand? Hurting inside, I pulled free and with a whistle for Noah to follow, left the tent.

Chapter 3

Escape from Helam

The dream was vivid. In it I stood on the mountainside looking at Helam. The city was deserted. No smoke wafted into the blue sky; no sounds came from empty streets. Everyone had gone from the city. Then, as part of my dream, a quiet voice came. "I will ease the burdens the Lamanites put upon your shoulders, that even you cannot feel them upon your backs while you are in bondage, that you may know that I, the Lord God, do visit my people in their afflictions."

I woke with a start. What did the dream mean? I pondered it for a moment as I looked around. The tent was completely dark except for faint sheen of starlight coming through the open flap. Smells of sweat, anise, and cooking grease—familiar smells of the tent—scented the air. I could hear Father's even but heavy breathing in the rear section. I lay back and slept once again.

At breakfast Father excitedly announced the Lord had spoken to him during the night. When he quoted the words the Lord had spoken: "I will ease the burdens the Lamanites put upon your shoulders...." I looked at Father in stunned silence. They were the same words I remembered from my dream!

I was puzzled. Was this a message from God? If there was a God, had my unbelief been wrong? If there was a God, was He truly interested in us? I mentally shrugged as I ate my porridge and wheat cakes. Mother and Zoram indicated they heard the same words in their dreams. I was even more puzzled by this thing which was more than mere coincidence.

I asked Nehor about it that afternoon. He gave me a big grin.

"I don't know," he said. "I heard the words, too. In fact, everyone I talked to said they heard in their dreams that their burdens would be lighter."

"Does that mean there is a God? And that he does speak to people?"

"I don't know what it means," Nehor sneered. "But I do know I'm not going to sit around waiting for some god to free us from the Lamanites. If we're going to be free, we've got to do it ourselves."

I continued my task of carrying rocks, but I thought often of Nehor's words. Would God, if there was a God, just let us remain as slaves to the Lamanites? Didn't He care about our sorrows and feelings? I sadly contemplated the past few months. First was the kidnapping of Ruth. Many times I still lay awake long into the night thinking of my vow and wondering if I could ever fulfill it. Then Helam's remains had been found by a work crew looking for balsam trees. I had not been near Annah's tent since that time. I knew she must be very miserable, first losing her daughter, Ruth, and then her husband.

Nehor and I had not raided the Lamanites for some time. Not because we had quit, but because the Lamanites had really toughened up. Their patrols roamed the city day and night. No one was allowed out of his home after dark. Those caught were never heard of again. As part of Lamanite reprisals, Amulon had announced that no Nephites could pray openly. That didn't bother me—I didn't pray anyway—but I saw it was a problem for Father.

He had aged greatly since Helam's death. His eyes were more lifeless and it seemed to me he had lost more of his greying hair. The only bright spot had been this morning when he had appeared so radiant at the breakfast table because of his "vision."

The cheerfulness of the Nephite workers surprised me. Many carried huge packs of wood or stone but I heard no complaining. Again, doubts assailed me. Had I been wrong about God? Was He actually helping us?

As each day passed people became more cheerful. I asked my brother, Zoram, to explain. He looked at me with understanding.

"Little brother," he said, "people's burdens truly have been made light. I am sure that soon the Lord will release us from bondage."

I wasn't prepared to believe that. "But the Lamanites are stricter than ever," I said.

"That's true, but it doesn't matter. My own burdens are made lighter. Whatever the Lamanites pile on I carry with ease."

I walked away shaking my head. I would have to be convinced. As I left, two Lamanite guards came from the city gate and walked towards the tent. I stepped aside and watched them. Moments later they stepped from the tent, my father between them.

I could feel my heart beating in my chest. Were they going to take my father as they had taken Ruth?

As they passed through the gate in the city wall I plunged back into the tent. Mother sat on a stool, her hands in her lap, eyes closed. I was about to speak when I realized she was praying. I waited. She opened her eyes and gazed around the tent. When her eyes met mine she smiled.

"Father has been called to appear before Amulon," she said. "Apparently Amulon is angry at our people's seeming indifference to his harassment."

Father came home an hour later, his eyes sparkling. He told of standing up to Amulon and the anger Amulon showed. I was convinced my father had been a coward when the Lamanites took over the city but now he had showed courage before Amulon. Had I misjudged him?

The next morning I received another surprise. Father greeted us at the breakfast table with astounding news. He said the Lord had again spoken to him. The Lord told him that the time had come for us to be delivered from bondage. I had never seen anyone so excited as Zoram was when he heard the news.

On this important day I was lucky to be assigned the same work detail as Nehor. We cleaned fish nets on the beach. The day was warm and pleasant and everytime the guard was distracted we talked.

"What do you think of Father's vision?" I asked Nehor.

He shook his head. "I'll believe it when I see it."

"But Father has told everyone. He says that tomorrow is the day we leave."

Nehor sneered. "You are stupid if you think Amulon and the Lamanites will sit back and watch us walk away from the city. They are too lazy to do any work, and if the work isn't done they don't eat." He shook his head in disdain. "No, I wish it were true, but I don't believe it. The only way we will ever free ourselves from the Lamanites is to get enough weapons and fight our way out."

"If we leave tomorrow, will we need our weapons?"

"Yes. We won't be able to get away without them."

"When will we get them?"

"Tonight."

I waited for the Lamanite guard to move further away, then whispered. "How shall we do it?"

"We'll take Aaron and Jacob to the cave and bring back all we can carry. In the morning we'll be ready to fight."

"Shouldn't we tell Father or someone so they can help us get the weapons?"

Nehor looked at me coldly. "No. They are ours. We will get them ourselves. We took them from the Lamanites and I'm not turning them over to anyone."

He licked his lips and looked past me at the guard, then whispered, "Meet me at the wall just after dark, before the moon comes up."

"What about Aaron and Jacob?"

"I'll get them. Aunt Lea will just think they are sleeping at our place."

We were silent after that. Each had his own thoughts as we cleaned moss and driftwood from the nets.

At our evening meal, Father laid out plans. He and Zoram would fashion packs. Mother and the girls would then pack them for our journey. We would be very limited in the belongings we could take with us. Zoram, being the strongest, was to carry our small tent. Each of us would carry a pack.

I was assigned to get our small herd of goats ready by getting ropes to string them together. Father was afraid they would run off into the forest. I thought Father had lost his reason. Trying to sneak away from the Lamanite guards was one thing, but to take along bleating goats? Maybe Nehor was right. We would have to fight our way out of the city.

Just after dark Father slipped away into the forest. I knew he would be going after his precious writings. I was glad he was gone. Now I could make my way to the wall behind Aunt Lea's house. Whistling for Noah, I hurried down the hill in the dark.

"Sssst."

Shadows appeared on top the wall. Noah growled. Nehor and the other boys dropped silently beside me in the sand. I was glad it was going to be a moonlit night. Traveling to our hideout was scary even in full daylight. We slipped away from the wall and into the forest while it was still dark. The forest was dark, damp and musty. We waited there and made plans. Finally, the moon came out. We broke out into the grassy sward on the hillside. The moon bathed us in its soft rays. The scream of a jaguar broke the silence. I jumped, then reached down and petted Noah. He was getting old but was still a comfort.

By soft moonlight we struggled up the mountainside. I didn't notice until we were half-way up that Noah was no longer following us. I thought of the time just three years before when Noah had been so frisky as we climbed the mountain. I hoped he was all right.

We had no fire for a torch, and when we arrived at the cave we had to feel our way in to get the weapons. We gathered all we could carry and piled them outside the cave on the boulder.

I counted them. We had fifteen swords, two axes, and ten bows with arrows—not nearly enough to arm our people against the Lamanites, but still better than none at all. We loaded them up and started back down the mountain. I wondered as I walked what the morrow would bring. Quietly we cached the weapons in the forest behind our tent.

I waved good-bye to the others and went to our tent. Noah was there. He followed me as I slipped out to the goat pens. As quietly as I could I put lead ropes on each of the goats and tied them to the fence. Soon I was back in the tent watching my family work. Moonlight was the only light they had. Father and Zoram worked without talking. Mother and my sisters, Netta and Leesa, kept up a constant whispering chatter. They were still whispering when I fell asleep.

Zoram shook me awake. "It's almost time for us to go."

Sleepily I looked around. "Where's Father?"

"He went into the city to gather the people."

"The Lamanites will kill him."

Zoram shrugged. "The Lord will protect him."

The weapons. The ones we had brought from the mountain. Should I tell Zoram? Since he was the best swordsman in Helam I decided he should know. I motioned to him.

"Come with me," I whispered.

I led him around the tent and to the edge of the forest. Lifting a large fern I showed him our cache.

He whistled between his teeth, reached down and picked up a sword. Hefting it in both hands, he asked, "Where did you get these?"

I saw no need to lie. "From the Lamanites. We hid them in a cave on the mountain."

He looked at me with a look of new respect. Carefully putting the sword back, he pulled the fern down around the weapons, again hiding them.

"Do you think we will need them?" I asked.

"I don't know. But we must let Father know about them when he comes back."

Father was beaming broadly when he arrived at the tent. He spoke rapidly. "The people are meeting at the south gate. We must move quickly."

Zoram said, "Father, before we go Alma has something to show you."

Father followed us into the forest. Again I lifted the fern displaying the weapons to his view.

Father looked at the swords and bows, then looked at me. He didn't even ask where they came from. He knew.

"We'd better take these with us," he said. "Bows and arrows will be excellent for hunting game, and we will probably need swords and axes to cut a trail through the forest."

He put a hand on my shoulder. "Son, I don't approve of how you obtained these weapons, but thank you for getting them. They will be a great help to our people."

I kept one bow and a quiver of arrows for myself and a sword for each of the other boys. Zoram selected a long sword. Father took the rest of the weapons for the people. I knew that Nehor would be angry at me for giving everything away, but I didn't care. Father was leading us out of slavery, just as the Moses I had read about led the children of Israel out of Egypt.

"How do we get past the Lamanite guards?" Zoram asked as we gathered our things together.

Father smiled broadly again. "The Lamanites are all asleep at their posts. There are none to stop our leaving."

By the time we arrived in the open place before the south gate most people were already there. I noted with grim satisfaction that this was the very place where the Lamanites had stood and humiliated Father and Helam three years ago when they took over the city. In my fourteen-year-old mind I felt that was real justice!

Father took the lead as we departed the city. There must have been several thousand people with their herds of goats. Some carried huge packs; others took little with them. I wondered to myself if this is what the children of Israel looked like as they left Egypt.

We went around the lake, then east into the forest. Father stopped at the forest's edge, letting people pass him. I supposed he wanted one last look at the city. I kept my herd of goats moving, but Noah was just too slow. I finally picked him up and put him across my shoulders. If necessary, I thought, I will carry my dog, Noah, wherever we go.

All day we cut our way through forest. I was pleased that we had stolen the swords and axes. Without them I thought we would have been in deep trouble. Vines and undergrowth choked the forest floor. We were going through new country, away from the land of Nephi—creating our trail as we went.

After struggling through forest all day, I was excited when we broke out into a long broad valley. The sun, hidden by tall trees, was almost setting. Father called a halt and instructed us to put up our tents and gather wood. I was glad to stop. I had carried Noah most of the way and was very tired.

I helped gather wood until darkness set in, then watched as the men built a roaring bonfire. Father asked for volunteers to watch the goat herds and I offered. I didn't feel like sitting by the fire listening to people talk.

I sat on a little hill in the dark, goats all around me, regretting my quick decision. I could hear shouts and laughter as people celebrated their new freedom. Songs of praise and thanks to the Lord drifted out to me and finally there was a loud shout. Mother told me later that the shout was the people acclaiming the valley as the Valley of Alma. Everything seemed so peaceful, but I was worried about the Lamanites. Wouldn't they be following us by now? How long would our new-found freedom last if they caught up with us? The few swords and bows we had would be almost useless against trained and well-armed warriors.

The next day was cool and pleasant. Hummingbirds dipped and weaved and hovered. Warbling of tanagers, orioles and thrushes heralded our passage. Monkeys chattered and spirited gossip of cuckoos and parrots came from the long crescent of pine woods that flanked our descent.

As we hiked northward through the long valley the wind tousled my hair. Fresh dew on the grass wet my sandals and legs. Smells of clover and crushed grass blended with that of meadow flowers. Aroma of pine droppings was wafted from the hills. I was glad to be alive, and free! The thought was exhilarating.

Two rabbits, flushed from their burrows by our passage, bounded from a patch of maguay plants, and bounced away, kicking up tiny spurts of dust. They, too, seemed to enjoy their freedom.

Freedom. Was ever a word more wonderful than that one? No, even if the Lamanites found us and dragged us back, at least we were free now. Freedom was what Nehor and I had plotted and schemed about for three years. Freedom was ours and we hadn't even had to fight the Lamanites to get it. That was still confusing to me. Did it mean God was up there or even down here with us as we trudged downward through the broad valley named after my father, Alma?

Soon the little river we followed became wide and deep. Game was plentiful along the way, giving me lots of practice with bow and arrow. Chattering and squalling birds of every color nested in the trees; fish were plentiful in the river. On either side of the valley were jumbled hills and plateaus.

The further we traveled, the thicker became the forests. Our chopped-out trail was hemmed in by huge trees, draped with hungry, life-sucking parasites; the very density of the trees creating beautiful hanging gardens of bromeliads, vines, and flowers.

Walking through the forest was like walking in perpetual twilight. Rare rays of sunlight which succeeded in slipping through the shadowy treetops appeared as strands of jewelry. Bands of chattering monkeys cursed us as they traversed through the treetops above us. Brilliantly colored parrots mocked our passage with raucous voices. Insects made an unceasing highpitched whine around our heads. Air became more hot and humid; the forest floor was damp and spongy underfoot.

Nehor was angry with me for giving away the weapons, but we were still friends. Every day, with Aaron, Jacob, Abelon and the other boys tagging along, we sought adventures: hunting for frogs in the forest depths, fishing for big, lazy catfish in the river, searching for birds' eggs high in the trees. We even tried imitating monkeys, swinging from tree to tree on the lianas.

I had never been more than a half day's walk from Helam. How exuberantly alive I felt to be exploring new country. Father seemed to fear for our safety but I shrugged it off. It was so good to be free: to roam without worrying what the Lamanites would do if they caught us. My only fears were big cats; we had seen several black-spotted leopards skulking through the forest and at night we often heard wailing cries of jaguars. When I wasn't exploring with my friends, I trudged along behind my family with Noah on my shoulders.

Noah didn't explore with us. If I didn't carry him he limped along behind the goats, often getting far behind. I really worried about him. Father told me he was just getting old. Zoram had given him to me on my first birthday and I was almost fifteen. That would make Noah only fourteen. Was that old? He was still my best friend.

"*Aarrghh!*" The roar came from behind us. Noah barked.

Noah! I hurried back.

"Alma, wait!"

I ignored Nehor's warning shout.

I found Noah backed against a tree, his gray fur matted and pink with blood where a cat's claws had raked him. I almost reached him when I heard a hiss, almost a snake sound. I turned my head and looked right into the yellow eyes of a huge jaguar. It crouched to spring when Noah darted between us. The cat swiped him with a paw, sending him hurtling through the air. Noah landed in a heap.

Angrily, I grabbed a stick and turned to face the cat. Before I could move it sprang at me. I could feel its hot, fetid breath on my face. I fell backwards, the cat on top of me.

"Father!" I shouted.

I was terrified. With both hands I held the cat's twisting head, pushing its slobbering mouth away from my face. It's claws raked my shoulders. I rolled, trying to turn it away.

I remembered no more until I awakened in father's arms.

His eyes, as I looked up into them, showed genuine concern.

"Father," I whispered, "my shoulder feels as if it is burning up."

He nodded, rocking gently back and forth, holding me not like a fourteen-year-old but as a child.

"Noah?" I whispered hoarsely.

Father shook his head.

I closed my eyes, fighting back tears.

I heard Father call for Mother before I slipped back into unconsciousness. I half-consciously remembered feeling Father's cool hands on my forehead, hearing words of blessing. For some time I didn't know what was happening. I awakened in the night, my whole body aching, sweat pouring from me. Lying there, listening to the night sounds of the forest, I became aware of someone beside me. I turned my head. Mother, her head nodding with sleep, sat on a stump by my pallet. Tears welled in my eyes. I turned and blinked them away. It was good to feel loved.

Though I felt somewhat better by morning, Mother would not let me walk. Father had a litter made and I was carried through the forest. Nehor and Aaron carried one end, and Abelon and Jacob the other. Mother walked beside me, sometimes holding my hand, sometimes just brushing flies and mosquitoes away.

I lost track of time, drifting in and out of sleep, half-dozing, lulled by swaying of the litter. A shout awakened me.

"The city! There is the city!"

Chapter 4

Nephite Warrior in Zarahemla

What is wrong with me? I sneaked a glance at Father. He has surely given up on me, I thought.

I clenched and unclenched my fists under the table and tried to relax, not wanting Father to see how tense I was. Here I am, I thought, sixteen years of age and unworthy to sit in the presence of my father. Besides, I still don't even know what I really want out of life. Deep inside me I knew much of my frustration came from my failure to achieve my own life goals.

I was really mixed up. I had rebelled against Father but sometimes I still had desires of becoming a minister and missionary like him. When I was eight—when Father baptized me—I committed myself to that purpose. To be a church leader was all I then desired; now I'd discarded that dream and through my sins made its attainment forever impossible. Why?

Was my rebellion because of the devastating, heart-breaking experience of seeing Ruth torn from our people and dragged off? Did I rebel against Father because I still felt he acted cowardly before the Lamanites? Or were those merely excuses for my behavior? Was something inside of me causing me to act the way I did: lack of self-confidence? envy of Father who is so loved by the people? my feeling that I could never be as good as Father?

What makes me do the things I do? Why do I feel helpless in governing my own life?

These questions agonized me for the thousandth time as I nervously stirred my corn-meal porridge. I glanced across the table at Father, then quickly looked back into my bowl. I closed my eyes and pushed the bowl from me. How could I eat?

I looked up surprised when Father spoke, gently breaking the silence.

"Alma, something troubles you. Please tell me what it is. Perhaps I can help."

I tried to hold the tears back but couldn't. Uncontrolled, they rolled down my face. Words tumbled out from my lips.

"Father, I know you want me to be like you, but I can't. I don't know how. You are a person that people love and enjoy being around; people look up to you with respect."

Father reached over and gently brushed the tears from my cheeks, making me feel even worse. I noticed Father's eyes were also brimming.

I continued between sobs. "I don't care whether I am rich or famous. I just want people to know that I'm alive, that I can be a leader. I want people to treat me like they treat you...with respect."

I knew I wasn't making much sense. Blindly, I pushed away from the table and rushed from the house.

* * *

Our first year in Zarahemla had passed quickly. Helam had been a quiet town but Zarahemla almost vibrated with excitement. There were many fun things to see and do. I spent most of my daytime hours at King Mosiah's school of scribes. When I could I helped Father on the new church he was building.

Nehor was busy doing other things, but he was still my friend. I enjoyed being with him and others I had known in Helam, but now I felt a restlessness. I wanted to be me—whatever that meant.

While training as a scribe, I became acquainted with King Mosiah's four sons. All were enrolled in the school of scribes. Aaron, the oldest, was two years older than I and very serious. He knew that someday, when his father died, he would be king of Zarahemla. I think that responsibility frightened him. I understood him, though, because sometimes I had similar feelings. Since my brother, Zoram's, only desire was to be a warrior I knew that someday Father would want me to be high priest just as Aaron's father wanted him to be king.

Ammon, Mosiah's second son, was my age. He and I were almost the same size although he was a little broader-shouldered and bigger-chested. We differed in other ways. His brown hair cascaded around his expressive face, with deep blue eyes flanking a straight pointed nose. My black hair and brown eyes contrasted sharply. His chest and back were covered with brown, curly hair whereas my body was almost hairless. Though almost totally unlike in our appearance, we were alike in our feelings. He and I developed a bond of friendship the first time we met. We talked often of things we had done as boys.

Omner and Himni, the younger brothers, were tagalongs. Everywhere Ammon and I went, they came along. We tolerated them. Besides, someone had to do chores and be fetchers.

In the land of Helam, my scribe training had been in Hebrew. The Zarahemla school taught reformed Egyptian. I had difficulty memorizing the thousands of pictures but Ammon helped me. After once getting the word-pictures in mind, I discovered Egyptian was easier and much shorter; one page equalled over thirty pages of Hebrew.

Ammon and I loved to explore. As often as we could, we left our studies and sought out the jungle and river. The oppressive heat, quite different from the land of Helam, was especially miserable in the city. Temperature varied little from day to night and the waters of the river really helped to relieve us from screaming yellow sun.

Ammon's brothers usually followed us as we explored both sides of the River Sidon. We fished, hunted mud turtles, and swam in the river. In one place the river had undercut a huge bank, forming a deep pool—a perfect swimming hole. Scrambling up the bank, we'd poise on the edge, then dive into the dirty water below. Sometimes we just tried to see who could stay under the water longest. We made a slide down the bank, threw water on it until it was slick, then stood at the top, threw ourselves into the slide, and careened into the water. We had a great time splashing and swimming.

Nehor sometimes explored or swam with us, but he didn't really like being out of the city. He was more serious than I and didn't like taking time for play. Zarahemla's streets became his territory, and he roamed them with young men who had ideas similar to his own.

Sometimes after swimming we sat and visited about serious matters like religion or the kingship. When Nehor was with us our talks were especially serious. He talked of gods you could see instead of an invisible god; gods you could hold and touch instead of one who was distant. His eyes lighted with strange zeal when he talked of the power religion gave to men.

"Your father," he said while focusing his pale eyes on me, "is as powerful as King Mosiah."

I looked at Ammon and his brothers.

"Priests have great power over people," Nehor continued. "They should be paid well for what they do."

"But father doesn't get paid," I said.

"Your father, by playing on people's emotions, could be the wealthiest man in Zarahemla."

"But father is not interested in riches."

"That's why I say he is foolish."

Another night, when Nehor wasn't with us, I asked Ammon his feelings about religion.

"Your father and his people all seem faithful. What happened to you? Why haven't you accepted the teachings about God?" I asked him.

Ammon answered. "My grandfather, King Benjamin was a good king and taught the people about religion, but I was too young to understand his teachings." He shrugged. "And hearing it second hand from my father...well, it just sounds too farfetched. All that stuff about coming back to life just doesn't make sense."

Himni added, "And when they teach that a god will come to earth and take the form of a man...." He shook his head. "Somebody must have dreamed that up."

"So," Aaron finished, "this religion thing just isn't for us."

I nodded. I was confused about my own religious feelings and the brothers' reasoning made sense.

Occasionally we talked about girls. Since Ruth's kidnapping I never had a girl friend. Nehor boasted of his conquests: the girls he knew and had made love to. One night he asked Ammon and me to join him at a place he knew—a place where we could visit some girls.

Ammon looked at me and shrugged. Why not? I nodded acceptance. We followed Nehor to a part of Zarahemla I had never seen. I had never been out of the Nephite sector; now we were deep in the area where the people of Zarahemla lived. Streets were filled with trash. My nose wrinkled at smells of human waste and garbage. Our footsteps sounded hollow as we threaded our way down a dark alley to a building with a single torch lighting its entrance. By the time we arrived I was having real doubts and was hesitant about going inside.

"Aw, come on," Nehor prodded. "This will make you a man."

Reluctantly Ammon and I followed Nehor. The room, decorated with jaguar skins piled deep on the floor, was dimly lighted by a single, smoking lamp. There was no other furniture. Several girls, lips painted with berry juice, features indistinct in the dim light, lounged in various provocative positions on the floor. Two men, absorbed in what they were doing, didn't even notice our arrival.

My muscles tensed as I prepared to bolt back through the door. Smell of stale wine and cheap perfume almost gagged my nervous stomach. Nehor, apparently sensing my hesitation, put his hand on my arm. An older woman, her teeth yellowed and worn short, approached us.

Nehor whispered something to her, nodded at us, and produced some copper coins. She grinned, exposing more of her rotting teeth.

"Come with me, dearie," she said. Her hand grasped my wrist.

I tried to pull back but she held tight, the grin broadening in her ugly face. I looked back at Ammon. He shrugged helplessly. I walked in a daze, feeling I had lost control over my own actions. We entered a small cubicle off the main room. A girl, tawny-haired in the dim light, lay nude on the floor furs. The old lady patiently pushed me towards her. The girl reached up, grasped my hand, and pulled me down beside her.

* * *

I pushed the thought of the girl from me and returned my thinking to present. Here I am, running from my father's presence. Drums played inside my head. A voice throbbed there for the thousandth time, "I have sinned. There is no hope for me. I am lost to the Church and to my family. I can never now be like my father."

As I fled the house and Father's presence, I made a decision. I had to get away; I could no longer face Father.

I thought of Zoram, serving as a warrior in some frontier town, protecting it from the Lamanites. That's what I could do, I thought. I could become a warrior, and by so doing, perhaps I could fulfill my long-time dream, too. I could find Ruth, if she were still alive.

"Ammon, I think I am going to join the army and be a warrior."

"A warrior!" Ammon looked shocked.

"I need to get away. Father has given up on me. Mother thinks I'm rebellious. Maybe by getting away I can amount to something."

Ammon smiled at me in his perceptive, quiet way. "You're feeling guilty, aren't you?"

I nodded.

"Me, too. The more I think about it, the more I believe you may have solved our problem. The army may well be the perfect solution."

"At least it will get us out of scribe training," I said dourly.

"What about Aaron and my younger brothers?"

"What about them?"

"I wouldn't want to leave them behind. I think they would join with us. None of us would have to learn a trade, and Aaron can learn about the military so he will be a better king."

I could tell we were talking ourselves into it, but the more we talked, the more excited I became. We could be totally on our own. Once more I could be free! And I wouldn't have to face Father every day with my guilt.

Ammon told his brothers what we planned. All decided to become warriors with us, even Aaron. Our decision was made. We separated to talk to our respective fathers. I didn't envy them breaking the news to the king, but he and Father both gave reluctant permission.

Enlisting was easy. We walked to the warriors' barracks near the north gate of the city, made our intentions known, and were soon in training. I was surprised. The army even took Omner and Himni, as young as they were.

Wearying war games, weapons instruction, and drill consumed most of our time. We carried hide shields and wooden swords and learned to march in formation, our feather banners waving in front. Drilling in the hot sun was devastating. Between the sun and the humidity many warriors toppled over during drill. The uniform that was put on in the morning would be soaking wet from shoulders to knees within a few minutes.

Drummers beat a slow cadence as we marched. We learned to march forward and to the side, to pivot and wheel as a group. We were being welded into a fighting force.

Hour after hour Arbuch, our old and scarred instructor, ran us through sword practice. I sometimes felt awkward, but for Ammon sword practice seemed to come easy. Since Ammon and I were close to the same size, old Arbuch often paired us against each other. Day after day we thrust, chopped, and hacked, our wooden swords beating on each other's shields until our arms ached from exhaustion and our ears ached from Arbuch's yelling.

Arbuch was so pleased with Ammon's swordplay he pulled his own metal sword from his belt and handed it to Ammon. Ammon thrust and parried, the sword glinting and winking brightly in the strong sunshine. I looked down at my wooden sword. I wondered if I could ever be a valiant warrior.

After sword practice we learned to use the sling. I liked it better than the sword. For long hours we practiced whirring the sling around our heads, releasing a thong at precisely the right moment. The stone, discharged at great momentum, sped to the target. I was good at the sling, but Ammon was better. He seemed to excel in everything we did, but I wasn't envious. He was my friend.

We tossed spears at cloth dummies, shot arrows at wooden targets, and bludgeoned imaginary enemies with our axes. In but a few month's time, we were considered trained warriors and were sent on our first assignment to the city of Manti.

Manti was the border city sitting on the main trail between the land of Zarahemla and the Lamanite's land of Nephi. The city, located near a mountain pass between two of the tributaries which became the Sidon River, was dominated by huge mountains on east and west. Manti's climate was much more moderate than Zarahemla's. In fact, it reminded me somewhat of Helam. Instead of rain forest, the land about Manti was forested with pine trees.

The city was beautiful but small, with several towering temples and a large amphitheater and game court. A strong wall gave some protection to its inhabitants. We were housed in barracks near the south wall.

Since we were now full–fledged warriors, we were issued armor: thickly quilted cotton toughened by being soaked in brine, which extended from neck to knees. The armor was supposed to protect us from the enemy, but we hated it; it was hot and scratchy and sweaty.

Having real weapons was exciting: black metal swords, shields of tightly woven wicker covered with leather, long powerful bows with a plentiful supply of arrows. Each day we practiced with our weapons.

Each day we became more proficient at warrior skills—skills to be used for killing the enemy.

Manti was a peaceful place to be, even though it was our city of first defense against any Lamanite attack. But after once settling into military routine, days passed in boring sequence. We had served as warriors in Manti for a year and a half. Every day monotonous same: get up, roll up our pallets, sweep the barracks, eat a tasteless breakfast of fruit and corn mush, sword practice, guard on the palisade, lunch of fruit and nuts, archery practice, marching drill, dinner of roast monkey or peccary, roll out our pallets, go to bed.

Standing guard on Manti's wall, I almost wished the Lamanites would come into the land to give us battle, just to have something to do. An attack would relieve our boredom and give us real weapon practice.

Ammon, his brothers, and I, spent much time hunting for wild peccary and fishing in the mountain streams. Being in the woods gave me much time to think about my life. I didn't want to be a warrior all my life. And now that I'd sinned I felt I couldn't be high priest even if I wanted to. If fact, I made up my mind that since I had sinned I might as well continue sinning because I was damned anyway.

I knew Father loved me and wanted me to be part of his life. His life, though, was wrapped up totally in the Church, and I wasn't happy about that. I needed to have freedom to do the things I wanted to do. I laughed to myself as I thought that. I wanted freedom and yet I had given up my freedom to the army. The army, just like the Church, was a prison for me—fencing me in. I didn't want to be inhibited. I wanted to make up my own rules.

As the high priest's son, I was constantly being watched. I didn't like being watched. I was concerned that someday Father would want to call me as high priest over the Church. I wasn't worthy of that calling. Besides, I didn't want to be high priest. I was determined to silence my inner voice and discover life for myself. So far I had been very disappointed in what I found out. I was really mixed up and didn't know what I wanted. I knew one thing: I didn't like being a warrior and being assigned to such a place as Manti.

I wrote letters to Nehor and other friends in Zarahemla. Nehor's short return note indicated a continuing rebellion against the Church. Apparently he was gaining many followers and they were actively harassing those in the Church. He pleaded that we join him in his cause of overthrowing the Church and setting up a church of our own.

I wondered what Father was doing to counter the threat Nehor and his group posed. Would he tolerate this rebellion and persecution? Or would he fight?

I read Nehor's letter to Ammon and his brothers one day as we sat near the river on the tormented high roots of a cypress tree. Hundreds of tiny frogs peeped around us. Frogs fell from their perches and flopped awkwardly in the water, where, miraculously, they were transformed into purposeful, deft darts skimming across the surface.

As I read the letter an air of tension settled upon us. Ammon nudged me in the ribs and broke the silence with a laugh.

"I can see Nehor now," he chuckled. "He wants power, fame, and money. His desire is to have a cushiony priest's position as head of his own church where people support him in a kingly manner."

"And we?" I asked. "What do we want?"

Aaron, serious as ever, chimed in. "Even with this god, Zimpoc, that Nehor has created, how can he fight against the mightiest king amongst the Nephite nations?"

As Aaron spoke, I wondered what I would do when my warrior enlistment was over. Would I go to Zarahemla and join Nehor in his fight against my father's Church? I spoke up. "Right now, all Nehor has are words."

"I have never seen anyone slain by words," interjected Himni.

"All movements begin small," said Ammon quietly. "I feel Nehor's words will have great impact on this land." He sighed.

I thought I knew the feelings going on within him. Here he was, ostensibly a warrior serving in his father's army, sworn to defend the kingdom. As my friend, he was also a would-be disciple of Nehor committed to revolution against the Church and his father. I was son of the high priest of the Church, a warrior of King Mosiah, and possibly a disciple of Nehor's god, Zimpoc. Ours was a confused loyalty. What loyalty did I owe the king? Or my father? Or the Church? What loyalty did I owe myself?

Chapter 5

Gods of Flesh

A roar of greeting came from a hundred open mouths. Nehor raised his arms high above his head, his hands clenched.

"It's time to arm ourselves. We are at war against the Church of God! Small bands of Zimpoc priests in each city shall attack church goers until none dare go to church. We shall grow stronger each day, until, like King Noah of old, all power shall be ours."

Nehor's oratorical skill was spell-binding. Even I, who had heard the same thing many times, was captivated by his power. I looked around to see how his rhetoric was being received.

Ammon's face reflected the gravity of the moment. He whispered to me. "I believe he will do it. Religion will be his means."

Ammon is right, I thought. Religion is a tool, a way of controlling people's minds. For years I had looked upon religion as a weakness—an opiate for the masses. If people wanted a religion, we would create one for them—one they could believe in. Let them use it for a crutch; what difference did it make? Nehor said through people's belief we would get rich. Yes, we would use Nehor's religion to our advantage.

"Zimpoc," Nehor screamed, "shall be the god of all the land."

"Zimpoc! Zimpoc!" chanted the crowd.

Nehor stepped down from the raised platform and walked quickly to where we were standing while the crowd continued its chant.

Aaron faced him. "Nehor, are you sure this is the right thing to do?"

Nehor looked at him coldly. "Are you having second thoughts?"

"No, but I am concerned as to what this will do to father's kingdom. I...."

Nehor interrupted him, his eyes glinting icily. "Your words are the words of a weakling."

Aaron flushed. "Our lives are at stake. I just want to make sure we are doing the right thing. Isn't that right, Alma?"

I didn't want to be drawn into this conversation. I looked at Ammon who seemed to be waiting for my answer. I shrugged.

"I agree with Nehor. Only by having a strong religion like the religion of Zimpoc can we unite the people. Right now some follow my father, some follow other gods, and some have no religion. We shall make sure everyone in the land of Zarahemla follows Zimpoc."

"Or else...?"

"Yes, or else!" I shouted. "We have delayed long enough. Now is the time to strike for what we believe."

I said the words with as much force as I could, but I knew it was a lie. None of us really believed in the god we had created. It was all a lie. Zimpoc was a god of plaster and stone whom we had brought to life.

I envied Father his conviction. He really believed in the God he preached about.

Nehor was looking at me, a half smile on his face.

Ammon chuckled in his scraggly beard, "Wise words from son of the high priest." He turned to Nehor. "What do we do next?"

Nehor swept his arms in an arc, indicating the crowd around the fire. "This is the cadre. We will split up and disrupt the churches in every city. These shall be the priests of Zimpoc."

The sons of Mosiah and I were the only ones remaining around the campfire. Nehor had agreed that we stay together. The others had already left for assignments in various cities. Nehor, with Lamanite escort, had set off for the land of Nephi. He was not going to be satisfied with converting just the land of Zarahemla but included the Lamanites in his plans as well.

"What makes Nehor so zealous?" Aaron asked. "He is more radical about religion than your father."

"Yes," Omner added. "This started out to be for fun, but Nehor is really serious about this Zimpoc thing."

"His heart is in it," I said. "You can see it in his eyes."

Himni stirred the fire. "We have committed ourselves to something that may destroy us as well as the Church of God."

Ammon laughed mirthlessly. "Why do we struggle so? All is planned."

I thought for a moment. "I suppose we can say it is god's will that we do what we do."

Aaron sighed. "Yes, if Zimpoc has a will."

I regarded him curiously. "Aaron, several times you have said things which indicate an unwillingness on your part. Are you with us or not?"

He hunched his shoulders and looked me square in the eye. "Alma, you speak of loyalty to Zimpoc. Are you sure the worship of Zimpoc is what you want, or is it that you just want to attack your father through Zimpoc?"

I looked at him in surprise. He didn't know it, but perhaps he had come close to the truth.

"Doesn't the disunity of this country bother you?" I asked lamely.

"Yes, but I make no pretensions. I do not speak of Zimpoc like you. If Nehor helps us unite the country by getting all of the people to worship one god, fine. If not, I feel we should go it alone."

"Nehor says we will triumph over the church of God," I said, "and I believe him."

"And if not, what then?" Aaron persisted.

"We will make sure it happens," I said doggedly. "We are too far into this thing to think of backing out now."

Ammon gave me a long look. "No one is thinking of backing out. But we do need to be united in our thinking."

"Meanwhile," Aaron said with a curious smile, "think over your own motives, Alma."

Feeling a need to straighten out my thinking, I left Ammon and his brothers in Sidom and returned to Zarahemla. Church services were being held in the plaza before the temple. I didn't let Father know I was there, but I wanted to hear him speak once more. The crowd seemed immense. I stood in the back of the temple plaza and listened. Father stood in front, straight-backed, commanding, so sure of what he was saying. I wished again that I could be like him, but I couldn't. I had already sinned too much.

His words cut through me like a knife, "I ask of you, my brethren of the church, have you spiritually been born of God? Have you received His image in your countenance? Have you experienced this mighty change of heart? I say unto you, can you imagine that you hear the voice of the Lord, saying unto you, 'Come unto me ye blessed, for behold, your works have been the works of righteousness upon the face of the earth?'"

I could take no more. I walked away from the meeting, moved restlessly through the streets. I was angry; angry at Father, angry at myself, even angry at God. I shook my fist at the heavens and shouted, "God, leave me alone."

I was shocked by my own defiant words. But I had said them. I couldn't call them back. I felt cold inside. I still had a deep sense of guilt, but no longer did my conscience whisper to me like it had.

Next morning, with new resolve, I started back to Sidom. I would become as great a speaker as my father, I promised myself.

In Sidom we threw ourselves into the work: street meetings, word-of-mouth campaigns, debates with local teachers and priests. Nehor's plans were carried out to the letter. Synagogues became objects of abuse. Meetings were disrupted. People were beaten on their way to church. I never had to beat on anybody. There were plenty of men around who enjoyed such things.

Nehor had returned from the land of Nephi, and had set up headquarters in Ammonihah. I traveled there to report our progress. Amlici was with Nehor when I entered their chamber. I looked at him pointedly. I had never liked the man whom Nehor had appointed second-in-command. He stood there now, a sneer on his face. His face was a study of contrasts. Balding head, with a frizz of hair around his ears accentuated his high wrinkled forehead. His hawk nose dominated his arrow-shaped face, along with down-turned mouth. I had never seen the man smile. His deep-set dark blue eyes were unreadable.

Nehor saw my look and smiled. "You know Amlici?"

I nodded. I had met him at one of Nehor's meetings.

"Amlici was a warrior. He knows the fine art of fighting. He will be the leader in our task of suppressing the people."

As Nehor stepped forward and embraced me, he asked of my father.

I looked at him with surprise. "I know not of him. I haven't seen him."

Nehor smiled, but his eyes remained cold. "That is just as well. By now he has undoubtedly received reports of our activities."

"Let's get on with his report," Amlici cried.

I saw Nehor's warning glance. It would not do to offend Amlici at this point.

Nehor sat on a bench, his hands folded in his lap, appraising me with his cold eyes.

"Tell us your report," he said. "What is happening in Sidom?"

I told Nehor of our meetings, of torchlight parades through the city, of creating a huge statue of Zimpoc on the outskirts of the city where people came by hundreds to hear us preach of this new God.

He nodded excitedly during my report, then rubbed his hands together gleefully.

"It is happening," he said to Amlici. "Not only in Sidom, but in Melek, in Ammonihah, in the land of Nephi. Soon we will also challenge the church of God in Gideon and Zarahemla. Then...."

He left the thought unspoken. I finished it in my mind. Then we will have overcome all that my father had fought and taught for all his life.

Nehor's eyes bored into mine. "What of your friends, the sons of the king?"

"They are loyal to you," I said. "Without them we could not have accomplished what we have done in Sidom."

"Even Aaron?"

"He is with us, even though he might sometimes have doubts."

"We cannot afford doubts. Does he communicate with his father, Mosiah?"

I shook my head. "No. No one has communicated with anyone in Zarahemla. We have been too busy establishing Zimpoc's church in Sidom." I thought of Aaron, how alike we were, and with many similar problems.

Nehor interrupted my reverie. "These are perilous times for the land of Zarahemla. It is essential that we give Mosiah no provocation."

"He gets no word from us."

"I feel Alma, the high priest, is much more dangerous to our cause than Mosiah," Amlici said.

I felt my face burning, yet I dared say nothing in my father's defense. I calmed my feelings and asked, "Why do you say that?"

"Mosiah is too far removed from the people." Nehor interjected. They look to him for big decisions, but the real leader of the people is your father. It is Alma whom we must sooner or later deal with."

Amlici laughed without mirth. "Give him enough rope and he will hang himself."

I saw nothing funny about the situation.

As I journeyed back to Sidom, I was troubled. I allowed my mind to drift. Nehor knew my father better than anyone else in Zarahemla, other than myself. As an orphan, Nehor had spent as much time in our home and tent as he had with his Aunt Lea. He knew father's inner strength and determination.

Though I had broken from my father, I wanted no physical harm to come to him. Amlici was a hatchet man. He could be very dangerous. If it came to danger to Father, I would warn him.

The River Sidon was high, forcing me to swim. I was glad that I had learned to swim as a lad. The river was empty, except for the decomposed body of a tapir, bobbing on its back, four legs stiffened and upthrust. Sidom's walls extended almost to the river's banks. I slipped inside the city and searched out the sons of Mosiah.

* * *

Rainy season returned. I moved to Zarahemla, attempting to organize our church among Mulek's descendants. It was while preaching to them that word of my mother's death came to me. I sat down heavily. Several years had passed since I had taken time to see her. That neglect now weighed on my soul. Another sin. I thought of her sweetness, her bandaging of cuts when I hurt myself, her compassion for every living thing. I knew that she really loved me, and I had hurt her.

At the burial I stood with my sister, Netta. The funeral was a large one. I missed seeing Zoram, but he was off somewhere fighting Lamanites. Leesa did not make it from Melek in time. My attention was brought back to mother's grave—a cold empty hole in the ground. With experienced hands an attendant slowly lowered the blanket-wrapped body into the damp earth.

I watched my father, standing there so self-righteous. Who did he think he was? That was my mother in that hole in the ground. My feelings were so bitter I could not even cry. I clenched my fists as I listened to his empty words. Words like "resurrection," "spirit world," "eternal life," had no meaning to me. Father spoke of the coming of a God named Jesus Christ to earth to redeem all mankind from their sins. I shook my head. How could anyone take from me my sins?

A slight cough made me turn. Netta was frowning as she looked into my eyes—eyes devoid of tears and filled with anger. I shook my head and turned from her, jaw raised in defiance as I looked out over the crowd. Disconsolate feeling weighed upon my soul. I was lost. I didn't belong here.

While the grave was being covered, Father came to me and tried to put his arm around me to console me. I looked at him angrily and turned on my heel. I left the cemetery, hoping that I would never see him again.

* * *

I continued preaching in Zarahemla. Ammon and his brothers were always with me. Amongst the Nephites we had no success. They were too involved with the church of God, and Zarahemla was too close to the palace for disruptive tactics. Our reception by the Zarahemlaites was better. Undercurrents of contention had always existed between the Nephites and the original settlers of Zarahemla. Many Zarahemlaites felt they were discriminated against by the ruling Nephites. We played on those feelings, building a core of believers.

I knew Zarahemla well, having spent my youth from fifteen there. For Ammon, it was his home from birth. We used alleyways and back streets, avoiding palace guards and warrior patrols. Ammon and I had favorite places where girls and wine were plentiful. After all, I excused myself, one has to relax after so much time teaching and preaching to people. I tried to rationalize that no longer did I have a conscience to bother me with feelings of guilt. I was a free man, free from constraints, free from conscience, free from poverty. More converts joined our movement; church coffers filled rapidly. Nehor had been right, we were becoming rich.

Nehor visited us in Zarahemla. His hair and beard were longer than ever; his eyes were hard and wild. He waved a rolled piece of bark paper before us.

"Have you seen this," he growled.

We shook our heads. I was curious as to what Nehor had brought.

"It has been brought to our attention," he mimicked, "that certain people are persecuting members of the church of God. Our king, the great Mosiah, has issued a proclamation that this will cease. The proclamation is to be read in all cities throughout the land."

He waved the proclamation above his head. "Read it Alma."

I looked at Ammon, then at the roll of bark paper. I read.

"BE IT HEREBY KNOWN THAT NO ONE IN THIS LAND SHALL PERSECUTE ANOTHER FOR HIS BELIEFS. THE LAWS OF MY FATHER, BENJAMIN, CLEARLY STATE THAT THE PEOPLE OF THIS LAND SHALL HAVE FREEDOM TO CHOOSE THEIR OWN BELIEFS, AS LONG AS THOSE BELIEFS DO NOT INTERFERE WITH THE BELIEFS OF ANOTHER.

"NO PERSON SHALL DENY THE RIGHT OF SOMEONE TO BELONG TO ANOTHER CHURCH. THERE SHALL BE AN EQUALITY AMONG ALL MEN. LET NO PRIDE NOR HAUGHTINESS DISTURB THE PEACE OF THIS LAND. LET EVERY PERSON ESTEEM HIS NEIGHBOR AS HIMSELF. LET EVERY MAN LABOR WITH HIS OWN HANDS FOR HIS SUPPORT, INCLUDING ALL PRIESTS AND TEACHERS."

I could feel sweat running in rivulets down my spine. My shirt chafed my skin and I felt a strong urge to scratch but I stood motionless. Again I glanced at Ammon to see his reaction to the proclamation. He shrugged, his gaze fixed on my own eyes.

I handed the proclamation back to Nehor.

His eyes gleamed with hate. "Our movement has finally got the king's attention," he said.

"What will we do?" I asked.

He turned slowly to me. "We will continue our plans. Zimpoc will soon be the god of this entire land." He smiled evilly as he tore the proclamation to shreds. "This paper has given us freedom to act."

"But what of the guards and the warrior army?"

"As I have said before," said Nehor, "the Nephite army cannot be everywhere at once. We will preach for Zimpoc until the control of government is in our hands. Until then, stay out of reach of the army."

Ammon finally spoke. "The proclamation of my father—you say it gives us more freedom to subvert the government it tries to protect?"

Nehor gave a hard smile. "And more. It guarantees freedom of religion. It gives us permission to exist and to continue undercutting Alma's church."

"But what of our persecution of the people?"

Nehor's hands formed a deliberate steeple. "We just don't get caught." He looked piercingly at Ammon. "Your brothers. Are they still with us?"

Ammon stood and paced to the other end of the room, then turned, facing Nehor. "My brothers are loyal to the cause. You will not find us shirking our responsibilities."

Responsibilities, I thought to myself. That's a word Father had often used. I tried to put the thought from my mind. Why is it that I still have doubts? I had occasionally heard Father's preaching, but I paid little attention. He had his life to live; I had mine. I loved speaking to the people. The endless scribe training I had been subjected to as a youth was now paying off. I could use words to influence and persuade. I learned to use flattery to sway the people to my way of thinking. I remember Ammon once saying that I was a "man of many words."

Chapter 6

Angel of God

Slap!

I no longer felt the pain of the blows. My mind reeled, seemingly disconnected from the limp body held up by hemp rope. For several days I had been locked up in this hut, many hours of which I had been tied to the post.

Flickering torches lighted faces of the men in the room. I knew many of them—men who until just recently had been my followers. I now saw them for what they really were: men anxious for personal riches who had rebelled against the Church and now persecuted its members for profit. Nehor, himself, once closest friend and now high priest of Zimpoc, stood before me. It was he who slapped me.

Nehor was a brawny man, heavy through shoulders and chest. His blonde hair was pulled back from his face in a single braid. Piercing blue eyes peered intently, almost madly, through his reddish-blond beard.

"I'm sorry to do that," he was saying, "but you need to come to your senses. You and I can still rule all of Zarahemla." He smiled broadly so his full set of white teeth showed through his beard. "Zimpoc will yet be the god of all the land of Zarahemla."

I closed my eyes, trying to shut out Nehor's words, but I could no more escape his words than I could escape this hut in which I was imprisoned. In the time I had been held captive I had meticulously gone over every inch of my jail. The room had solid, two foot thick, mud walls with no windows. The roof was held up by heavy mahogany timbers. The only creatures which seemed to have no trouble escaping in and out were the hordes of fleas and lice which now infested my naked body. My skin was raw from scratching.

Nehor's voice droned on. "We are rich. We dress in the finest clothes, live in the finest houses." He paused. "Don't throw all that away just because you claim to have seen a so-called angel."

Angel. Nehor's words triggered thought in my tired mind. Dwell on angel. Shut Nehor out. My mind drifted back in time to when the angel appeared to me.

* * *

The day had been beautiful. White, fleecy clouds flowed eastward through azure sky. I had never felt so alive, so strong, so capable. Ammon, Aaron, Omner, Himni and I were traveling from Sidom to Gideon. We had experienced great success in Sidom: huge crowds worshipping their "new" god, Zimpoc.

Nehor had remained in Sidom to strengthen our "church" while we went to Gideon to start anew our pattern of conversion. We laughed, joked and planned our prosperous future as we walked. Soon every city would be in our hands. No one, not even our fathers, could stand against us.

The only two cities where we had little influence were Gideon and Zarahemla. We were confident these, too, would soon come to our way of thinking. Some "persuasion" might be needed among some of the members of the church of God, but we had many men who could do that.

Several hours distant, the ridge we would have to cross was clearly silhouetted, the sun's bright burnished paten resting on its summit. To the west the sun's level distinct rays probed at a wooded ridge and blue–purple flanks of distant mountains behind it. Near at hand, every flower–clotted gully, every scented stand of fern and sapodilla filled me with delight. A breeze from behind us carried the delicate scents of anise and marjoram. What a great day to be alive!

The earth shook beneath our feet, interrupting our laughter. I suspected another earthquake.

"Zimpoc is shaking the earth again," Omner quipped.

As Omner spoke, the earth shook even harder, then a cloud blotted out sun and sky. Air was stifling, hard to breath. We couldn't see. We were suddenly frightened. This was no ordinary earthquake.

A burning light shone through the blackness, blinding at first. I covered my eyes with my hand, then as I looked again I made out a man–like figure in the midst of the light, standing in the air. A thunderous voice came from the apparition, loud, rumbling, and unintelligible. I pressed the flat of my hand to my temple. Could this be real?

The angel, for now I believed him to be such, spoke directly to me. I finally understood the words.

"Alma,...."

I fell to my knees and covered my eyes with my hands. My head hurt and I could not stand to look upon the shining person. He spoke again.

"Alma, arise and stand forth."

Holding to a tree for support, I arose shakily to my feet. No longer was I aware of anything except the shining being before me.

"Behold, your father has prayed with much faith concerning you, desiring above all else that you might be brought to a knowledge of the truth. The Lord has heard his prayers, and the prayers of his people. I have come to convince you of God's power and authority, that those prayers might be answered according to their faith.

"Alma, unless you want to be destroyed, seek no more to destroy the church of God. Remember the captivity of your fathers in the lands of Helam and Nephi, and remember what great things God has done for them, for they were in bondage and He delivered them.

"Alma, again I say to you, go your way and seek to destroy the church no more that the prayers of your father and his people may be answered. Do this, even if you will of yourself be cast off."

The angel continued talking, his voice rumbling and shaking the earth beneath me. I felt dizzy and then must have fallen unconscious. I heard no more.

* * *

Slap! Slap!

My mind returned to the present with the dull pain of the blows. Nehor stood before me, his cold eyes filled with malice. Warm blood, salty tasting, ran from my nose across my lips, dripping to my bare chest.

"Pay attention to what I say." Nehor licked his lips. "Either you are one of us," he paused for emphasis, "or you are no more. Which will it be?"

I managed to smile through my cracked lips. "Nehor," I rasped, "nothing you can do to me will even come close to the pain and torment I have already felt. I have literally endured the pains of hell. Can your punishment match that?"

Nehor looked at me with loathing, then turned away to the others. "It is no use. He is no longer one of us."

I hardly heard him. My thoughts still focused on that marvelous experience with the angel.

* * *

After losing consciousness when the angel spoke to me, I felt almost as if I were dreaming. I remembered the angel's declaration to me before I had lapsed into unconsciousness. Though I was unaware of what was happening around me, my mind was alert. I kept hearing the angel's words. My soul was harrowed with terrible nightmares. I dreamed of being cast into a burning pit which I thought was hell. The burning seared my skin. I had never felt such pain.

Then in my dream another being spoke to me and told me I was to appear before God. The thought of me, a sinner, standing before God filled me with horror. A sinner such as I? In my dream I saw myself praying that I might not be brought before God. It would be better to be banished, both soul and body, than to stand in the presence of God and be judged.

As my sins burned me as if with hot coals, I felt I could endure the pain no longer. At that moment I thought of my father's teachings when I was but a child. He talked often of a Jesus Christ—the Son of God—who would come to the earth and take upon himself the sins of the world. Again at the funeral of my mother, when I pretended I wasn't paying attention, he talked of this same Jesus Christ.

I cried out in my dream, "Oh, Jesus, thou Son of God, have mercy on me, who am in the gall of bitterness, and am encircled about by everlasting chains of death."

Suddenly, miraculously, the pains left me. No longer was I tormented. In my unconscious state I stood and looked around with great relief. Everything radiated and pulsed with brilliant light. My soul was filled with joy. Whereas, before, I had been dwelling on my sins, now I could remember my sins no more.

I looked more closely into the radiating light and saw God sitting on His throne, surrounded by great concourses of angels singing praises to Him. I felt myself yearning to be there with them, praising God with all my heart. The sounds of heavenly choirs softened until all I could hear was the drone of many voices.

I opened my eyes. No longer was there a dream. I didn't know how long I had been unconscious, but now I lay on a pallet in the church—I recognized it as the church in Zarahemla. My father, on his knees beside me, prayed. Tears dripped into his graying beard. Surrounding me were others whom I recognized as priests of the Church; priests that I had been fighting against just a short time before.

One cried, "He awakens!"

Father looked at me, his eyes luminous. He put a hand under me, helping me sit up. I smiled and winked at him, the first time in many years. He blinked back tears, then winked back, a smile breaking his face.

I felt very weak but I needed to stand. I struggled to my feet, helped by several priests. Father, looking frail and old, stood beside me, his arm around my waist.

I spoke, "Brethren, be of comfort." I looked around at them. Doubt showed on many faces. I couldn't blame them for distrusting me. "I thank you for your prayers in my behalf." I turned to Father, resting my hand on his shoulder. "Not only the prayers you offer now for me, but also the prayers offered over the years by you and your people that I might return to the truth.

"I have repented of my sins and have been redeemed of the Lord!" I breathed deeply, attempting to control my emotion. "The Lord, in his mercy, has given me another chance. After much tribulation, even through repenting almost unto death, the Lord has snatched me out of the everlasting burning which I had earned through my sins. And now, I am born of God."

I was weak and leaned heavily on Father's shoulder for support. Standing close to him, I continued. "The Lord told me, *Marvel not that all mankind must be born again; changed from their fallen state to a state of righteousness, being redeemed of God, becoming His sons and daughters. Thus they become new creatures. And unless they do this, they can in nowise inherit the kingdom of God.*

"Brethren, I testify to you that unless a person is born anew, he must be cast off." I looked around, then added softly. "I know, because I was about to be cast off." I looked at Father. "However, I have been redeemed from the gall of bitterness and the bonds of iniquity. I was in the darkest abyss, but now have beheld the marvelous light of God. My soul was racked with eternal torment, but now my soul is pained no more.

"I had rejected my Redeemer and denied that which had been taught me by my father." I felt his squeeze as he pulled me tighter to him. "Now I know the Lord remembers every creature He has created and manifests himself unto all."

I paused as I tried to find the right words to express my deep feelings. "I now know that all men shall stand before God to be judged at the last day. At that time every knee shall bow and every tongue confess. All those who deny God will confess that the judgment of an everlasting punishment is upon them. They shall quake, tremble, and shrink beneath the glance of His all-searching eye."

Father sniffed as tears ran down his cheeks. I gently wiped them with my fingers. The spirit was so strong, many priests quietly cried.

* * *

My attention was drawn back to my present predicament. Nehor and his priests conferenced in one corner of the room, apparently deciding what to do with me. Nehor was a violent man and I sincerely believed he would kill me. Even as a child he hated opposition. His work in persecuting the Church also proved that. I was ready to meet my God.

And yet, words of my father came to me, words he spoke during our captivity in Helam. At that time I brushed them aside as being trite. Now I could almost hear Father saying them: "Where there is life, there is hope." And I did have hope.

For over a year, ever since my conversion, I and the sons of Mosiah had been teaching hope. Wasn't it hope which helped people change their lives? Wasn't it hope that gave them faith in a God they couldn't see? Wasn't it hope which opened up the communication channels with that God? As missionaries attempting to undo the evils which we had earlier committed, we had constantly taught hope, faith, and repentance.

As I stood before Nehor and his cronies, my thoughts turned to my friend, Ammon, and the other sons of Mosiah. I wondered where they were and if they were having success. I prayed they had not been taken prisoner as I had.

Amlici and Zarahemnah, the men who captured me while I was preaching in Sidom, walked up and stood before me. A descendant of Zarahemla, Amlici was now one of Nehor's priests. He grabbed me by the hair, raised my head, and spit in my face. Zarahemnah laughed at my discomfiture. Anger welled within me, then I relaxed. Father's example during our captivity in Helam came to mind. I would not let myself use Nehor's tactics. If the Lord desired me to be free, He would provide the way. Amlici drew back his knee and brought it up sharply into my groin. The pain was intense. If I had not been tied to the post I would have doubled up in agony. As it was, the sweet peace of unconsciousness once more engulfed me.

* * *

A spattering on my face. My eyes opened to the rain, then closed. My groin throbbed and my head ached. When I tried to move, pain shot through me. I was lying in water. Pushing with my heels I raised my head higher. Somehow my head had stayed out of the water or I would have drowned. I tried to think, to bring back what happened. Nehor, and Amlici.

While unconscious, I must have been dumped in the swamp to die. But I was alive. The Lord protected me. I mentally braced myself for the effort, then rolled over. Pain from my head stabbed through me, but now I was able to get my hands under me. Reaching out I grasped a tuft of marsh grass. Handhold by handhold I dragged myself through the dark, brackish water. Green scum joined by putrescent leaves and bulbous water lilies, parted before my slow, painful crawling.

Finally I was on semi-solid ground. My head felt heavy and I had to stop. I passed out, awakened, and crawled again. At a low-branched tree I tugged myself up until I was in a sitting position. Soft raindrops still fell on my face. I was weak and wet but alive. A breeze blowing across my wet body exacerbated my shivering.

During brief moments of consciousness, I thought of Father. I smiled. This was one episode I wouldn't write to Father about. Each week since starting our missionary work in the land of Zarahemla I had faithfully written. My letters told of our activities, even some of my sermons.

What I hadn't told Father were the troubles we had encountered. Nor had I told him of Nehor and his priests and their fight against our words.

Each week I waited anxiously for Father's letters. Never had I felt closer to him; I was glad to have a father once again.

In one letter Father asked: "Is Nehor still preaching dissension? Has he not changed his ways to follow the teachings of God?"

I wrote back: "You ask about Nehor. It is sad for me that he still leads the opposition to our message. He has continued teaching of Zimpoc, the snake god, but like myself a few, short months ago, I am convinced he is more interested in senines for Nehor than converts for Zimpoc." Now I could add a postscript to my letter about Nehor.

I had written, "We are exhorting the people to keep God's commandments. As we preach in each city we confess the sins we have committed against God and the people. Then we tell them of the angel who visited us to tell us of the one true God. We finish our sermon by declaring that the Lord reigns and it is He whom they should worship."

* * *

I must have slept. Flies landing on my bruised body and the sun's heat on my face awakened me. The rainstorm had passed, and now I felt stronger. A breeze was still blowing. It carried to me the scent of decaying vegetable matter. I also smelled smoke—as if from a campfire. A movement caught my eye. A gray lizard, yellow-gray tail raised high, walked gingerly before me. Sensing my presence, it darted into a cave of damp leaves, its tail still obvious.

I started to push myself away from the tree where I was resting. I must find Ammon and his brothers, I thought. They will be concerned about me. But even as I thought it my eyes closed again in sleep.

I was awakened by voices. They seemed far away. Day had become night while I slept. Through tree branches overhead stars dotted the black expanse above me. The voices seemed to move away, then came back again.

"I tell you, I have a feeling he is close by." With a start I recognized Ammon's voice.

"But why would he be here, outside of the city?" That was Aaron.

"I don't know, but I still have a feeling." Ammon again.

I opened my mouth to cry out, but no words came. Again I tried.

"Ammon." Even to myself my voice sounded weak and disembodied. No one could hear me. They were still talking.

"Ammon!" stronger now.

"Alma! Alma, is that you?"

"Over here," I called.

Brush crackled beside me. A white face materialized out of the blackness.

"Alma, is it really you?"

"How did you find me?" I asked weakly.

"I'm sure the Lord led us here, but that's a long story. Let's take care of you first. Aaron, Himni," he shouted. "Over here."

In what seemed but a few moments, fire crackled in an opening between trees. A squash, opened and steaming, sat on hot rocks. Omner spitted a monkey and soon the smell of roasting meat filled my nostrils. While dinner cooked, I told my friends of what had transpired; how Amlici and Zarahemnah had lured me into meeting with them then overpowered me and put me in the mud shack. I also told them of Nehor's arrival and his words to me.

After a filling meal and a good night's sleep my strength quickly returned. We returned to Sidom to teach the people. Within a short period of time I had fully recovered from my experience. I put it out of my mind and concentrated on preaching the word. Days sped by as we preached to the inhabitants of Sidom and Melek.

Two years quickly passed. Through our missionary work we had done all we could to undo our wrongs. Now it was up to the Lord and my father's priests and teachers. With Ammon and his brothers, I returned to Zarahemla. Father was overjoyed to see me.

Chapter 7

Missionaries

The babble in the throne room was intense. King Mosiah, chin in hand, watched and listened, a look of amazement on his face. Aaron, his face red from the exertion, plead with him with little success. I looked around the room. Ammon, Omner , and Himni stood behind Aaron, giving him moral support. Ringing them were several friends: Muloki, Ammah, and others whose names I did not know.

Aaron gestured helplessly, "Father, you must understand. This isn't something we are casually thinking about. This is what we feel we have to do. Please?"

"But why?" roared Mosiah. "The kingship is yours. I am getting old and want one of you to take the responsibilities. Think of me."

A commotion at the door drew my attention. Father and my sister, Netta, came into the room. Father winked at me and smiled. He looked so happy. I don't think he has frowned since my conversion.

He walked up and stood, head-bowed, before Mosiah. "You sent for me. What is it, my king?"

"It is these sons, that's what it is," sputtered Mosiah. "I can't talk any sense into them. I have asked that they stay in Zarahemla and help me govern the kingdom, but all they can talk about is missionary work. And now it is to the Lamanites!"

"What do you want me to do?" Alma asked.

"Talk some sense into them," Mosiah said.

Father turned to Aaron. "Tell me your desires," he said.

It was Ammon who replied, "Father Alma, for the past two years we have felt the joy of missionary work. By teaching people in the land of Zarahemla about the true God, we feel we have paid for our wicked acts and our sinfulness. We would like to leave the rest of the teaching to the priests whom you have appointed."

Father nodded. "Go on."

"We have asked our father," Ammon nodded towards the frowning Mosiah, "to grant permission for us to go to the land of Nephi so we can preach about God to our brothers, the Lamanites."

Father looked at Mosiah, who frowned back.

Ammon was still talking, "We desire to bring the Lamanites to knowledge of the Lord. Perhaps we can cure them of their hatred towards the Nephites."

Omner added, "Through teaching them about God, perhaps we can help avoid further fighting and contention."

Aaron again spoke, "We are desirous that salvation should be preached to every creature. We cannot bear to think that any human soul should perish." He blinked back tears as he continued. "Even the thought of people having to undergo endless torment brings us great sorrow."

"So," Ammon concluded, "we have asked Father's permission to go to the Lamanites and teach them. So far, we have gotten nowhere."

Father asked, "What can I do?"

Mosiah leaned forward. "I want you to pray and see if God will tell us what to do. You are the high priest and this is a religious matter."

Father nodded. "I will inquire of the Lord." He motioned to Netta, glanced again at me, then the two of them left the room.

We busied ourselves with small talk while waiting for Father's return. More than an hour passed. Sun had set; lamps in the throne room cast flickering shadows on walls and threw a pall of smoke towards the ceiling. The crowd hushed as Father and Netta walked back into the room. Head high, Father walked directly to Mosiah's throne. Despite his years he stood there straight and tall, without bowing.

"The Lord has spoken," he said.

Heads craned. Every eye watched Father.

"Well, what did he say?" Mosiah asked.

"The Lord said, *Let them go up, for many shall believe on their words, and they shall have eternal life; and I will deliver your sons out of the hands of the Lamanites.*"

Mosiah slumped in his seat, his head in his hands. An excited chatter erupted in the room as everyone seemed to be talking at once.

I watched Mosiah. Eyes closed, he nodded, looking suddenly old and tired.

"Yes, I must admit God said the same to me." His shoulders sagged. "I hoped I was mistaken, but if it is to be, it is to be."

He abruptly faced his sons, "When do you plan to leave?"

"As quickly as possible," Aaron said.

"What of the kingdom? I am an old man. Who of you would be king?"

All four sons answered, almost in chorus, "Not I."

I stepped to where Father stood. "Father, my heart burns within me. I desire also to go to the land of Nephi."

Father put his arms around my shoulders, drawing me to him.

"My son," he said, "I am already past the age when most people die. My eyes are dim and my hands are shaky. I can no longer keep the records of this people. The Lord has told me that you are to remain and be my hands and eyes."

I bowed my head. Not being able to go with my friends was difficult for me to accept. Perhaps in the land of Nephi I could find some trace of Ruth and partially fulfill the promise made so many years before.

I put the thought from me. "What would you like me to do?" I answered, but my heart really wasn't in my question.

"Since Nephi's time someone has been appointed to keep our history. Writing of God's dealings with us is important, so future generations may learn from our experience. God wants you to be His scribe. I also am selfish. I want you to remain with me."

"Whatever you wish, Father."

Ammon and his group of missionaries took several days preparing for their journey. It was also a time of preparation for me. I moved my things into a spare room at Father's house so I could learn record-keeping from him. Living in Father's home would also permit me to be ready in case something happened to him.

The evening came when the missionaries were to depart. My heart was saddened as I looked at them. I wanted to go with them so badly. Hundreds had come to see them off. Some probably came just out of curiosity. Others felt the zeal of Ammon and those who would go with him. The crowd met in the square before the Zarahemla temple—the church where I regained consciousness after my experience with the angel. Torches flickered around the square. People talked and cheered. A general spirit of revelry filled the air, but I didn't feel it. I looked at Mosiah. He also seemed morose and sad.

Father stood on the steps of the temple. Before him were the missionaries: Ammon, Aaron, Omner, Himni, Muloki, Ammah, Abram, and several others. Heads bowed as Father moved from one to the other, laying his hands on them and blessing them.

I dipped my brush in paint and wrote, "It has been over five hundred years since father Lehi left the land of Jerusalem. Today the sons of Mosiah leave for their mission to the Lamanites."

* * *

I looked at the calendar stone before me. An entire year had passed since Ammon and his brothers departed for the land of Nephi. King Mosiah had conferred upon me all of the records and commanded me that I should keep and preserve them. That, in addition to the responsibility of keeping a current record of all that happened, kept me so busy that time had flown. I laughed to myself. I was getting almost as dedicated to record-keeping as Father.

A commotion in the square disturbed my thoughts. I put down my brush and walked to the door, thankful for an opportunity to stretch my cramped legs. Coming out of the relative dimness of the church into the bright sunlight of the square momentarily blinded me.

Someone shouted, "Alma."

I didn't recognize the voice but as he came nearer, I recognized Abram, one of Muloki's friends who had gone to the land of Nephi with the missionaries. Accompanying him was a woman, tall, slender, dark-hair tinged with gray. She looked familiar to me. Her eyes were large and expressive, her skin white and creamy-looking, as if she had spent little time in the sun. She reminded me of someone, but whom?

Abram shouted, "I have a letter from Ammon." He motioned to the woman, "And a present for you."

The woman looked at the ground, obviously embarrassed. She was beautiful. I was intrigued.

"What present?" I queried.

"Aaron told me to bring Ruth to you...."

Ruth? My mouth dropped. I didn't let him finish the sentence. "Did you say Ruth?"

"Yes, Aaron said you would know what to do."

I stepped quickly to the woman's side, tilting her chin up with my hand. "Ruth, is it really you?"

She nodded mutely, tears welling in her dark eyes.

More than twenty years had passed since Ruth was sent captive to the land of Nephi. She had been but a girl and now she was a woman. During all of those years I had never stopped dreaming about her and my unfulfilled vow to somehow rescue her—and here she was before me.

Taking her hand, I led her through the door of the church, Abram forgotten. We had much to talk about.

"Mother and father?" she asked.

"Both dead," I said as I held her hand. "Your father died at the hands of the Lamanites, and your mother from the fevers. I'm sorry."

She murmured, "It is what I expected."

"And you? Tell me what has happened to you." I couldn't take my eyes off her. She was more beautiful than any woman I had ever seen.

She shrugged. "The Lamanites took us to the city of Nephi and made us priestesses in their temple."

"And that's all?"

"For twenty years we have performed their temple ceremonies for them. Because we were priestesses none were allowed to molest us."

I breathed more easily.

"Each day we lighted the lamps, cleaned the temple, and conducted ceremonies for the Lamanites. Amulon's priests were in charge, and...."

I impatiently interrupted her. "No one bothered you, or...."

Ruth smiled for the first time since I had seen her. "No, the priests protected us."

I grasped both her hands in mine. "Ruth, for more than twenty years I have longed for you. As children we talked of marriage and family. I never married because of my vow to you. Will you be my wife?"

She tried to hold back her tears, but they came anyway. I put my arms around her, feeling her shake. Her soft, sweet-smelling hair blanketed my face.

"Will you still have me?"

"Oh, yes," she responded, holding tightly to me.

I walked her from the temple to Father's home. Netta was there and soon they were happily visiting.

I left her for a moment and hurried to the palace library to see Father. I burst in on his reverie.

"Father," I cried. "Remember Ruth, the daughter of Helam, who was taken by the Lamanites?"

"Yes, I remember." He leaned back against the wall, his eyes looking out blankly as memories of his best friend engulfed him. "Her kidnapping led directly to Helam's death," he said quietly.

I nodded and tried to change the subject.

"Aaron and his brothers have been very successful converting the Lamanites. They also found Ruth and have sent her home along with letters for you and Mosiah."

"Ruth here? Letters?"

I helped Father to his feet. Together we went down the long hall to the throne room. King Mosiah sat there, several scrolls on his lap. He looked up as we approached.

"They are all safe and well," he said, his voice husky.

"Just as the Lord promised," Father said.

"Yes, just as the Lord promised. Alma, Aaron sends you greetings. He reports they have many converts including one of the Lamanite kings."

Father shook his head in wonder. "Even a king," he said. He looked at Mosiah. "Alma tells me that Ruth...."

Mosiah impatiently interrupted him. "Yes, they sent Ruth and all the Nephite women home with Abram and a Lamanite escort. The women have served for all these years in the temples in the land of Nephi. I sent them to their homes for reunion with their families."

"All but Ruth," I added softly. "She no longer has a family except for me."

Father nodded sadly, "Oh, that Helam and Annah were alive to see their daughter again."

"Father," I said. "Ruth has consented to be my wife."

Without a word Father turned and buried his face in my neck. I could feel his tears on my bare shoulder.

I was anxious to read Aaron's and Ammon's letters, but they would have to wait. Finally, Father regained his composure.

"When will be the wedding?"

"As soon as possible. But we have waited twenty years, I suppose a few more days won't matter."

Father celebrated his seventy-sixth birthday by marrying Ruth and me. The wedding was a state affair. The huge church of Zarahemla was gaily festooned. Garlands of flowers and ropes of blossoms hung in every likely place.

Ruth became involved with the most minute details of the wedding preparations. She spent hours fussing over her clothes, agonizing over her hair, even becoming involved in the kitchens in preparations for the wedding feast. She seemed to be attempting to exhaust herself in a sea of activity, alternating activity with fits of extreme shyness when she retired to her room and would see no one, not even me.

Father's house of stone was large enough that we decided to make our home there with him and Netta. Servants labored endlessly to clean the house and have it ready. A steady stream of priests from outlying cities came to pay their respects.

The morning of the wedding day began with a sky the color of a dove's breast, cleansed by a soft whisper of rain. I had spent most of the previous day on my knees in the church, praying for worthiness. The church was filled with people as Father performed the simple ceremony uniting Ruth and me as husband and wife. Ruth was dressed in a simple gown of white linen. Clasps of gold gathered the gown at her breast and shoulders, and her glossy, black hair was entwined with flowers.

Looking at her, I saw the most fragile of my dreams now becoming reality.

As evening spread its long shadows across the city, Ruth became very quiet. I helped her say good-bye to the guests. Our bridal chamber was ablaze with candles, the new linen sheets scented with sweet herbs. It was our night, and ours alone.

* * * * *

Father seemed happy to finally get me married. At the time I didn't realize that part of his happiness was that he didn't want to make me high priest over the Church until I was married and "settled down." I learned soon enough.

Barely a week passed before Father called me to his room.

"My son," he said. "I am old and am no longer able to carry forth the duties of high priest over the Church. I desire to confer those responsibilities upon you."

I was greatly surprised. "Me? But father, what of Zoram? He is the eldest. Or what of your other faithful priests of the Church?"

"Zoram is busy off somewhere protecting our borders against the Lamanites. The other priests, faithful as they may be, have not the leadership you possess."

"But father, I am unworthy. People will remember my rebellion against the Church." I shook my head. "No, father, it would be better for you to choose another."

Father reached out, his bony hand on my shoulder. "My son, it is not I who calls you to this position. It is the Lord."

It was enough. The next week I sat in the church of Zarahemla, my father's hands upon my head as he conferred the responsibility and authority of the position of high priest of the Church upon me. I silently vowed that I would never shirk my duties; I would never let down in fulfilling the trust of my father and the Lord.

Chapter 8

Letter from Ammon

I am now in the land of Ishmael, Ammon wrote.

He told of carrying weapons on their journey "that we might provide food for ourselves while in the wilderness." He wrote how as they journeyed they fasted and prayed that the Lord would grant them His spirit, that they might be instruments in His hands in bringing the Lamanites to a knowledge of the truth.

The Lord spoke to them: *Be comforted. Go forth among the Lamanites and establish My word. Be patient in long-suffering and afflictions, that you may be examples unto them. I will make you instruments in my hands unto the salvation of many souls.*

When they arrived at the Lamanite border Ammon blessed his brothers and fellow missionaries. Then they separated, going to the various Lamanite cities.

As Ammon followed the well-marked trail leading to the land of Ishamel, the hairs on the back of his neck rose. He knew he was being watched. He kept his sword sheathed and his bow across his back, hoping that whoever was watching would know he came in peace. As he walked, he silently prayed. Father, I desire to serve Thee. Protect me with Thy love so I may do so.

He rounded a bend and stopped. Four Lamanites blocked the trail, their arrows pointed at his chest. He raised his hands above his head, palms to the Lamanites, in a gesture of peace. They approached him warily, roughly stripped his bow from his back and his sword from his side.

"Why do you come to Lamanite country?" one asked gruffly.

"I come in peace. I desire to be a teacher to your people," he replied.

"Teach what?" the same man questioned.

"Teach them to read and understand the writings of their fathers," Ammon replied.

"Hah," the Lamanite scoffed. "Nephites cannot be trusted. They have already stolen our heritage." He motioned to the others. "Bind him. We will take him to King Lamoni. He will know what to do with him."

Ammon meekly stood while his arms were trussed tightly to his sides. His legs were left free so he could walk, but a long lead rope was fastened securely around his neck with the other end in the hands of the Lamanite leader. They tugged him forward, and Ammon stumbled as he attempted to keep up. He found it difficult to keep his balance without free movement of his arms.

Several hours of stumbling along well-beaten trails brought them to the city of Ishmael. His captors led him through dusty streets. Soon a rowdy mob of young Lamanites followed, casting stones and verbal jibes at him. Dodging the stones the best he could, he ignored the jibes. The mob dropped behind when Ammon and his captors entered the gates of the palace. Ammon looked around. The buildings were old, apparently built years before by Nephites who later escaped to Zarahemla. Ammon wondered if this was one of the palaces from which King Noah had ruled the people.

He didn't have much time for speculating. His guard dragged him into the Lamanite king's chambers, pushed him forward and made him prostrate himself before the throne. He looked up.

The king was a large and well-built man. Black hair hung loosely over his shoulders and down his back. His dark eyes were piercing but not unfriendly. His coppery skin shone as if rubbed with animal fat. Sitting on the throne beside him was the queen. She was lighter in color, her eyes liquid and bottomless, without expression.

The king motioned with his hand. Ammon's captors hauled him to his feet by the rope attached to his neck.

"I am Lamoni," the king said. "This is my land and my people. Why do you come to my land?"

Ammon repeated what he had told the guards. "I am Ammon. I come to be a teacher of your people."

"You mean you have left your land to dwell with us?"

"I desire to live in your land, among your people, for a time—perhaps even until the day I die."

His answer seemed to please King Lamoni. He smiled at Ammon.

"Loose his bands," he commanded the guards.

As the ropes were taken from him, Ammon rubbed his arms to restore their circulation.

"I have many daughters," the king said. "Perhaps you would take one to wife?"

Ammon bowed before him. "My king," he said, "I am unworthy to take one of your daughters to wife, but I will be your servant. Whatever you desire of me, I shall do."

This also seemed to please the king. He motioned to a servant standing by the door. "Take this Nephite to quarters by the stables. He will help tend the sheep."

Ammon was intrigued by the stables. There were no horses in the land of Zarahemla. King Limhi had spoken of horses but this was the first time he had seen them. They were magnificent animals, as tall at their shoulders as he was. He had heard that horses had been brought once to

Zarahemla but did poorly. Ground was always muddy from incessant rains, but the worst problems were the big cats. Horses were favorite meat for jaguars and cougars. It had been impossible to keep a horse. Ammon hoped to be able to learn to ride one of these fine animals of the king.

Each morning Ammon and several Lamanite servants took sheep from the king's corrals to pasture near the waters of Sebus. The other servants refused to talk with Ammon, apparently hating him because he was a Nephite. He wondered how he would be able to teach them, but he trusted the Lord to provide. After returning the sheep to the corrals in the evening, Ammon and the servants slept on pallets of hay near the king's stables.

The third day of sheep-herding started like previous days. Ammon and Lamanite servants rounded up bleating sheep, started them from corrals, and followed behind. The thirsty sheep needed little guidance but headed straight for the waters of Sebus. The Lamanite servants were talking amongst themselves, when suddenly they halted.

"Aiiii," one cried. "Sheep stealers!"

Ammon looked where the man pointed. A group of wild-looking Lamanites, apparently finished with watering their own sheep, were running towards the king's flock. Yelling loudly, they scattered the sheep in every direction. Puzzled at this, Ammon looked at the other servants.

Most were fallen on their knees lamenting their fate. Ammon heard, "Now the king will slay us."

Ammon pulled the nearest servant to his feet. "What do you mean the king will slay us?"

The man was weeping, but he cried, "Each time the flocks have been scattered before, the king slew those servants who permitted it." He gestured at the running sheep. "Our flocks are scattered and I don't want to die."

"Why do these men scatter the sheep?"

"They steal the sheep by driving them to their own lands."

Ammon tried not to show his excitement. Here was the way to get his message to the king. I will help them round up the flock, he said to himself, and by so doing they will be grateful to me and I can teach them.

Aloud, he said, "All is not lost. The sheep are thirsty and will probably not get too far from water. We'll gather the sheep and return them to the king as if nothing had happened."

Encouraged, the servants leaped to their feet and followed Ammon as he ran to head the sheep. By noon they had the flock together once again. Ammon saw those who had scattered the sheep coming again. This time he knew what to expect.

He shouted to the servants, "Circle the sheep and keep them from scattering. I will take care of the robbers."

About twenty Lamanites made up the outlaw band. Ammon ran towards them, scooping up rocks for his sling as he ran. He was thankful for the extensive warrior training he had received as a youth in Zarahemla.

Clubs in hand, the smirking Lamanites waited expectantly for him. He was only one man and they were twenty. Those are good odds, he thought. What the Lamanites don't know is that the Lord is on my side. When he was within sling range he stopped. Whirring the sling around his head, he released.

Whap!

A Lamanite, hit in the temple by a small stone, crumpled. Before others could move, a second man was hit. Then a third. Angrily the remaining robbers ran towards him. Ammon kept slinging stones, each one accounting for another Lamanite. Not one stone missed its mark. Six Lamanites lying still on the ground were evidence of his marksmanship.

When the remaining Lamanites were so close that his sling was ineffective, he dropped it into his pouch and drew his sword. Angry Lamanites came on, clubs raised high. Again he silently thanked God for his warrior training and for the strength with which the Lord had blessed him. The outlaw leader came at him with raised club. Ammon parried and thrust. The Lamanite, strong and quick, backed Ammon against a tree. Ammon danced lightly on the balls of his feet, waiting his chance. He saw his opening, stepped forward and slipped his sword between the Lamanite's ribs. The robber's expression changed from anger to surprise, then he slumped to the ground.

Ammon leapt over the body, engaging two more Lamanites. He had no desire to kill any more. As one raised his club against him Ammon dodged and swung. His sword cut through skin and bone, lopping off the Lamanite's arm. Blood spurted from the stub as the severed arm fell to the ground.

More Lamanites charged Ammon, and again he was quicker. Each time a Lamanite raised a club to strike him, Ammon chopped off his arm. Those who were not wounded had apparently seen enough. They looked at the destruction Ammon had caused, turned, and ran. Ammon chased them beyond the pond, then walked back to the king's flock.

Servants looked at him, fear in their eyes.

"Come," he said, attempting to act nonchalant. "Let's get the flocks watered and return to the palace before it gets dark."

Obediently, the servants moved the flocks to the water. From the corner of his eye Ammon noticed with pleasure that they kept looking at him and whispering amongst themselves. Truly, he thought, the Lord has opened a way by which I can teach this people about Him.

With the other servants' help, Ammon drove the king's flocks back to the corrals. He was secretly amused. Several servants had gathered up severed and bloody arms. Grisly souvenirs, he thought.

After securing the sheep in the king's corrals, the other servants left. Ammon remembered the king had commanded them that morning to prepare horses for a ride to the land of Nephi. Apparently King Lamoni's father was king over all the land and was having a great feast to which Lamoni was invited.

Ammon fed and groomed the horses, then hitched them to the king's chariot. When everything was done, he went to report. The king looked at him with an expression of fear and awe. Ammon decided to wait for a better time and started backing from the room.

"Wait," shouted a servant. "Rabbanah, the king desires you to stay."

Ammon went forward and knelt. "What do you desire of me, oh king?"

The king did not answer, but continued staring at him. Ammon wondered, is something the matter? Have I offended the king in some way?

After a long pause, Ammon asked again, "What do you desire, oh king?

Still the king didn't answer. Ammon glanced around at the other servants. All stood stiffly, avoiding his glance. He looked back at the king and uttered a silent prayer. Father, bless me to know what to say. A small voice in his consciousness whispered, *King Lamoni thinks you are the Great Spirit because of what you did today.*

Ammon, filled with the warm, sweet spirit of the Lord, asked, "King Lamoni, are you silent because I defended your flocks from outlaws? Are you disturbed that I killed seven of them with my sword and sling, and cut off arms of others to defend your flocks and servants? Is this what has caused your silence?"

The king nodded without speaking.

Ammon bowed low. "You shouldn't marvel, my king. I am but a man who desires to serve you. Whatever you desire me to do, which is right, that will I do."

Whispering, King Lamoni finally spoke. "Who are you? Are you that Great Spirit of whom our forefathers have spoken?"

"I am not," Ammon said.

"Then how do you know my thoughts?" the king asked. "And tell me where you gained the power you have shown by killing and crippling a dozen strong men. Tell me about this power. I will give you whatever you desire."

"King Lamoni, will you listen to me if I tell you by what power I do these things?"

"Yes," the king answered. "I will believe all your words."
"Do you believe there is a God?"
King Lamoni shook his head. "I don't know what that means."
Ammon rephrased the question. "Do you believe that there is a Great Spirit?"
"Yes."
"This is God. Do you believe this Great Spirit, who is God, created earth and heavens?"
"Yes," the king said. "I believe He created all things which are in the earth. I don't know the heavens."
"Heaven is the place where God dwells with all His holy angels."
"Is it above the earth?" the king asked, leaning forward intently.
"Yes, and God looks down upon all men. He knows their thoughts and intents of their hearts. By His hand we were all created."
"I believe all you have spoken," King Lamoni said. "Are you sent from God?"
Ammon bowed again, then looked the king in the eye. "I am but a man, but God has called me to teach these things to you, that you and your people may know the truth. God gives me knowledge and power according to my faith and desire to serve Him."
Ammon taught the king and his servants about creation, about Adam, and the fall of man. Then he taught Lamoni about sacred scriptures and records. He told him the story of Lehi, the king's great forebear, who had left Jerusalem.
He unfolded the story of their wandering in the wilderness and about Laman, Lemuel, and the sons of Ishmael. He told of their rebellion against Nephi and of Nephi taking the sacred records with him as he fled from them.
Lamoni listened intently, his eyes never leaving Ammon's face.
Ammon concluded his teaching by telling the king of the plan of redemption, and of the Savior who would come to earth.
Silence filled the hall when he had finished. The king's face was flushed. Ammon felt the Spirit of God and knew King Lamoni also felt it. He waited.
King Lamoni physically shook himself, as if to wake himself up.
"I believe all you have taught me this night." He looked around the room, as if for support, then fell to his knees. "O Lord, I pray that you will have mercy upon me and upon my people according to the mercy you have shown to the people of Nephi."
Ammon was not prepared for what happened next. As soon as the king had uttered his prayer, he fainted and rolled to the floor. Ammon quickly summoned servants and together they lifted the unconscious king and carried him to his bedroom.

The queen screamed in horror. "He is dead!" She sat on the floor by his body, rocking back and forth, keening a tremolo with her lips and tongue. Her sons came and sat by her, unsure what had happened.

Ammon tried to console them, to convince them the king was not dead but only unconscious. They would not believe him. They were convinced the king was dead.

Ammon left the king's bedroom, returned to the stable and unharnessed the horses from the chariot. He had done all he could this night. Now it was in the Lord's hands. As he knelt beside his straw pallet, he prayed that God would preserve King Lamoni and whisper to the queen that he lived.

Two days and two nights passed. The king remained unconscious. King's courtiers attempted to have Lamoni buried, but the queen would not permit it. Through tear-reddened eyes she watched continuously by his bed. Servants brought food and drink, but she would not eat. One of the handmaidens was wife of a servant who had been with Ammon at the waters of Sebus. She told the queen of Ammon's powers.

The queen, Artibus, summoned Ammon.

"My servants have told me you are God's prophet and have power to do many mighty works in His name."

He nodded.

"If this is so, I desire you to go to my husband who has been as if dead for two days and two nights." She wrung her hands in misery. "Some say he is dead and should be buried, but I feel he still lives."

Ammon rejoiced. Thank you, Lord, he prayed silently, for giving opportunity to show Thy power. I know Lamoni is merely carried away by Thy spirit.

He followed queen Artibus into the king's bedroom. Lamoni lay almost as Ammon had left him two nights before. A servant sat by the bed sponging the king's lips. Another waved a fan in rhythmical cadence over the king's head, keeping flies away.

Ammon took the queen's hands in his and led her to the bed. "He isn't dead but sleeps in God's presence. Don't bury him. Tomorrow he will awaken."

He looked into her brimming eyes. "Do you believe what I say?"

"I have no one else to believe," she said simply. "My servants tell of your power. I believe you."

"Blessed are you because of your faith," Ammon said. "Queen Artibus, I have seen no greater faith among the Nephites."

"Thank you," she said. "I shall watch with my king until tomorrow when he will rise."

At first light, after feeding the horses, Ammon was summoned again into the king's bedroom. With the queen he waited for Lamoni to awaken.

The king's eyelids fluttered, his eyes opened and he gazed around the room. He smiled when his gaze rested upon his wife. Ammon helped him to sit up. Lamoni reached for the queen's hand.

"Blessed be the name of God," he said. He squeezed Artibus' hand as he looked at her. "And blessed are you, my dearest. As surely as you live, I have seen my Redeemer. I know now that He shall come to earth, be born of woman, and shall redeem all mankind who believe on his name."

He swooned. Ammon tried to catch him but the king fell backwards onto the bed. The queen, apparently also overcome by the Spirit, fell beside him. Ammon knelt beside the bed and prayed. His heart was so full. The Lord had manifested His spirit so abundantly upon these people.

He felt light-headed and had difficulty breathing. His head fell forward upon the bed.

When he awakened the room was filled with people. The tumult and shouting reverberated from stone walls and ceiling. He arose and looked around. At his feet a large Lamanite, sword in hand, lay as if dead. The queen, talking and gesticulating, was before one group of people, the king before another. Even the queen's servants were talking with people. He caught a few words: "salvation," "God's presence," "spirit of God." Ammon smiled. Truly their hearts were changed. They had accepted the Lord.

* * *

"And so father and friends," Ammon wrote, "The Lord prepared a way that the people of Lamoni could be converted. Many came forward to be baptized. Others declared angels had ministered to them. The Church was established and the Lord has continued to pour out His spirit among them. We see that His arm is extended to all people who will repent and believe on His name.

"Father, please tell Alma of a woman named Abish. She is the daughter of Malkish and Arina—Lamanites Alma converted while in the land of Helam. Through her many people experienced conversion in the palace of Lamoni. Now let me continue with my story."

* * *

After Ammon established the Church in the land of Ishmael, the king desired to go to the land of Nephi so Ammon could meet his father—king over all the land.

In his stable room, the voice of the Lord came to him: "You shall not go to the land of Nephi, for behold, the king will try to kill you. Instead, go to the land of Middoni. Your brother, Aaron, and his friends, Muloki and Ammah, are in prison there."

Ammon hurried to the palace and bowed before the king.

"King Lamoni, you desire that I go with you to meet your father in the land of Nephi. I cannot. My brother and friends are imprisoned in Middoni. I must go there and free them."

"Then I will go with you to Middoni," Lamoni answered. "The king there, Antiomno, is a friend. I will help you get your brother and friends from prison." He leaned forward, a perplexed look on his face. "But who told you your brother was in prison in Middoni?"

Ammon smiled. "The Lord whispered to me."

"It is enough!" the king cried. He clapped his hands and when servants appeared, commanded that they should prepare two chariots for travel to Middoni.

Ammon had not been outside the city since he first entered the land of Ishmael. Road networks branched in several directions from Ishmael. Lamoni pointed out the road which led to the land of Helam and Jerusalem, and the other road to the lands of Nephi and Middoni.

People crowded the road, many with large burdens on their heads or backs. Ammon and King Lamoni stopped for lunch beside a river. They enjoyed the fruit and bread which servants had fixed, then prepared to resume their journey.

"Wait," Lamoni said.

Ammon looked where Lamoni pointed. Dust rose in the distance. A chariot, sunlight glittering from fine-hammered gold finish, came towards them. Harness and chariot glimmered with precious stones. Ammon admired the sleek, well-groomed horse.

"It is my father," Lamoni whispered.

"The king?"

"Yes. Stay behind me," Lamoni said. "He will be upset."

"Hold!" a gruff voice shouted.

The chariot pulled up beside them. Ammon looked at Lamoni's father. He and Lamoni looked much alike. The old king was heavier, paunchy jowls sagging from the sides of his face, hair gray and receding from his forehead. A purple robe hung loosely from the king's shoulders, exposing large bare chest and heavy arms. He was an imposing figure.

His eyes snapped in anger. "Lamoni," he said. "Why didn't you come to the great feast? You and my other sons were to be guests of honor."

He seemed to notice Ammon for the first time and shouted angrily at Lamoni. "And where are you going with this Nephite, one of the children of a liar?"

"Father, I am sorry to have missed your feast," Lamoni said. "But I was unconscious at the time; under the influence of the Great Spirit."

He motioned to Ammon. "Now we go to Middoni to free brother and friends of my friend, Ammon."

"You call this Nephite a friend?" the king retorted angrily. "And you would free Nephites from prison?"

Stepping down from his chariot he strode angrily towards them. Hands on hips, he stood directly before his son. "Don't you know yet that all Nephites are liars and sons of liars. Their forefathers robbed our fathers and now this one comes among us to rob us once more."

He curled his lip in contempt. "Take your sword and slay this Nephite and then return with me to the land of Ishmael."

Lamoni stubbornly said, "Father, Ammon saved my life. I shall not kill him but shall continue to the land of Middoni where we will release Ammon's brethren. I know they are just and holy prophets of the true God."

"True God!" his father shouted. "I will show you." He pulled his sword from his belt and raised it as if to strike Lamoni.

Ammon pulled Lamoni back and faced the angry king. "You will not slay your son. But if you did, it would be better for him to die than you. He has repented of his sins. But if you should die at this time, in your anger, your soul could not be saved."

He pulled his own sword from its scabbard, resting its point on the ground before him. "Besides, if you killed your son, who is innocent of any wrong-doing, his blood would cry from the ground condemning you to God and you would lose your soul."

"Yes, I know my son is innocent. It is you who should be destroyed," the king shouted. Again he raised his sword, this time to strike Ammon.

Ammon deftly parried the old king's blows. With a mighty swat he knocked the sword from the king's hand. Fear was written in the king's eyes as he stood helpless before Ammon.

The king dropped to his knees. "Please spare me for my people," he pleaded.

Ammon raised his sword above the king's head. He heard Lamoni's sharp intake of breath behind him.

"I shall kill you unless you grant to me my request."

"Anything," the king gasped. "Even to half of my kingdom."

"I don't desire your kingdom," Ammon said. "If you will free my brethren from prison and guarantee that Lamoni may retain his kingdom, I shall spare you. Otherwise, I shall kill you now."

The king stood, piecing together what dignity he could muster. "Because this is all you ask for my life, I shall grant it gladly. Your brethren will be released from prison and Lamoni will retain his kingdom. I shall govern him no more."

The king looked at Ammon, his eyes puzzled. "But I don't understand. Why didn't you take the kingdom when I offered it to you?" He didn't wait for an answer. "Please come to my kingdom in the land of Nephi and teach me what you have taught Lamoni. I am desirous of learning."

"I shall do that." Ammon said, his heart full. Once more the Lord's power had been manifest in preparing someone to receive His word.

"Good-bye, my son," the king said. He turned to Ammon, the puzzled look still in his eyes. "And good-bye, Nephite." He wheeled and entered his carriage and was off in a cloud of dust.

Lamoni and Ammon, without speaking, mounted their chariots and continued their journey to Middoni.

In Middoni, Lamoni quickly explained the situation to King Antiomno, and then he and Ammon hurried to the prison. Ammon was appalled. Aaron and his brethren stood naked before them. Aaron's once strong, handsome body was lacerated and skeleton-like. Scars attested to numerous beatings. Red welts showed where rough ropes had bound. The others were in similar condition.

After making sure his brethren were cared for, Ammon and Lamoni returned to the land of Ishmael. Ammon had tried to talk Aaron, Muleki, and Ammah into coming with them, but Aaron felt they should continue teaching the people in Middoni.

In Ishmael, Ammon tried to once again be Lamoni's servant, but Lamoni would not.

"No," he said. "You shall be a priest to my people. We shall build places of worship and you will train priests."

Lamoni called his people together. "No longer are we governed by my father. Here in this land you are a free people, able to worship God according to your desires."

* * *

Ammon ended his letter. "I pray that all of you are well in Zarahemla. The Lord has truly blessed me in working with this people. I will remain here as long as is necessary to bring them to full understanding of the Lord's way."

* * *

King Mosiah put down Ammon's letter. I silently sat before him, thinking of all Ammon had said. Thankfulness filled my heart as I thought of God's goodness. Surely no one was as blessed as we. In my heart, I envied Ammon and his missionary work. I did not have long to contemplate. Mosiah picked up Aaron's letter and read aloud.

Chapter 9

Letter from Aaron

"Before we parted at the borders of the Lamanite lands," Aaron wrote. "Ammon blessed each of us and imparted the word of God unto us. Muloki, Ammah, and I followed a trail leading westward. The map given us by Alma showed this to be the path leading to the Waters of Mormon where Alma baptized his people.

"Two days' journey brought us to a city, which we found to be named Jerusalem, after our father Lehi's home. Muloki, Ammah, and the others left me at the city gates where I was to labor. The others were to direct their missionary efforts in the villages surrounding the city.

"Many white-skinned people were in the city. Lamanites and whites mingled freely, which made it easy for me. Later, I would find the light-skinned people would be my downfall."

* * *

The letter continued, telling of Aaron's amazement at the many beautiful buildings in Jerusalem. The city was in some ways even more beautiful than Zarahemla. Pyramids reared apexes to the sky; government buildings of stone stood in stark contrast to stick shacks of the poor; city walls were high and strong.

He wandered freely around the city, talking with people, observing the sights. Synagogues and other places of worship seemed abundant.

More interesting than the buildings were the different cultures and peoples Aaron observed. Three distinct peoples seemed dominant: white-skinned, light-skinned, and Lamanites. Some subtle questioning gave him information that the white-skinned people were Amalekites, descendents of Amaleki and his followers. Amaleki had remained behind when Limhi led his Nephite people to Zarahemla.

The other light-skinned people were descendants of Amulon and the priests of Noah. The priests, as remembered from Alma's writings, had married Lamanite women, and their descendants were a mixed breed, proud of their genealogy.

The dark Lamanites were also a proud people. The three groups seemed to get along well together, even though differences were apparent. Aaron noted the hardness on people's faces. Little love or consideration was shown to others. People pushed and shoved and demanded their own way.

The synagogues were always crowded. Aaron attended each day, attempting to get close to the people, waiting for the right teaching moment. He listened in the synagogue, recognizing the worship of Zimpoc, the snake god, and other religious dogma which he himself had taught just a few years before. Nehor's priests are here, he thought.

Aaron was impatient. He had been in Jerusalem for almost a month and had not been able to teach anyone the message he had brought from Zarahemla. One day in the synagogue, the opportunity presented itself. He stood and began preaching.

"Men and women of Jerusalem," he began. "Your city is named after the city where our father, Lehi, was commanded by an angel of God to preach repentance to the people. He was forced to leave that city and flee here, to a land of promise.

"An angel also appeared to me, commanding me to call people to repentance. I have come to your city for that purpose. Repent and worship the true God or you shall perish."

A rumble of talk greeted his remarks. In the front of the synagogue an Amalekite, apparently one of the priests, rose to address him.

"What is this you have testified?" he said in a disparaging tone. "Do you mean to tell us you have seen an angel? We are a good people. Why don't angels appear to us? Are we not as good as you?

"You have called us to repentance and threatened that if we do not repent we shall perish. How do you know the intent of our hearts? How do you know that we have anything to repent of? How do you know that we are not already a righteous people?"

He swept his arm around him. "We have built sanctuaries such as this throughout the city and assemble together often to worship God. We believe God will save all men."

Aaron looked around the room, then addressed the Amalekite leader. "Our forefathers taught that the Son of God would come to earth to redeem mankind from their sins. I know that this will come to pass. Do you believe this will happen?"

"We do not believe that you know any such thing. We do not believe in these foolish traditions. We do not believe that you or anyone else knows of things which will come in the future, nor do we believe that your father and our fathers knew concerning the things of which you speak."

Aaron then began quoting scriptures from the brass plates and the writings of Nephi. He told them what had been prophesied concerning the coming of Christ, the resurrection of the dead, and that there could be no redemption for mankind except through the death and sufferings of Christ, and the atonement of His blood.

The longer he spoke, the angrier the mood of the people. He saw his cause was hopeless. No one really listened, but instead were talking loudly against him. He began to fear for his life. Pushing through the grumbling people he exited the synagogue.

He looked to the heavens. Free air certainly smelled delightful.

Everyone he spoke to rejected his message. Days of preaching on street corners only earned him bruises and verbal abuse. Discouraged, he left Jerusalem.

Near the city he entered the village of Ani–Anti. He found Muloki, Ammah, and several other friends teaching there. His friends were having no more success than he had in Jerusalem.

"My friends," he said. there is little chance of success with such a hard-hearted people. Let's go to the land of Middoni."

The city of Middoni was located on the southwest shore of the Waters of Mormon. Aaron looked with excitement upon this place where Alma had first baptized his people. But his excitement was limited to the location. The people, as hard-hearted as those in Jerusalem, rejected them and their message. Few believed. Several times Aaron and the other missionaries were stoned. Finally, they were bound and cast into prison. Several months passed before they were freed by Ammon and King Lamoni.

"Ammon told me the king over all the land lives in the Land of Nephi. The king has asked that someone come and teach him," Aaron told his companions. "Our lack of success in Middoni has prompted me to call on the Spirit. The Spirit says go to the land of Nephi."

Taking Muloki and Ammah with him, Aaron announced himself at the king's palace. They were ushered into the throne room. He looked around. With the exception of several servants, they were alone with the king. Aaron and his friends bowed low before the king.

"Behold, O King," he said, "I am the brother of Ammon, and these are my friends, whom you freed from prison. We have come to the land of Nephi to be thy servants."

"Rise," the king said. "You will not be servants, but I insist that you teach me. I have been very troubled by the generosity of your brother and the greatness of his words. Why didn't he come up from Middoni with you?"

"The Spirit of the Lord directed that Ammon return to the land of Ishmael to continue teaching the people of your son, Lamoni."

"What did you say about the Spirit of the Lord?" asked the king. "This is something which has troubled me. Another thing which troubles me is what Ammon said: 'If you will repent you will be saved, and if you will not repent, you shall be cast off at the last day.' What does it mean?"

"Do you believe in God?" Aaron asked.

"The Amalekites say there is a God, and I have given them right to build sanctuaries where they could worship. If you say there is a God, then I will believe."

Aaron rejoiced in the king's attitude. "As you live, oh king, there is a God." he said.

"Is God that Great Spirit that brought our fathers out of the land of Jerusalem?" asked the king.

"Yes," replied Aaron. "He is that Great Spirit. The same Being who created all things in earth and heaven. Do you believe this?"

"Yes, I believe," responded the king. "I believe the Great Spirit created all things. Please teach me about these things, and I will believe your words."

Aaron, assisted by Muloki and Ammah, taught of God's dealings with man from the creation of Adam to the present time. They taught the king God's commandments, the atonement of Christ, and how Christ would break the bonds of death through His resurrection. They painted for the king a picture of eternal life where sting of death would be swallowed up in hope of glory. When they finished teaching, there was silence for long moments in the throne room.

The king stirred himself. "What shall I do that I may have this eternal life of which you have spoken?" he asked.

Before Aaron could answer, the king asked more questions.

"What shall I do that I may be born of God? How can I root the wicked spirit from my breast so I can receive the Spirit and be filled with joy, that I might not be cast off at the last day?"

He looked around the empty throne room. "If necessary," he said quietly, "I will give up all I possess, even my kingdom, that I may receive this great joy."

"Giving up your kingdom is not necessary," Aaron said. "If you really desire eternal life, you must have faith in God and repent of your sins. If you do this, with a belief that you will receive, you will receive whatever it is you desire."

When Aaron said this, the king prostrated himself on the floor and cried to the Lord.

"Oh, God that Aaron has told me about; if there is a God, and if Thou art God, please make Thyself known to me. I will give away all my sins to know Thee, that I may be raised up from the dead and saved at the last day."

Aaron and the other missionaries knelt with eyes closed during the king's prayer.

"He falls!"

"The king is dead!"

Cries of the servants interrupted Aaron's meditation. He looked to where the king had knelt. The king had swooned to the floor. He lay as if dead. The servants ran over to look at him. Some, apparently frightened, hurried from the room.

Aaron, Muloki, and Ammah stood over the fallen monarch, wondering what they should do. As they stood there, the queen, apparently roused by servants' cries, swept into the room. She ran to the king, looked up angrily at Aaron and his friends.

"Take these men and slay them," she screamed shrilly. "They have killed the king."

The servants held back. Finally one answered the queen. "Don't command us to kill these men. "That one," he pointed at Aaron, "is mightier than us all. If we attempt to kill them he will kill us."

"Then go call the guards that they might come and kill these murdering Nephites."

Aaron, feeling the urging of the spirit, walked to where the king lay, reached down, and raised him from the earth.

"Stand," he said.

The king stood, looked around the room with gleaming eyes. Then he called the queen and servants to him.

"I have seen God," he said. "He has forgiven me of my sins."

* * *

"Father," Aaron wrote. "Never have I felt the Spirit of God more strongly. The room seemed filled with the Spirit. After waking, the king immediately began to teach the queen what he had learned; the servants listened and they, too, were converted. In fact, the entire household of the king was converted to the Lord.

"A mob gathered outside the palace, shouting that we be brought forth and killed. The king stepped out on his porch and taught them and they were pacified towards me and my brethren. He then had each of us preach and many more were converted.

"That afternoon the king sent a proclamation throughout the land that we were to pass unmolested through the land and teach in any city. He commanded his people that we were to have complete freedom to teach in the synagogues; that no one was to lay hands on us. He did this, father, that the word of God could go forth to his entire people without restriction.

"For the past few months we have traveled from city to city, from one house of worship to another, establishing churches, and consecrating Lamanite teachers and priests to carry on the work.

"One of our big thrills was when we went to the temple in Nephi-Lehi and found ten Nephite women serving as temple priestesses. We were especially excited when we found that one of them was Ruth. Alma had told us of her capture by the Lamanites. We have sent home the women with Abram, who is bringing these letters to you.

"The Lord is directing our work among the Lamanites. We will continue to have great success."

* * *

King Mosiah leaned back in his chair. Hints of tears remained on his cheeks; his eyes were still wet.

"Better to be missionaries than kings," he whispered.

Chapter 10

Chief Judge of Zarahemla

I planted and harvested, hunted, fished, and in other ways provided for Ruth, my father and Netta. In addition, I counseled with priests from throughout the land, taught the Gospel to all who would listen, and performed every other duty as high priest over the Church.

By candle and torchlight I studied and wrote. I memorized scriptures, read great stories of my ancestors, Lehi, Nephi, and Jacob. I copied carefully in my own hand from the plates in the king's library. Abinadi's words which Father had written were of special consequence to me. Through those words Father had been converted. I read and reread King Benjamin's powerful sermon, much of which I committed to memory.

As Mosiah and my father translated the twenty-four gold plates, I often sat and listened, thrilling at the words of Ether as he recorded God's dealings with the Jaredites; shuddering at the carnage and destruction during the many times people turned from God. I sensed as I heard Ether's words that they were intended for our people—a warning of what would happen if we were not faithful to God's teachings.

One dreary, rainy afternoon Mosiah called me to his throne room. Father sat to one side, leaning on his cane. The king cleared his throat.

"Alma, realizing your father and I are getting old, I have given much thought to what to do with the records of the Nephite people. Come with me."

I helped Father to his feet and followed the king to the record library. Once again, though I had been here many times, I was thrilled at what I saw. The stacks of plates filled with the history of our people and God's teachings to them enthralled me.

"The treasures in this room," the king said, "represent God's dealings with man from the beginning."

I nodded.

"I am king and seer, not the prophet as your father is, yet I have seen in vision that these records represent salvation for millions of people who will read them and come to a knowledge of the Savior."

Mosiah paused as he picked up a stack of small plates and cradled them lovingly in his hands.

That I Were An Angel

"On your father's advice, I have decided that all records should be turned over to you, and that you should be the custodian as well as scribe."

Mosiah and Father both watched to see my reaction. I was astonished. Keeper of the records! I looked at Father. A tired smile wrinkled the corners of his mouth.

"Well, do you accept this calling?" Mosiah asked.

I bowed before him. "Yes, of course," I responded. "Being custodian and scribe of the Lord's records is more responsibility than I have earned, but I accept gladly."

Father's voice rumbled. "God's dealings with his people must be recorded. You are best prepared for that assignment." He smiled. "Remember how, as a youth, you wondered why I insisted upon your taking scribe training? And how you resisted?"

I remembered well. Father's wisdom and planning were evident in my life. Oh, the waste of youth, I thought. How often we rebel against those things which are best and right for us. How often we think we are wiser than our parents.

Once again I looked around the room filled with plates and Nephite memorabilia. I was humbled. All things in the room would now be my responsibility.

Mosiah handed me the interpreters in their golden bow.

"These have been prepared from the beginning of the earth and have been handed down from generation to generation for the purpose of interpreting languages. Whosoever has these stones is called seer."

"Me, seer?"

"Yes, my son," Father said. "You are now not only chief priest but seer for this people."

I was overwhelmed.

"With these records and these interpreters goes awesome responsibility," the king continued. "As your king I command you that you shall keep and preserve all the records and treasures. In addition, you shall keep a record of God's dealings with this people. And when the time comes for you to die, you are to confer the records onto a righteous priesthood holder who will carry on the work."

I turned to father, taking his hands in mine. "I shall do so," I replied humbly. Bowing my head, I continued. "I have dedicated the rest of my life to the work of the Lord. I will treasure and preserve His records. I will be His scribe."

* * *

Events during the next few years rolled forward as rapidly as jagged tongues of lightning strike through the sky. Mosiah sent to the people a proclamation changing the form of government from a kingship to that of judges.

Our first son was born. I named him Helaman. He is truly the light of my life. Ruth and I spend hours playing with him on the rug. He is so tiny but so strong. I didn't realize one's love could be expanded so much. First I loved my parents with all my love. Then my love expanded to Ruth and she filled my life with sunshine. Now my love has expanded once more to encompass this little one, this precious gift from God.

I had a difficult time tearing myself away from him to devote time to the records and my other duties. I just wanted to play with this little one whom God had given to us.

Ruth walked up behind me as I copied records at my desk. "A messenger is at the door."

I reached up and pulled her face down to mine, giving her a loving kiss.

She pulled away and laughed—the little tinkling laugh which had thrilled me since I was just a boy. I looked at her. As usual, her dark eyes were inscrutable, but laugh lines creased her glowing face.

The message was short. "I desire to see you at the palace." The note was signed by King Mosiah.

Mosiah had aged greatly in the few months since I had seen him. His hair was white, his face sallow in color. He motioned me to come closer.

"Alma," he said, his voice lacking in strength. "I have done all I could before my death to make sure the government is organized well. With your father's help we have set up the process of government and have appointed judges throughout the land. All is done except for one thing."

I waited patiently for what the king had to say.

"Alma, I know you are already heavily burdened—chief priest over the church, keeper of the records, scribe—but I must ask you to do one more thing. With my sons gone I have no one else. Alma, I am appointing you to be the first chief judge, subject to the ratification of the people."

Mosiah's words came as a shock. Chief judge over all Zarahemla? I nodded acceptance.

Several weeks passed as people in every city throughout the land were given opportunity to cast their votes.

"The last votes are in," Ammorihah, my assistant judge announced.

"And?"

"The people have unanimously acclaimed your appointment."

"Unanimously?" I smiled at his enthusiasm. "I suppose we must then get on with governing the land," I said. "Zarahemla is too large to be governed as King Benjamin governed. He insisted on not being paid to rule. Our first task is to set up a fair wage for each judge, including myself."

From that day on my daytime hours were devoted to the judgeship, with time squeezed in the evenings and on the Sabbath for my role as high priest, record keeper, and scribe of God's church.

I very much appreciated Ruth. Her patience and long-suffering enabled me to work through this hectic time. I watched little Helaman, now almost a year old, and wondered if I was spending enough time with him.

We held a family gathering at father's house to celebrate his eighty-second birthday. Everyone was there, all four children and ten grandchildren. I had been chief judge for just two months. What an enjoyable time I had visiting with my brother and sisters whom I had not seen for years.

"Alma, come quick." Netta's voice had an urgency to it.

Zoram and I rushed inside.

Father lay back in his chair, his eyes open and staring, a smile on his face. I put my ear to Father's chest, then straightened up.

"He is gone."

Leesa hurried in. She saw Father's lifeless body, dropped on her knees before him, grasped his cold hands in her's. She placed her cheek against his legs, rocking gently back and forth. When she looked up through her tears, though, it was with a soft smile.

She turned to me. "I feel mother's spirit here."

"I, too." I looked at Father's body without really seeing it. Instead, I saw Alma, the high priest, teaching, baptizing, blessing people.

"He has finished his work," I said. "He has joined mother in the kingdom of his Father."

Death is always balanced with life. Ruth came in, heavy with our second child. I took her hand.

"Father is dead."

She grasped my hand as she looked down at my father's lifeless body. "He is at peace. He died secure in his knowledge of the coming of the Lord." She squeezed my hand. "Even more important, he died knowing that his family was all righteous."

* * *

I stayed close to home as time for Ruth's delivery approached. She was almost past the age of child-bearing and each pregnancy was difficult for her. Being high priest and chief judge took much time, but being with Ruth was more important.

"It's another boy," the midwife announced.

The words brought joy to my heart. Another son!

I picked up the tiny red baby and cradled him in my arms. He was dark-haired and round as a squash. He never stopped crying.

"I name you Shiblon," I said. "With a voice like that you shall be a great missionary to this people."

A month after Shiblon was born, Mosiah died. I inscribed the records:

And now Alma, my father, died, being eighty-two years old, having lived to fulfill the commandments of God.

And Mosiah died also, in the thirty-third year of his reign, being sixty-three years old, being five hundred and nine years from the time Lehi left Jerusalem.

* * *

The babble of voices quieted as I took my seat behind the hewn-rock table in the room which served as court. I was dressed in a plain, white tunic and wore a headdress of feathers. The headdress was the only ostentation I allowed myself.

One defendant after another appeared before me. Most were accused of stealing, lying, or some other petty offense. By afternoon I had cleared my docket of all the routine cases. The final case of the day was one I had been dreading. For the first time since being appointed chief judge by King Mosiah, I was to try a man for murder. Many sleepless nights had already preceded this case. The man to be tried was no ordinary man.

"Bring in the prisoner."

The guard hurried to obey.

The door opened on a large man, naked to the waist. He swaggered in, his muscles coiling and flexing. Blonde hair hung in ragged strands below his shoulders. His face was almost covered by a reddish-blonde beard and huge mustache. Icy-blue eyes—eyes sometimes wild and irrational—showed through the beard, and now swept back and forth across the court, finally resting on me. His lips curled upward in a half-smile of greeting, tilting the heavy mustache on his upper lip, revealing his straight-white teeth.

He stopped before the hewn-rock table behind which I sat. In an eloquent gesture, he held up chained hands, then dropped them. His voice was firm and quiet when he spoke.

"Alma, old friend, we meet again."

I hoped no emotion showed in my voice as I responded.

"Yes, Nehor. I'm really sorry that it couldn't have been under different circumstances."

He shrugged, then turned to gaze at the audience. Most cringed under his intent gaze. He turned back to me.

"Let's get on with it."

I nodded to the clerk. "Read the charge."

The clerk, a long roll of bark paper stretched between his hands, stepped forward.

"This man, Nehor, has gone about among the people, preaching what he said was the word of the God, Zimpoc; accusing the church of teaching false doctrines; declaring that every priest and teacher should be paid for his ministry and should not have to labor for his sustenance but be supported by the people."

"Go on," I prodded.

"He preached that all men would be saved at the last day and men need not worry but should lift up their heads and rejoice. He teaches that Zimpoc created all men and also redeemed all men, and all men should have eternal life without any effort of their own."

Alma interrupted. "What he preaches, as long as there is no force applied, is his right. What specific charges are there against this man?"

"Murder, your eminence."

I leaned forward, looking Nehor in the eyes.

"How do you plead to this charge, Nehor?"

"I only preach that which you, yourself, preached a few short years ago. I cannot help it if an old man got in my way."

The first of what he said was true. But my life had changed. I wished with all my heart that Nehor also would have changed. Wearily, I continued.

"If there are witnesses, they will step forward."

Three men stood and walked forward, warily skirting Nehor.

"You each saw what happened?"

The three nodded wordlessly.

"Who will speak for you?"

The man on the right, a tall, beardless, dark-haired man nervously raised his hand. I motioned him closer to my table.

"What is your name?"

"Mosiahah, your eminence."

"Can you tell me exactly what happened?"

"Your eminence, this man, wearing costly robes and apparel, came to Gideon to establish a church to his god, Zimpoc. On his way into the city, he met Gideon, priest of the church your father established.

"Gideon stopped him and told him to leave the city. This man became very angry, drew his sword, and began striking at Gideon."

"Did Gideon defend himself?"

"No, your eminence. Gideon was an old man. I understand he was a warrior in his youth, but now, as a priest, he carried no weapon. He was helpless and defenseless before this man's attack."

"And?"

"Before anyone could stop him, this man," he pointed at Nehor, "killed Gideon."

I looked at the other two witnesses. "Is there anything you would add?"

Both shook their heads.

"Do you witness to what Mosiahah has said? Has he told the truth?"

Both nodded, whites of their eyes showing as they glanced sideways at Nehor.

"Were there other witnesses?"

"Yes, your eminence. By the time this man drew his sword, several hundred people had gathered around listening to Gideon contend with him. We could not stop the killing, but did capture the killer," he said smugly.

I looked over the crowd in the court chambers. "Is there anyone else who will stand as witness, either for or against the accused?"

No response.

I looked sadly at Nehor. He looked back defiantly.

"Nehor," I said, "how often I tried to reason with you. How often I attempted to persuade you to repent and become part of the Church of God. With your temper I felt sure that someday you would put yourself in the position in which you now find yourself."

Nehor stood unflinching before me, cool eyes fixed on my own.

"Nehor, I feel that I partially share your guilt for being partners with you in introducing priestcraft to this people. But for five years I have worked to erase the damage I did as a dissenter from the Church. I also tried to turn you away from the course you had chosen."

I shook my head in frustration. I could tell I was getting nowhere with this man who was once my closest friend.

"Nehor, you are not only guilty of continuing to teach priestcraft after King Mosiah proclaimed against it, but you have endeavored to enforce it with the sword." I spoke more to the audience than to Nehor as I continued. "If priestcraft were to be enforced among this people it would prove their entire destruction.

"You have shed the blood of an innocent man, a man who did much for this people. Gideon was instrumental in bringing the people of King Limhi out of bondage. He was a loyal priest and supporter of my father.

"Nehor, if we were to spare you, Gideon's blood would come upon us for vengeance. Therefore, you are condemned to die, according to the law."

Nehor looked at me, a fierceness showing on his face and in his narrowed eyes. He grimaced, lips drawn tightly over clenched teeth. "You should have drowned in the swamp," he said grimly.

I motioned the guard to lead him away. As they left the chamber, my head drooped. I sat there while memories of experiences Nehor and I had shared raced through my mind. It was finished. There was nothing I could do. Justice must be done. It was too late for mercy.

Nehor's sentencing had been my responsibility. The sentence was carried out by Amnor, chief of the palace guard. He took Nehor to the top of the hill Manti. There, before he died, Nehor acknowledged he had been teaching contrary to the word of God. None of Nehor's followers were there as Amnor's sword severed his head from his body.

Though he was now dead, Nehor's influence and false teachings lived on. His followers thrived; many liked the riches of the world. Priestcraft continued to spread. I was kept busy punishing those who stole, or those who lied, and the occasional murderer. But the real criminals, those who would steal a man's soul, or lie about his salvation, or kill his dreams, roamed free. They preached false doctrines to get riches and honor.

Persecution continued. Reports came in daily of faithful church members threatened by those who disliked their humility or their quiet faith. Church members were taught to be peaceful, and to not fight back, but many fights still occurred outside the churches.

I had been chief judge for two short years, and already it seemed as if society were falling apart around me. How could I possible continue to govern this land?

And yet, there were faithful members of the Church. The priests of the Church taught and lived the commandments as they had been laid down by my father and king Mosiah. They worked alongside their congregations, then on the Sabbath dropped their hoes and picked up the scriptures. Most members were faithful and gave of themselves for others. There was peace within the Church, regardless of the forces of evil which continued to attack.

Because of the members' faithfulness the Lord blessed them. They became rich with things of the world: an abundance of flocks and herds, bountiful crops, gold, silver, precious stones, and beautiful clothing and tapestries. The exciting thing to me was that even in their new-found wealth, people did not turn away the needy and hungry. They did not set their hearts upon their riches, but accepted them as gifts from God which could be shared.

It pleased me that those in the Church became much more wealthy than those who followed Nehor's teachings. Zimpoc's followers indulged themselves in sorceries and idolatry. They were a lazy people, hoping to get riches from other people's labors. They wore expensive clothing, spent their time in pursuit of wickedness, and committed many transgressions. Anyone caught breaking the law was punished. Such quick enforcement of the law brought us a fairly peaceful existence for the next few years.

It was during this time of peace that our third son, Corianton, was born. He was a wiry child, dark and beautiful like his mother. In fact, as he lay in his crib, he seemed to me to be the exact image of what Helaman had looked like just a few short years before. I shook my head in wonderment. I was now forty-three years of age, and in just five short years I had been ordained High Priest over the Church, given responsibility for the records, married Ruth, made Chief Judge, and had three children. Also in that period of time my father and King Mosiah had died.

* * *

Peace could not last forever. In my fifth year as chief judge, the law could no longer contain the trouble. Amlici, Nehor's chief lieutenant and Zimpoc's chief priest, had built up his following each year since Nehor's death. Now he and Zarahemnah challenged the whole system of judges which Mosiah had established such a short time before.

"You are disturbed." Ruth said quietly.

We were sitting on our front porch watching the children play in the yard. Little Corianton was on Ruth's lap, cooing softly as she stroked his head.

"Yes," I sighed. "Amlici's followers clamor for him to be made king. If he were king, I know what will happen. He will make the worship of Zimpoc the state religion. The Church of God will exist no more."

"I thought Mosiah, in his wisdom, set up the structure so all changes in government, including the election of judges had to be made with the voice of the people."

"Very true, but that's part of the problem. I am afraid Amlici will use that very procedure for destroying our orderly system of government. He and his people are campaigning, using force and coercion where necessary, to woo and sway the people to his way of thinking. Forums throughout the land feature debates between those favoring kingship and those in favor of retaining the judges."

Ruth reached over and took my hand. "I am sure the Lord will see that righteous men are kept in office."

I sincerely hoped she was right.

After months of debating the people voted.

I almost ran home to give the news to Ruth. "People overwhelmingly supported a continuation of the system of judges. I was thrilled that even in the face of threats of violence, people voted wisely."

Ruth just smiled. She didn't say, "I told you so." That wasn't like her, but she had predicted what would happen. The Lord wouldn't let us down.

But Amlici and his followers did not accept the people's mandate. I was greeted one day by my nephew, Aha, son of my brother, Zoram. He had traveled speedily from the borders of the land near Ammonihah.

"The Amlicites have gathered in Ammonihah," he said, "and have consecrated Amlici to be king."

"I feared this would happen."

"But that is not all. Amlici has commanded his people to take up arms and march against Zarahemla."

"What of your father, Zoram, and the border guards?"

"Father is leading his small warrior army from Melek to Zarahemla. He sent me ahead to warn you."

"Good," I replied as thoughts raced through my mind. "I will raise the army here while he is coming. We will prepare ourselves to put down this uprising."

The next days were hectic. Runners raced through the land of Zarahemla with a call for the people to arm themselves. Warriors were gathered from throughout the land and converged on Zarahemla. Captains were appointed over the different bands. Warriors were armed with swords and cimeters, bows and arrows, stones and slings.

I appointed Nabob chief captain over all the armies. Zoram was captain over his band, and I appointed other captains to command their individual bands.

Word came from Amlici that his army would meet us in battle on the hill Amnihu, east of the river Sidon. I would have preferred more familiar terrain, but we were committed to fight him regardless of location. I was familiar with the hill Amnihu. It was one of the places I had explored with Ammon so many years before.

I went home to say good-bye to Ruth and the boys

"Why do you have to go to battle?" she asked. "You are chief judge. Stay in Zarahemla."

"No, my love, this is the first real challenge during my short term as chief judge. I must lead my people myself. Amlici will be in front of his army. His leadership must be challenged."

"Are you the only one that can challenge it?"

"Yes. There is none other. I will go to battle in the name of the Lord. With Him at our head, we will win."

Chapter 11

War With The Amlicites

A phalanx of shining spears pierced the sky on the plain before Zarahemla. Reflected sunlight glinted from thousands of swords. Bright colors of dyed armor dominated the plain. Huge feather banners were unfurled in front of the army and multicolored cloth flags marked the separate companies of warriors. Captains of companies stood at attention. The Nephite army was ready for battle.

Nabob, chief captain, had organized well. He stood before me now, awaiting the order to march.

Emotions of fear and excitement competed within me. I was determined not to show any fear. In my youth I had trained as a warrior but had never seen battle. As a mere child I had harassed the Lamanite guards in the land of Helam but I had never killed anyone. Now I was leading the Nephite army into a battle where there would be much killing. My sword hung heavy at my side.

I was glad my brother, Zoram, and his two warrior sons were here. They had made good time from the border near Melek. I had been tempted to appoint Zoram chief captain, but Nabob was senior. It would not do to show favoritism. I looked to see Zoram's company on the right edge of the mass of armies. Lehi's and Aha's companies were next to his. The battle would not be easy and I appreciated the experience of men such as Nabob and Zoram.

The army, ponderous in size, started forward on my command. We marched northward, paralleling the Sidon. Several hours of hot miserable marching brought us to the ford. Flies rose in furious swarms at our approach. Sweat poured from cheeks and nose tips. Warriors came to a halt as the river loomed before them.

Nabob drew a deep breath and yelled, "Forward!"

Warriors clambered off the bank and dropped into the dirty, foaming water. I went with the first group, bracing my feet as I felt the tug of the sluggish current. The muddy bottom was slick but gave good footing. On the far bank I climbed out wet and bedraggled. The army followed us, clambering up the bank, men sorting themselves back into their fighting groups. A huge snake, startled, whipped its immense, trunk-like body away from our intrusion.

Mosquitos, flies and tiny hopping insects rose out of the high grass at the stream's edge as men's feet disturbed it. Heat lay on the jungle like a blanket. Birds became quieter, and, as if to compensate, the cicadas gradually augmented the shrill whine of their call.

Rain came, pitting the swirling dark water, adding to the misery of already soaked warriors. As I waited for the rest of the army to cross, I analyzed my thoughts. I was not now afraid. The Lord had promised me that I would not die; wounds mended and bruises disappeared. I rehearsed in my mind what had transpired.

Amlici's decision to meet us in battle on the hill Amnihu, a day's march north of the land of Gideon, would give him terrain advantage. Amnihu was unfamiliar ground to my warriors. Terrain would be the only advantage Amlici had. The Lord was on our side! I grinned fiercely. Let Zimpoc show Amlici's army his power!

My thoughts were interrupted by Nabob's shouted orders. "Make camp."

Crude brush huts and a few tents soon lined the bank between the river and the edge of the forest. It was our purpose to attack Amlici and his army at first morning light. Better to attack when our army was rested than after a full day's march through the heat. Soon smoke rose from thousands of campfires, the smoke blending with the gray, muggy overcast.

All night it rained. When morning dawned it still rained. I looked out of the tent opening at the falling drops. This must be a rain like the rain before Noah's flood, I thought. Our men, dressed in cotton armor, would be soaked and miserable.

Creeping dawn brought hot sun which melted away the rain clouds. Blue–purpled mountains to the west stood out in stark relief. Soon the jungle steamed. Men formed up after eating their meager breakfast, wet and wrinkled hands holding tightly to swords slick from drenching moisture.

I walked stiffly between groups of warriors, wet armor clinging to my body. Men stood around, bodies drooping dejectedly. Only their eyes showed life. Nabob appeared, stripped to the waist, massive muscles of arms and chest rippling as he moved. He walked easily, ignoring rain and mud. He turned to the warriors and grinned. Spears stood straighter in the air. I could see men stiffening shoulders, gaining confidence just to have him at their head.

We led the troops forward through the jungle. The rain had stopped but sheets of water, like rain, continued to drip from overhanging trees and lianas. Scent of copal was rich and choking. It entered my lungs and I could not seem to expel it. My breath became short.

Armor chafed our bodies. I saw Nabob's wisdom in stripping for the march. Warriors trudged through the jungle ignoring the water.

We were getting close to the hill Amnihu. My heart beat rapidly in my chest. Muddy, slippery ground sloped less gently upward. Keeping one's balance on the slippery slope would be difficult enough, let alone attempting to chop with a heavy sword.

Movement of our warriors slowed to a crawl. I heard warriors panting behind me as they clambered up the hill. The ground here was drier. Naked rock pushed through the ubiquitous carpet of vegetable matter. Seeming to sense the enemy's nearness, warriors moved more quietly. There was little talking and no joking. Perhaps they wondered, as I did, just how many would be killed this day.

The warriors followed a low ridge that wound deviously, sometimes doubling back on itself. We were now several hundred feet higher than our last night's camp. Pure sunlight appeared at distant intervals through gaps made by an occasional fallen tree. But the heat had not diminished. Neither had the cacophony of jungle sound.

I glanced quickly to left and right to see if my men were advancing. The forest's shade didn't hide the grim faces and high-held weapons.

There. Far to the left came the first sounds of battle. Warriors started passing me in their rush to get at the enemy.

Front ranks reached tight-packed ranks of Amlicites. Clang! Swords shocked upon swords. Suddenly, I felt sick inside. These were our brothers. Nephites were fighting Nephites. Then the thought left me. Amlici and his people rebelled and took up arms against us. If Amlici won this battle, that would mark the end of the Church and our people.

We pushed forward. The noise was deafening and when I looked again I saw the charging mass of Nephites spreading away on either side in a human tide. The warriors, seeming in a desperate hurry to get to the Amlicites, yelled, urging themselves on. I rushed on with a wave of warriors, finally seeing the enemy close before me.

I was shocked. Amlicite warriors had not shorn their hair like the Lamanites, but their foreheads were painted red. They were fierce-looking. Their combined shouting of "Kill! Kill!" was deafening and made any sort of thought impossible. I raised my sword. A volley of arrows clattered around me. I was thankful for my armor. Several warriors before me tumbled back down the hill.

Emboldened, the Amlicites started down towards us, their wild eyes and piercing screams reawakening the fear in me. Some men huddled behind trees for safety, cowering before the enemy, but there was no safety except in pressing the attack. I moved forward. Swords flashed, spears lunged and withdrew like steel tongues.

"Attack! Attack!" Nabob cried.

An Amlicite's painted head appeared directly in front of me, but his yell was cut short as my sword fell brutally on him, splitting his head open. I had no time to feel shock or remorse. Other enemy warriors charged towards me and my men.

Nabob was beside me, urging his men on, hundreds of warriors hit the slope, climbed through the trees, only to be repulsed again and again by the Amlicites on top. Yet, still more warriors pushed up the hill, hurrying as if there were safety in the milling, scrambling, horde which bulged at the top. Fresh groups charged, holding swords high, trampling over dying and dead lying in the mud.

Screams of dying men were all around me. Chop and parry, chop, thrust, hack and parry. Swords, spears and muddy ground were red with blood. The ground was slick with it. It seemed ages since we had met the Amlicites, but still the fighting continued.

The sun, hot and piercing through the forest, was almost straight overhead before I felt any easing of the battle.

"They're pulling back," someone shouted.

As Amlicites retreated down the backside of the hill, our warriors followed in hot pursuit. Never had I seen such a slaughter.

Rain started again, sweeping down across the hill. Broken swords and bodies littered the slope; where bodies had fallen unrecognizable dark smears spread in the already dark mud. Sounds of retreating fight floated back; sounds of men clawing each other to death in the mud were muffled by the rain.

I stood on the hill with remnants of our army. Nabob was dead. He lay backwards on the moist loam, his arms wide, his eyes staring at nothing, an arrow lodged to the feathers in his bare chest. I was angry. Why should good men die just so someone could have power.

I recognized Zoram's voice from the top of the hill shouting for men to join him.

"This way. This way."

The remaining warriors quickly surrounded him. The thought crossed my mind that now he would be chief captain. We pressed our advantage, moving down the hill after retreating Amlicites. We stayed on their heels, slaying them with a fierce slaughter.

Darkness was thick around us by the time we reached the valley of Gideon. Zoram organized teams of warriors to return and care for wounded and bury the dead. The rest of the warriors were put to work setting up tents and shelters.

I sat on the tortured, elevated roots of a cypress tree. As though orchestrated, hundreds of tiny frogs began to peep. High above, flapping of wings indicated birds were getting settled for the night.

While camp was being set up, I called for volunteers for a special assignment. Five warriors stepped forward: Zeram, Amnor, Manti, Limher, and Moroni. I knew none of them. All looked impressive in their armor, faces eager for any assignment. Zoram stood with me.

"All are excellent warriors," he said. "The least experienced is the youngest of the five, Moroni, a quiet, modest youth who never complains."

I looked them over, my eyes resting on Moroni. He looked to be no more than sixteen. All were young, seemingly unfazed by the battle we had fought. In contrast, I was exhausted. Forty-four years was not old, but years of relative inactivity had taken their toll. I wondered how Zoram was holding up.

"We have to be certain about the enemy's location. I need scouts for a reconnaissance," I said.

"We'll go, sir," they responded in chorus.

I smiled at their youthful enthusiasm. Several had cuts and other minor wounds, but they were undaunted.

"Four scouts is enough for the reconnaissance," I said. I pointed to Moroni. "You stay. My aide was killed today in the battle. You will be my aide. I need someone I can depend on."

"Yes, sir," he said. He was obedient to my wishes but disappointment was obvious in his voice.

What loyalty! I thought. Oh, that I could have been as loyal to my father as Moroni is to me.

I turned back to the four.

"Amlici's army is still before us," I said. "By now they have pitched their tents and camped for the night. Find their camp. Follow them. Capture some prisoners. Do what is necessary to find out their plans."

The scouts did not return that night. At dawn our army was ready to move out. By the time the sun was a quarter way up the sky I was worried. Where were they? Why hadn't they returned? Had they been killed or captured? I fussed at the men. We could wait no longer.

"Form your warriors into companies," I commanded Zoram.

We started through the valley in the direction the Amlicites had gone the night before.

Noon came before the scouts returned. Zeram and his men were muddy and red-eyed from their hurried march. Without summons, they came directly to the head of the column where Zoram and I stood.

Zeram saluted, his fist smacking sharply against his armor.

"Sirs," he reported, "we followed the camp of the Amlicites past Gideon, all the way to the land of Minon on the way to the Land of Nephi."

He shook his head. "To our great astonishment we saw a great army of Lamanites marching towards the city of Zarahemla. We thought they would immediately destroy the Amlicites, but to our surprise, the Amlicites joined with them."

"Joined with the Lamanites?" Zoram asked.

"Yes. They conferenced for some time, then the Amlicites fell right in with the ranks of the Lamanites."

"Then what happened?" I asked.

"We didn't stay long to watch. They continued marching towards Zarahemla and we hurried back to report."

"This is the kind of treachery I should have expected from the traitor, Amlici," I said. "He has made arrangements with the Lamanites to conquer Zarahemla." I shuddered. "If they had won yesterday's battle they would have swept through the land, leaving nothing but death and desolation."

Manti nodded soberly, "They destroy everything in their path. Those who haven't been killed are fleeing before the Lamanite army, driving their flocks before them."

"Unless we make haste to stop them," Zeram said, "they will take Zarahemla and destroy our families."

As I thought of that consequence, I looked over my army. The men stood waiting, anxious to continue after the Amlicites. I nodded to Zoram. He called the captains and explained what the scouts had told us.

"Prepare your troops for a forced march." He commanded. "We must block the Lamanites. When we get to the River Sidon be prepared to attack. This time we will not only be defending our freedom but the very lives of our wives and children."

I was proud as I saw how quickly our warriors moved out.

"Go. Go. Go." A fast chant started in the middle of the ranks. Soon the entire column was chanting.

The warriors moved with rustle of cloth and clinking of sword against bow shafts. A sense of urgency propelled them. Ahead was the enemy. As we drew closer to the river a silence spread through the ranks.

There was no sign of the Lamanite army, only muted jungle sounds. The enemy was across the river and must be close now. The heavy forest along the banks of the river blotted out half the sky.

To the right and across the river was a slight elevation, a grass-covered knoll. Lining its base was a windrow of massed logs and vegetable rubbish deposited by the current. To the left the stream veered away and on its bank was a level stretch of sand no more than twenty paces across and several hundred paces in length. The beach was familiar to me. As a teen I had played and swum here often with Ammon and his brothers.

The rain, which had eased off during the morning, now came with increased vehemence. The river was flooded, foaming white and high but we had to cross in order to defend Zarahemla. How to do it without all of our men washing down to the ocean? How much time until the Lamanites met us?

Zoram sent a work party into the jungle. Under his direction, men selected strong lianas for a lifeline. Several men stripped naked swam across the Sidon, lengths of lianas tied to their waists. On the other bank they tied the lianas to trees, forming lines the men could hang to as they crossed the cresting water.

Rain had flooded fields and forest west and north, and still the wind shrieked at us, bringing more water. Everything was fouled with mud. My only consolation was that the rain and mud would slow the Lamanites' march. I prayed that the Lord would give us time to get our armies to the west bank before the Lamanite army came upon us.

Darkness came while our men crossed the river. I swam strongly across the swift-moving current, while continuing to pray. Finally the last man was across. Men were in the water again, their swords cutting the lianas free to tumble downstream in the current.

Zoram placed his armies across the fields and approaches leading to Zarahemla. He commanded the right side of the line. I was on the left—with the river my left flank. The narrow strip of beach by the river was to be our fighting ground.

We spent a miserable night on the west bank of the Sidon. With no tents or shelters the drenching rain scything across the ranks of huddled men added misery to fear. The fear was palpable; I could smell it. And behind us, not a two hour's walk, was Zarahemla, sheltering our wives and families. There could be no retreat.

Morning brought a miraculously clear dawn. Cheers rose in the throats of the warriors. I inspected my men. The inspection was not to check their bedraggled uniforms, but to grin at them and encourage them, because today these warriors would be called upon to fight a great fight, to write a page in the history of their people, to defend their city and their families.

Tension mounted as the sun arched up in the sky, imagination making fears real. Where were the Lamanites? When would they attack?

Shouts from the top of the river bank drew my attention. A warrior pointed upstream. There, filling the opening, from river bank to forest were the glistening bronze bodies of the Lamanites, white Amlicites interspersed among them.

I watched the assembling Lamanites and Amlicites as they crowded along the river. There seemed to be no obvious leaders. It was as if the combined army had a mind of its own.

Earlier I had placed our best archers in front. They squatted now on one knee, their arrows nocked. Like some beast saved from imminent drowning, the Nephite army heaved itself out of the mud, forming into ranks behind the officers. The archers and swordsmen waited quietly, watching the assembling Lamanite army.

A sudden feeling of comaraderie seemed to flow through the ranks. It was a warmth, a feeling of difficulties that would be shared. I felt close to the men and could see that other leaders were having similar feelings.

Scraps of tattered clouds dotted the blue sky overhead. Two tiny black V's, condors flying high above, drifted across the sky. The sun was so hot the sword in my hand felt like it had just come from the oven.

"Hold your arrows," I cautioned. "Wait until they are close. Pass the word." The whisper went down along the line. The archers stood at ready.

A conch horn's dismal sound shattered the stillness. At this signal, the Lamanites advanced. When I judged they were within arrow range, I commanded, "Release arrows."

Volley after volley hissed into the air, searching out targets in the horde of onrushing bodies. Hundreds of Lamanites died but those behind just stepped over the bodies and kept coming. As those whom the arrows missed struggled towards us, our swordsmen fell upon them. The river bank became a massive sink of death.

A cry brought my attention back to the task at hand. Waves of Lamanites and Amlicites were coming out of the forest close at hand and now threatened the right flank.

I shouted to Moroni and pointed.

He nodded his head in understanding and pushed through the warriors, gathering them with him as he rushed to fill the gap. Nerves of steel were required to move towards that screaming horde. I gained even more respect for our brave Nephite warriors. The thought struck me, it takes more than nerves of steel, it takes discipline. And commitment.

Horrid sounds, messages of war, created a din around me. The sounds were frightening to my ears as the Lamanites burst upon us, coming in seemingly endless numbers. The Lamanites were naked except for loincloths, brandishing weapons of all kinds: bows and arrows with barbed tips, swords, clubs made of knotty branches, daggers, and lances that exceeded the height of a man.

With my men I formed a stout group, standing back to back, shoulder to shoulder, our swords hacking an opening in the ranks of the attackers. I was glad that my four young men: Zeram, Amnor, Manti, and Limher stood with me.

The enemy came in, jabbing with their lances, slashing with their daggers. When I hacked one down it seemed as if two more stood in his place.

An Amlicite standard bearer weaved his way towards our fighting group. He was a massively built man. Directly behind him was Amlici himself, followed by officers and guards. I had no trouble recognizing him and his lieutenant, Zarahemnah. My mind went temporarily back to the mud shack where I had seen them last: I as a prisoner; they as my captors and tormentors. I looked upon Amlici with revulsion: hideously painted face, slashes of red paint across his forehead and down his cheeks.

Beside me, Zeram loosed an arrow, catching the standard bearer in the throat. The yellow standard fell to the ground like a dying bird. I forgot about any of the others, concentrating only on Amlici. I stepped towards him, parried his sword and swung hard at him. He grinned wickedly and dodged my blow, slowly backing towards the river, pulling me away from the protection of my warriors.

Blow by angry blow I forced him into the swirling water. Then Amlici rallied, fighting me back to the crumbling bank. I stumbled in the shifting sands. With a wolfish grin, Amlici stepped forward for the kill. His sword flashed and I rolled and was once again on my feet.

I called upon God: O Lord, have mercy and spare my life that I may be an instrument in Thy hands to save and preserve this people.

As I prayed I felt my strength returning. Once again I forced Amlici back. I would never forget the look on his painted face as my blows rained down upon him. Nor would I forget that last blow slicing through his shoulder, his blood spreading into the water, his body floating downstream in the muddy current.

Wearily I climbed back onto the bank. The battle was raging elsewhere and I had a chance to rest. I became conscious of the smell. It was the smell of death—a blending of sweat and dung and ripped bowels and congealing blood. The dead were all around me, lying grotesque and still on the river bank.

I grabbed the arm and leg of a dead Lamanite and dragged him to the river, watching the body swirl and eddy and finally float out of sight. One after another body I cast into the river, clearing the bank so our warriors would have room to fight. The black humps of their bodies broke up the ripples in red and dark patterns.

Sounds of battle became louder. Fighting was again coming to me. I reluctantly picked up my sword and moved towards the Nephites who had their backs to me, fighting sword to sword with the Lamanites. My warriors were being forced back, the Lamanites inexorable in their pursuit. I recognized my guards, Amnor and Limher. Stepping quickly between them, I raised my sword and again commenced the work of death.

Lamanite after Lamanite fell to our swords, but still they came. Would it never end? Amnor was hit by an arrow and fell forward. He was hacked to pieces before he hit the ground. I didn't have time to mourn his death, but I was sickened. Amnor had been one of my bravest men.

The killing was terrible; truly a baptism of slaughter. The hideous faces of the enemy continued to come at me. I recognized the Lamanite king with his headdress of feathers and armor of brass. The rest of the Lamanites were naked except for their loincloth of fur. He fought in the midst of them, seeming taller. Finally Jeram and I stood before him, raining blow after blow upon him and his guards. Foot by weary foot we forced them backwards. Slash and parry, strike fast, parry returning blows—there was a sameness to what we were doing. It was as if my life had become nothing but a long battle; my sword an extension of my arm.

The Lamanite king fell back, sending his guards forward. My warriors and I fought our way through the mob of howling warriors to a low rise south of the main encounter. It was the place where I hoped to link up with Moroni and his company.

A hoarse voice boomed from the right. It was Moroni, rallying his men.

"Come on you God-fearing Nephites." His voice sounded hollow, as if he had been doing much shouting. "Stand and fight these heathens."

A cave-like opening in the high cutbank of the river gave some protection. I led my men there. We again formed up, shoulder to shoulder in the opening. As the enemy attacked, we created a heaping mound of fallen Lamanites before us. Din of battle never let up; not even to permit us to search out our wounded.

A conch-horn sounded. Lamanites started to fall back. They had lost hundreds of men but had still advanced without hesitation, eyes dilated and teeth bared.

Their retreat gave us breathing time. My arm ached from swinging the sword, and my head ached from the hot sun and lack of water. I glanced around at the beach. Bodies were piled everywhere. I detailed the warriors to finish the job I started earlier—casting the dead into the river. Several of my warriors were stretched out on the sand. Others were tending their wounds. Nearby another lay as if asleep, his dead eyes watching us as we prepared to meet another Lamanite assault.

It seemed like we scarce had time to draw a peaceful breath when the conch-horn sounded again. Somewhere a voice yelled a command, then a dull roar of voices as the enemy came forward. The voices rose to a fierce crescendo as they charged.

My archers were again poised and ready. "Release arrows."

The first row of Lamanites seemed to melt into the sand, but they were merely trampled underfoot by the oncoming horde.

Little flying insects no bigger than midges hovered over me like a buzzing cloud, settling in my sweat and more especially in the rivulets of blood, thickening and sticky, from the slashes and gouges in my skin.

Once again we fought man to man, sword to sword, sword to spear or axe. It seemed to me that the yelling, screaming Lamanites were unstoppable.

We fought for long minutes that seemed like days. Enemy archers aimed their shafts toward us in our place of retreat. Some caused bloody and painful wounds. There seemed to be hundreds of the enemy to our dozens and their arrows came whistling and singing in through the openings. How long could we hold out?

I felt a real brotherhood with my men. The feeling was one of desperate loyalty based on the fact that any might die at any time. I thought to myself, here on the borders of death, life follows an amazingly simple course. Life is limited to what is most necessary. All else lies in gloomy sleep.

My tired day-dreaming was interrupted. Three attackers held Zeram at bay. Manti sprang to his rescue, seized a Lamanite by the hair, brought a knee up into his face, smashing his nose. A hellish cry came from him and he reeled away, blinded. A second Lamanite I caught on the tip of my lance. The lance was so deeply embedded I was unable to withdraw it. Zeram kept his other attacker at bay, chopping the air with his dagger and defying him to come nearer. I smashed the Lamanite with the flat of my sword on the side of his head and he fell like a clubbed ox. Zeram turned to me with gratitude in his eyes. As he began to speak an arrow pierced me, high in the thigh where my left leg joins with my trunk. It passed through the flesh without hitting any vital parts. Another arrow caught Zeram in the neck, with part of the arrow protruding on both sides. Dazedly I looked at him. He tried to speak but no words came out, only a bubble and a gurgle. His eyes lost their sheen. I caught him as he fell, but there was no saving him. He tried to breathe but he was already choking on his own blood. All I could do was lower him gently to the ground. Then I remembered no more.

Consciousness came slowly. My face was right in the sand. I watched dreamily as my breath moved the stalks of grass before me. I noticed how fine was the sand. Turning my head, I looked up as if in a dream. Flocks of swallows swooped across the beach in close formation. Most beautiful of all was the dark greenness of the forest above me. As a cloud passed over the sun the color of the jungle deepened to an almost black hue, then as the shadows moved on the vibrant green color returned.

Vultures hopped around among the dead. I waved my arm weakly to keep them at bay. Their tearing and pecking noises gagged me.

The sun dropped below the trees to the west. Suddenly I was afraid. Had I been left here to die? Sounds of battle had ended. Where were my men? I tried to pull myself together. I knew my fears were unfounded. My men would not leave me to die here on the banks of the Sidon.

Consciousness came and went. I lay there in the slight depression, my forehead wet and my hair damp. Smell of death nauseated me. Sand stuck to my wet body. My hands trembled and I prayed softly. My only desire was to get up and leave this ghastly place, but my limbs seemed glued to the earth. I tried vainly to rise, but to no avail, so I pressed myself even tighter to the sand.

I was stupefied with exhaustion and thirst. The battle was like fog to me. I dozed. Twilight came and once again I began to tremble.

Chapter 12

High Priest

I opened my eyes, feeling snug and dry in the blanket which was wrapped around me. Above me I could see peak of goatshair tent. Legs and feet of men standing outside the tent were visible when I glanced sidewise. Bit by bit, the parade of events fell into place in my sleep-drugged mind. Battle beside the river. Wave after wave of Lamanites and Amlicites coming at our army. My loathing of all the killing; especially that I had to be part of it. I stretched my legs and the pain hit me. My leg!

Pain brought more remembrance. Feel of my sword slicing through flesh and striking bone; of Zeram falling beside me, of wet, glistening dark Lamanite bodies before me; of shorn heads and painted faces; of dark, fierce eyes staring at me from hate-filled faces. I felt my thigh. Healing leaves and cotton cloth swathed it.

Weak and perspiring, I lay back on my blanket. I had no idea how long I had slept. Somewhere I must have lost a day—lost the sequence of events. I lay in my blanket, listening to low voices of the men whose feet I saw, gathering from their conversation that the Lamanites were beaten.

I sighed with relief; Zarahemla must be safe.

When I awakened again, I felt the presence of someone inside the tent. As I attempted to sit up, a cool hand on my forehead pushed me back down. I looked up into the green eyes of Ruth. I sighed with contentment. Now I was happy. I took her hand in mine.

"I almost died back there," I said.

"I know," she whispered, her hand caressing my chest, fingers twining in the heavy hair. "If you had been killed, I think I, too, would have died."

The desire to pull her to me was strong, but I was still too weak. So I talked instead.

"Part of me did die, sort of," I said. "A part of my life is gone forever. Maybe that is what happens to someone in war. I have been dreaming about it. I still see Nabob lying there, blood streaming from his wounds. And...."

"Shh, rest now," Ruth whispered. Her voice seemed far away. I reached up and touched her shoulder. As she deftly changed the dressing on my leg she bent her head to rest her cheek on my wrist.

I raised her chin. "I love you, Ruth."

She tried to smile, but instead, only tears came. She leaned over and hugged me, her long black tresses falling over my face, her tears bathing my bare chest. Distressed, she pulled away, her breasts rising and falling. I could see she was trying to contrcl her emotions.

"I am sorry about Nabob," she said.

"He wasn't the only one." I again saw young Amnor and Zeram, hacked to death. "So many faces they become mixed up in my mind." I paused as thoughts of the horrible battle again flowed through me.

"It's like one of those ghastly nightmares you have as a child, and it stays with you all your life."

Ruth was silent, leaving me to my nightmare memories.

I must have dozed. When I awakened again the sun's glare on the tent was from the west. It was afternoon and I was suddenly very hungry. How long since I had eaten? Then I realized my hunger came from smelling food cooking.

The flap raised and Ruth came into the tent, a steaming bowl in her hands. She smiled when she saw I was awake. She propped me up with a pillow and knelt beside me, feeding me from the bowl. I prided myself in being self-sufficient, so tried to sit up in order to feed myself. I fell back weakly. Pride or not, I let Ruth feed me.

What a luxury eating was. What an incredible feast: stew, thick and savory with large pieces of meat floating in broth. I wolfed it down as fast as she could feed me. Food had never tasted so good. Ruth brought another bowl and a gourd of water.

A shadow fell over me. Looking up I saw young Moroni, unshaven and red-eyed. He smiled, his eyes showing his gladness at seeing me alive and well enough to eat. I motioned him to sit beside me.

"Tell me what had happened. What of Zoram?"

"He is well. He had placed the armies around Zarahemla in case of further attacks."

"And the Lamanites?"

"The Lamanites and the few Amlicites who survived fled westward to the wilderness. They were totally defeated."

I noticed the intensity of his eyes.

"How far did they go?"

Moroni shrugged. "I followed them all night until they reached the wilderness we call Hermounts."

"Isn't Hermounts infested with wolves and many jaguars?"

"Yes, Moroni said, a smile on his stubbled face. "Perhaps the animals will finish the job we started."

"That's enough talk for now," Ruth said. she hustled Moroni from the tent. As I watched him go I thought of all the statements I had heard in Zarahemla concerning the waywardness of our Nephite youth. Well, that was one worry I didn't share. I had met and fought beside too many young men who knew the proud history of their people and didn't shirk their responsibility.

Ruth removed the pillows and I gratefully lay down, my mind filled with concern that Lamanites and renegade Amlicites still roamed our land. Then I slept.

I was awakened by a soft hand on my forehead. Ruth stood by my bed.

"You are feeling better?" she asked.

She stroked my hair, running fingers through graying strands.

"You have suffered much," she said. "But if you are strong enough, Moroni has sent men to move you back to our home in the city."

Being home, with children, wife, and my own bed helped the healing process. I was nervous to be up and doing. I had progressed from bed to chair, and enjoyed sitting in the garden in afternoon sun. Ruth's flowers gave off a heady smell and I always enjoyed the smell of the freshly-turned soil.

I was there relaxing and reading, enjoying sun and smell of earth and flowers, when a furious pounding on the door interrupted my pondering of the scriptures. Ruth appeared at the garden door, jaw set, her face red.

"Moroni has returned," she said. "I told him not to disturb you but he insists."

"Let him come in," I said with a smile. "You can't protect me forever."

She turned on her heel, a huffiness in her manner. I smiled to myself. It is nice to be loved and protected.

Moroni marched in and stood before me at attention. I could see he was excited about something, but he stood motionless waiting permission to speak.

I motioned him to sit. He squatted on his heels in the dirt, a look of intensity in his youthful face.

"What is it?"

"Sir, another Lamanite army has come down from the land of Nephi. They are in the land of Minon and are marching rapidly towards Zarahemla."

I gritted my teeth. No more, Lord, I said to myself. Controlling me emotions, I asked, "The Land of Minon?"

"Yes sir. The Lamanites destroy everything in their path—flocks, herds, villages. They even tramp down the fields of grain. Those people who escape are fleeing before them."

"How far are they from Zarahemla?"

"Two days' march."

I closed my eyes and sat silent for a moment, pondering the situation. My injured leg was going to be a real hindrance.

"Where is Zoram?" I asked.

"His armies still protect the west area around the wilderness of Hermounts in case Amlicites and Lamanites return."

"How many warriors in and near Zarahemla?"

"We could probably raise few more than a thousand."

"Messengers must be sent to Zoram informing him of what is happening, and instructing him to bring part of his army."

Moroni flashed a brief smile. "I have already dispatched a runner. Zoram could be here by tomorrow evening."

"Tomorrow? By that time Lamanites could be attacking the city."

Moroni nodded grimly.

"We have only one choice," I mused. "Manti's and Limhi's armies must delay the Lamanites until Zoram arrives."

"Yes, sir."

Moroni stood, saluted, and quickly departed.

I leaned back in the chair. As much as I abhorred war, I longed to go with Moroni. Ruth came out and sat beside me. She ran the tips of her fingers gently up and down my arm.

"My dear," I said. "This is only my fifth year as chief judge and already we have dealt with murderers, adulterers, preachers of priestcraft, rebellion by Amlicites, and now face our second major battle with Lamanites."

I sighed. "Why do people continue to choose evil when rewards for good are so great?"

Ruth didn't answer but she squeezed my arm to show she was listening.

I really hadn't expected an answer. Prophets throughout the ages had asked similar questions.

Waiting was anguish. What was happening to Moroni and our armies? Had Zoram arrived in time to rout the Lamanites?

Four days later Moroni reported back to me. The armies had held the Lamanites in a delaying action until Zoram and his army arrived. Then Nephite armies drove the Lamanites back into their own countries. I silently praised the Lord. Maybe now we could once again have peace.

* * *

My wound healed rapidly under Ruth's expert nursing. Though I limped, I was soon busy fulfilling my responsibilities as chief judge and high priest.

Church assignments gave me great joy through the next years.

"The people seem more righteous," Ruth commented one day. "You seem to be spending more time at the river, baptizing."

"Yes," I responded. "Loss of many warriors has humbled people. So far this month I and my priests have baptized several thousand in the waters of Sidon. I now understood to some extent the joy Father felt as he baptized at the waters of Mormon and again at Sidon."

"As busy as you are, have you noticed how the children are growing?"

"How could I help but notice," I said proudly. I thought of my children. Helaman was almost eight, quiet and serious in demeanor. Shiblon was a jolly boy of six, who delighted in helping his mother. Corianton at five was thin, wiry, and had a tendency to be mischievous. I remembered the lesson of my father and no matter how busy the positions of high priest and chief judge kept me, I spent much time with the boys. I taught each of them the use of the bow, and we spent many happy hours along the river. We fished, swam, and hunted for peccary or hare.

I had continued the school of scribes which King Mosiah began. Helaman was now enrolled and showed great felicity in writing both Hebrew and reformed Egyptian.

The eighth year of my judgeship brought problems—not from without, but from within.

"I am really concerned about our people," I confided to Ruth.

"What seems to be the problem?"

"The Lord, fulfilling his promise, has prospered Church members for their righteousness."

"I have noticed that many of our people have become wealthy," Ruth observed.

"There's nothing wrong with wealth," I said. "The Lord has promised us wealth. And there are many who use their wealth to do good after the pattern set by King Benjamin."

"But the others?" Ruth waited for my response.

"You've noticed the others. They don't understand the purposes of wealth and have become proud. They dress in fine silks and linens and wear much jewelry of gold and precious stones."

"Yes," Ruth said. "I've noticed those at church who seem to flaunt their wealth before the poor."

"Through their actions we are now seeing dissent and persecution."

"But you have done something about it."

"Yes. I have instructed my teachers and priests to warn people to be true to their covenants of baptism."

"There are many who continue to impart of their substance to the poor and needy."

"And I am very proud of those humble followers of Christ who feed the hungry and suffer many afflictions for sake of the Christ who will come."

Letters came from Ammon and Aaron. As I read of their continuing missionary work among the Lamanites, my eyes misted.

"I sometimes wonder if the Lamanite converts are becoming more righteous than the Nephites," I commented to Ruth after reading Ammon's letter.

She grew serious. "The Lamanites are a faithful people, very loyal to their beliefs." She paused, apparently thinking of her years among the Lamanites as a temple priestess. "I wouldn't doubt that they would be more faithful than many of our Nephite people."

"They have had troubles."

"Troubles?"

"The renegade Amalakites and Amulonites continue to stir up trouble among the unconverted Lamanites. Ammon is fearful that a battle is imminent between his people and those who are antagonistic to the Lord's work."

That night I lay awake far into the night thinking of Ammon and his brothers and their missionary work. I was almost envious. I was frustrated. I was almost fifty years of age and felt I was accomplishing little for the Lord. The work of chief judge kept me so busy I could not spend the necessary time teaching people and leading the Church. There was no way I could fulfill both things well. I had been chief judge for more than eight years. Perhaps the time had come to give someone else the responsibility. I desired to devote full time to Church and family.

The next morning I approached Ruth about my thinking. "Ruth, dearest, I am thinking of giving up the chief judgeship."

She poured me a glass of guava juice and waited for me to continue.

"I am feeling the need to spend more time teaching the people and fulfilling my responsibilities as high priest over the Church." I reached over and took her hand. "I also feel the need to spend more time with you and the boys."

She smiled. "Alma," she said, "I love you and will support you in whatever decision you make."

I squeezed her hand. "I will inquire of the Lord."

I fasted for two days, spending much time in the temple on my knees. The answer finally came.

"I am to give up the judgeship," I excitedly announced to my family.

"Who will take your place?" Ruth asked.

"Father counseled me that government leaders must be righteous and holy men. Therefore, I decided to choose one of my faithful priests as chief judge."

"Who?"

"Nephihah, one of the elders of the Zarahemla church. During all of our trials he has been like a rock—never wavering."

"Have you asked him?"

"No, and even if he accepts the appointment, he must still be ratified by a vote of the people."

Nephihah agreed to accept the responsibility if it were given him. I sent noticed throughout the land, informing people of my decision to step down as chief judge, asking them to vote for Nephihah to fill that position. The vote, tallied by judges in each city, came back strong in his favor.

With relief I resigned my position and turned over the judgeship to Nephihah. I had served in that position for nine years. Now I could get on with the Lord's work.

My first task was to insure that I was in tune with the Lord. I fasted and prayed for many days, kneeling in the same forest clearing where Father had spent so much time on his knees. I poured out my heart to God, feeling in return the warmth and peace of his sweet spirit. I wrote down the words the spirit taught me.

Go forth and say unto this people: Repent, for except ye repent ye can in nowise inherit the kingdom of heaven.

Repent, all ye ends of the earth, for the kingdom of heaven is soon at hand; yea, the Son of God cometh in His glory, in His might, majesty, power, and dominion. Behold the glory of the King of earth and heaven shall very soon shine forth among all the children of men.

Behold, the axe is laid at the root of the tree; therefore every tree that brings not forth good fruit shall be hewn down and cast into an unquenchable fire. Remember, the Holy One has spoken it.

For the names of the righteous shall be written in the book of life and unto them will I grant an inheritance at my right hand.

Armed with the word of the Lord, I spent time with Ruth, writing and reviewing what I wanted to say to my people. After writing, Ruth helped me refine my words of challenge and exhortation. I was now ready to spend my time preaching and calling people to repentance.

In my sermons I challenged people of the Church. "Have you spiritually been born of God? Have you received His image in your countenance? Have you experienced this mighty change in your hearts?

"Do you exercise faith in the redemption of Him who created you? Can you look up to God with a pure heart and clean hands, having the image of God engraven upon your countenances?

"Do you look forward with an eye of faith? Can you see your mortal body raised in immortality to stand before God to be judged according to the deeds which you have done while in mortality?

"Can you imagine the voice of the Lord saying unto you in that day, 'Come unto me ye blessed, for behold, your works have been works of righteousness upon the face of the earth'?

"Or do you imagine to yourselves that you can lie unto the Lord? Can you imagine yourselves brought before the tribunal of God with souls filled with guilt and remorse, having remembrance of your wickedness and your defiance of the commandments of God?"

I taught in the streets and in the churches. Everywhere I could get a few people to listen I questioned them concerning their righteousness.

Humbly I asked my people, "Have you kept yourselves blameless before God? Could you say, if you were called to die at this time, that you had been sufficiently humble? Have you repented? Have your garments been cleansed from sin and made white through the blood of the Christ who will come to redeem his people?

"Are you stripped of pride? If you are not, you are not prepared to meet God. You must prepare quickly for the kingdom of heaven is soon at hand and only those who have humbled themselves and repented shall have eternal life."

I told them the Lord had invited all men to come unto Him. That His arms of mercy were extended to each of us and all we had to do was to repent in order to be able to partake of the fruit of the tree of life which Father Lehi had seen in vision.

I went forth among the people in Zarahemla, bearing my testimony, challenging them to do their duty, witnessing to them of Christ who would come.

"My people, I have spoken to you plainly so you cannot err. God has called me to speak to you. I am commanded to stand and testify to you the things which our fathers have spoken concerning the things which will come.

"And this is not all. I testify to you that I know that these things of which I have spoken are true. They are made known to me by the Holy Spirit of God. I have fasted and prayed many days that I might know these things of myself. And now I do know of myself that they are true, for the Lord has manifested them to me by the spirit of revelation.

"My people, I know Jesus Christ shall come. He is the Son, the Only Begotten of the Father. He will come to take away the sins of every man who steadfastly believes on his name."

I called upon everyone to repent and come unto God. Scribes wrote down my words and sent them to all the churches.

"I, Alma, having been called of God, command you who belong to the Church to observe to do the words which I have spoken unto you. You who do not belong to the Church I invite you to come and be baptized unto repentance, that you also may be partakers of the fruit of the tree of life."

Many repented and were stirred up in remembrance of their covenants. I ordained more priests and elders, laying my hands on their heads and blessing them to preside and watch over the church in Zarahemla. They gathered the people together often for prayer and testimony bearing. I asked them to fast and pray for those who had not yet repented and still knew not God.

Feeling the Church was in good hands in Zarahemla, with spirituality and belief reestablished, I traveled to Gideon. This city, home of my father's friend who was killed by Nehor, had always been a bastion of righteousness. Now, it too, was in the midst of struggle—struggle between those who had remained humble and faithful to their covenant of baptism and those who were departing from Church principles because of pride and sin.

I taught wherever I found people—in synagogues, on streets, even in homes of the faithful few. After preaching and baptizing for a full month, a large gathering was called for the Sabbath. In that meeting I would give my final sermon before departing the land of Gideon.

The plaza before the temple was full as I made my way up the steps. I looked over the vast assemblage. Here were people I had converted, older people who remained faithful from Gideon's and my father's time, those who were investigating the Gospel, and the idle curious.

"My beloved people," I began. "This is the first time I have been able to address you since being ordained as high priest. I have been wholly confined to the judgment seat.

"Now with Nephihah as chief judge, I have come to you with great hopes and much desire that I should find you humbled before God; blameless before Him. I trust that you are not lifted up in the pride of your hearts; I trust that you have not set your hearts upon riches and the vain things of the world; I trust that you do not worship idols, but that you do worship the true and living God, and that you look forward to the remission of your sins.

"The most important thing I can do is testify that the time is not far distant when the Redeemer will come to earth among His people. The Spirit has told me to tell you, *Cry unto this people, saying, repent and prepare the way of the Lord, and walk in His paths which are straight.* Behold, my people, the kingdom of heaven is at hand and the Son of God comes.

"The Spirit has told me that He shall be born of Mary, at Jerusalem, the land of our forefathers. She is a virgin, a precious and chosen vessel of the Lord, who shall conceive by power of the Holy Ghost and shall bring forth a son, even the Son of God.

"He shall go forth, suffering pains and afflictions of every kind that the words of Isaiah shall be fulfilled. He will die at the hands of his oppressors, and through his sufferings He will take upon Him our sins, that He might blot out our transgressions.

"Now I say unto you that you must repent and be born again, for the Spirit has told me that unless you are born again you cannot inherit the kingdom of heaven. Therefore, if you have not already done so, come and be baptized unto repentance, that you may be washed from your sins."

I entreated the people. "Come and fear not. Lay aside sins which now bind you down. Be baptized. Going into the waters of baptism will witness to Him that you are willing to repent of your sins and covenant with Him to keep His commandments. Whoever does this, keeping the commandments of God from this time forth, shall have eternal life, according to the testimony of the Holy Spirit which testifies in me."

I told them many more things, challenging them as I challenged the people of Zarahemla. I pleaded with them to walk blameless before God—to be humble, submissive and gentle; full of patience and long-suffering; temperate in all things; diligent in keeping God's commandments; praying often for those things, both temporal and spiritual, which they would need, and thanking God for his blessings.

The people of Gideon listened intently as I closed my sermon.

"May the Lord bless you. Keep your garments spotless. May the peace of God rest upon you, and upon your houses and lands, your flocks and herds, and all you possess, according to your faith and good works, from this time forth and forever."

I returned to Zarahemla. Over a month had passed since I had seen Ruth and the children. I was amazed how Helaman, Shiblon, and Corianton had grown in my absence. Shiblon was now enrolled in the school of scribes along with Helaman. I smiled at Shiblon's complaints. He hated being a scribe as much as I had when I was his age. Being with my family gave me greater satisfaction than anything else could do, and I most assuredly needed the rest. But I was still restless.

There were so many other cities I needed to visit. Nine years had passed since my father ordained me High Priest over the Church, and because of pressing problems of the judgment seat, my visit to Gideon was my first travel in that time. I needed to visit every city in the land.

Ruth understood my restless spirit. Here I was, fifty years of age, and yet I couldn't settle down. The Lord had called me to preach repentance unto the people and I just had to get on with it.

I said tearful good-byes to the three boys, a difficult thing for me to do. Little Corianton clung to my neck until I had to pry his hands loose and hand him crying to his mother.

Heading north out of Zarahemla, I kept the River Sidon on my right. For two days I walked towards the west mountains, finally seeing Melek before me. During my rebellious period, I had spent much time in

Melek. But that had been fifteen years ago. I hardly recognized the town now. The city wall was high. Piercing the sky behind it were several pyramids with temples perched high on top. These had been built by the Zimpoc worshippers. Now, with Amlici and his followers dead or scattered in the wilderness, the temples sat idle.

I stayed in Melek for two months, living with my older sister, Leesa. Her husband, Abelon had died several years before and her three girls were all married. Leesa lived alone and welcomed the opportunity of having me visit her.

I wrote to Ruth, "My missionary work in Melek has been very successful. People stream to the city from the entire area to hear the word of the Lord. I have preached repentance and baptism to the people and many have been baptized. Once again I am experiencing the joys of missionary work; the witnessing of the Spirit as people enter the waters of baptism and commit their lives to the Christ who will soon come."

Chapter 13

Amulek and Ammonihah

I tossed on my pallet, getting little sleep. My heart said to return to my family in Zarahemla; the Spirit whispered to continue my mission to Ammonihah. Since my conversion I had never disobeyed the whisperings of the Spirit. I sent another letter to Ruth, expressing my love, telling her of my feeling of urgency to preach in Ammonihah. In the letter I begged Ruth to give each of my children my love and tell them how much I missed them.

I thanked my sister, Leesa, and bid her good-bye, then left Melek for Ammonihah. Where the road forked outside of Melek—one road going to Zarahemla, the other to Ammonihah—I once again hesitated, but only for a moment. The Lord wanted me to preach in Ammonihah.

For three days I journeyed, seeing few fellow travelers. The way, through mostly treeless plains, was easy. In spite of my fifty years, I made good time and enjoyed the walk.

Ammonihah lay close to the mountain wilderness north and west of the Land of Zarahemla. Though I had never been over the mountains, I was told that beyond them was a narrow strip of coastal land fronting the west sea. Lamanites controlled the mountains and coastal plain.

I approached Ammonihah through a flat, treeless valley. The city itself lay in the low point of the valley alongside a river, with mountains west and a high plateau to the east. During the time of my waywardness—my rebellion against the Church—Ammonihah had been a stronghold of Zimpoc, the snake God. Only once had I been here, but I remembered the place well.

Before I entered the city, I found a quiet place and dropped to my knees. I earnestly prayed.

"Father, I pray that Thou will pour out Thy spirit upon the people in this city, that they might listen to Thy word; that I might baptize them in Thy name unto repentance."

Entering the city without challenge, I made my way to the square before the temple. I climbed the steps to the first tier. It was market day. People filled the square; stalls lined the outside edges along the walls.

I shouted, "Fellow Nephites, citizens of Ammonihah, I bring a message of great importance."

People turned to listen. A crowd began forming at the bottom of the temple steps. A group of men, richly dressed in colorful robes and feather headdresses, pushed their way through the crowd.

One—tall, well-formed, dressed in gilded robe with stripes of purple—held his hand up, silencing me. He shouted, "We know who you are. You are Alma, the high priest over the church you have established in Zarahemla and other cities. What are you doing preaching in our city?"

"I am teaching the word of God."

"We are not of your church," he retorted, his gray eyes flashing, "and do not believe in the foolish traditions which you teach."

"Are you the ruler here?"

He walked up the steps to stand beside me and looked back over the crowd. "I am Zeezrom, a lawyer of Ammonihah." He swept his arm out, indicating those who had come with him. "We are advisors to the judge of Ammonihah."

"Won't you and your people at least listen to what I have to say?"

"We don't want to listen. We are not of your church and since you have given up the judgment seat to Nephihah, you have no authority over us."

My heart was heavy as I faced him. I had traveled for many days to be here; I had been separated from my wife and children for several months; and now it seemed I wouldn't even be able to give God's word to this people.

From within me I called forth new strength.

"Fellow Nephites," I cried. "My desire is to tell you of God and His workings with his people. Now is the time for us to prepare to meet God, now is..."

I couldn't even finish the sentence. As if on signal, people began booing and throwing pebbles at me. I attempted to dodge but was helpless before such a crowd. Crossing my arms before my face, I turned to Zeezrom.

His face was hard as ever. He smiled at my discomfiture.

"Zeezrom," I cried. "Stay the hand of this people that I may preach to them."

For answer he spit in my face. At that gesture of revilement, the crowd became even more incensed. Dozens of men stormed up the steps, mauled me, then forcibly dragged me down into the midst of the mob. My hair was pulled, I was spit upon, my robe torn from my body. Even worse, the mob wrested my scrolls of scriptures from me. They dragged me, bruised and almost naked, through the streets and cast me upon the ground outside the gate.

"And don't come back," one cried as he kicked me in the ribs.

I picked myself up and limped away from the city. Beaten and discouraged I prayed as I walked.

"Why, Lord?" I murmured in my agony. "Why did You call me to preach to this city and then let the people do this to me? Why didn't You protect me so I could give them Thy word?"

No answer.

I turned downriver on the road towards Aaron, wandering almost aimlessly as I attempted to understand what had happened. The trail wound its way beside the river, through canyons and hilly tangle. Where the trail ran close to a deep eddy, I stopped and washed myself thoroughly. The coolness of the water soothed my hurts. After washing, I sat upon a large stone to dry, listening to sounds of the river as it swept past me.

Here I was, high priest of the Church in all the land, spit upon, stoned, mauled, and cast out of the city. With no scriptures, I would now have to rely on memory if I were to continue preaching. My mind still couldn't accept what had happened to me. Why didn't I just go home to Zarahemla? That would be the easiest thing to do.

I smiled at my own predicament. I had truly been knocked down, but I was not defeated. I analyzed my situation. I was naked other than loincloth and sandals; I had no food or any money to buy food; my face and body were bruised and scratched; I had lost my scriptures and my dignity. What should I do?

I decided to fast until the Lord gave me an answer. Should I return to Zarahemla, defeated by the Ammonihahites? Should I go on to Aaron and preach there, healing my wounds and my dignity?

Dense trees beside the river gave shade and protection. I gathered branches and built a rude hut. For three days I stayed in the hut; my only distractions the sound of the river and the chattering of monkeys and birds in the trees. I recalled my father telling me of his fasting for forgiveness and instruction while living in a cave in the forest by the city of Nephi. I would follow his example.

Earnestly, I petitioned the Lord for His direction. On the third day, hungry, weak, and sorrowing over the people of Ammonihah, I received my answer.

The day was bright and hot. I had just returned to my hut from bathing. On my knees, I prayed fervently. Attracted by a movement before me, I looked up. There, in the air, bright as sunlight, stood an angel.

I was startled and dropped my eyes, avoiding the glaring brightness of his being.

He spoke: "Blessed are thou, Alma. Now is not the time to be discouraged. Lift up your head and rejoice."

I attempted to keep negative thoughts from my mind, but couldn't help asking myself, what is there to rejoice about?

The angel read my thoughts. "You have much to rejoice about. You have been faithful in keeping God's commandments from the time I first appeared to you and gave you His message."

I sat transfixed by the personage standing in the air before me. Before, when he appeared, I had been so frightened I could not even look upon him. Now I took pleasure in his bright but kindly demeanor. His clothing, whiter than anything I had ever seen, dazzled in the sunlight.

The angel continued, "The Lord has sent me to give you another message. You are to return to Ammonihah and preach again to the people. Tell them that unless they repent the Lord will destroy them."

I was startled. Many thoughts crowded my mind. Go back to Ammonihah? Face that mob again? Then the thought struck. The Lord has given me the same assignment he gave Abinadi. I was to preach to a wicked people who wouldn't listen. Through Abinadi my father had been converted. Perhaps I, too, could touch the heart of one man—as my father's heart had been touched—then another people could be saved.

The angel was patient with me. When he saw I was listening, he finished his message, telling me the people of Ammonihah planned the destruction of people's liberty in direct opposition to God's purposes and statutes.

The angel disappeared. One moment he was there giving his message; the next moment he was gone.

Thrilled by the challenge I had been given, yet still reluctant to return to the city which had treated me so badly, I sat for a few more minutes ordering my thoughts. When I stood, I faced Ammonihah. I was determined to obey the Lord's command. I now knew that the Lord would provide clothing food and scriptures.

The return path was steep in places. I was weak from hunger and walked slowly, my mind filled with the angel's words. I had several immediate concerns. Where would I find something to eat? And where would I find clothes so I could continue my preaching?

I knew the Lord would somehow provide. Thought of the crowd's possible reactions as I appeared before them in nothing but loincloth brought a smile to my lips. As I retraced my steps up the winding path I could imagine people's incredulous reaction. I laughed to myself. It would almost be worth doing just to see their faces.

While I walked, the Spirit whispered to me to enter the city from the south instead of the main east gate which I had previously used. By the time I reached the south entrance to Ammonihah I was exhausted. The sun's rays, though it was only mid-morning, burned on my bare skin. Once inside the gate I leaned against the stone wall. The stones felt cool against my hot skin. I stayed in the wall's shade for a few moments while I regained my strength.

A man, small of stature but with a friendly face, entered the gate. The basket of corn he carried indicated a morning spent harvesting in the fields.

I hailed him. "Sir," I cried, "will you give a humble servant of God something to eat?"

The man turned, surprise in his eyes. He looked me over carefully, then his blue eyes brightened with intensity.

He carefully set down his basket and extended his hand. "I am a Nephite," he said, "and I know you are a prophet of God. You are the man I saw in a dream and an angel said to me, *You shall receive this man into your home.*"

I stepped to him and clasped his forearm. "I am Alma," I said, "a Nephite from Zarahemla."

He picked up his basket and motioned for me to follow. "My name is Amulek," he said cheerily over his shoulder. "Come with me so I can introduce you to my wife and children. My wife, Annadee, will feed you. Come, you will be a blessing to my house."

I followed Amulek through the streets. He was greeted with respect by everyone we passed. I was conscious of the amused glances passers-by cast me, embarrassed by my almost-naked appearance.

Amulek's wife, Annadee, greeted me warmly. She was a lovely brown-haired woman with sparkling bluish-gray eyes.

"Welcome to our home." She set a bowl of warm water before me. "If you care to wash after your dusty journey, I will fix something to eat."

The warm water felt good after so many dusty, sweaty miles. I quickly washed and dried my face and hands, then sat down and unlaced my sandals. I washed my dusty feet and replaced my sandals.

Amulek handed me a robe.

"This may be too small," he said apologetically.

"Thank you," I said as I pulled the robe over my head. I noticed that it only came to my knees, but once dressed I felt better.

Amulek motioned me to come to the table where three small children sat quietly staring at me. He solemnly introduced them.

"This is Sarah, our oldest." He nodded towards the blond-haired, blue-eyed girl. She looked to be about the same age as my son, Helaman.

He put his hands on the next girl's shoulders. "This is precious Mary who just turned four." Mary was a brown-haired child who looked much like Amulek. The same deep brown eyes and dark hair. I smiled a greeting at her.

"And this is Aaron," Amulek said. There was pride in his voice as he spoke. I knelt down beside the little boy. He was so like my Corianton. I solemnly clasped his little hand in mine as my own eyes misted. Oh, I missed my family.

Annadee bustled around the room much like my own Ruth. Her forehead had a sheen of perspiration, and several strands of hair straggled wetly down her cheeks as she set a plate of freshly sliced bread and meat and a pitcher of goat's milk before me.

Before eating, I offered a silent prayer to break my fast. The food was excellent and I ate until I was filled. The whole family watched me eat. Such a warm and homey place, I thought. Quite a different reception than I experienced the last time I was in Ammonihah.

"Thank you," I said as I put down the empty milk pitcher and wiped the back of my hand across my mouth. I looked at Amulek and Annadee. "With your permission, I would bless this house." I pushed away from the table and stood.

Amulek nodded.

Raising my arms towards the ceiling, I cried, "My God, I call forth Thy blessings upon this house; upon Amulek and Annadee and their children. Through Thee, I bless them with happiness and the accomplishment of all righteous goals. I bless them with purity of purpose and fulfillment of faith." I asked God for many other blessings for that family.

When I finished, everyone was silent. I said quietly, "I have not told you about myself. I am Alma, the high priest over the Church of God throughout the land of Zarahemla. God has called me to preach His word to the people of Ammonihah, but even though I spoke with the spirit of revelation and prophecy, the people here would not receive me. They cast me out and I was on my way to Aaron when an angel appeared to me and commanded me to return."

I looked at Amulek. "I am commanded to testify to the people of Ammonihah of their iniquities and call them to repentance. Unless they repent, this city will be destroyed."

Amulek nodded sadly. "Yes, I have known for some time of the wickedness of this people." He shook his head.

Attempting to overcome the gloom I had caused, I smiled at Annadee. "Thank you for dinner. I had fasted many days and was very hungry."

Dimples hollowed her cheeks as she returned my smile. "It is a pleasure to have God's high priest in our home." She called to the children. "Go and play," she said, tapping them lovingly as she shooed them out the door.

"Now tell me of your family," she said.

What a remarkable woman, I thought. She had seen my reaction to her children and knew my deep feelings. I accepted the offered chair, and told Amulek and Annadee of Ruth and my long wait until we were married. I spoke proudly of Helaman, Shiblon, and Corianton.

With her urging, I told of the visit of the angel and my conversion, of my father and mother. What a release of pent-up feelings as I shared my thoughts and life with this couple I hardly knew. I hadn't realized how much time had elapsed until Annadee got up to light a candle. The day had faded into evening. She stepped to the door and called the children.

That was the first of many delightful days spent in Amulek's and Annadee's home. I played with the children, growing to love them almost as my own. Most of my time was spent teaching Amulek and Annadee the Gospel. I started with the story of Adam and Eve found on the brass plates and ended with the writings of my father. For hours I discoursed the word of God to them, quoting scriptures, citing experiences. Amulek found bark–paper copies of scriptures, and we pored over them far into the night. In my prayers I thanked God that my father, Alma, had distributed words of King Benjamin and other scriptures to all the people.

Amulek asked many questions. We discussed each facet of the Gospel, including the coming of the Savior to the earth. I testified to them I knew He would come. Touched by the spirit, Amulek and Annadee both added their witness. Sweet spiritual moments were thus spent together. I felt close to this family—closer than I had felt to any except my own family.

Many days of such great outpourings of the spirit passed, until finally, one night in a dream, the angel spoke once again.

It is time to begin your preaching. Go forth and take Amulek with you. Both of you are to prophesy to this people the word of the Lord, which is: Repent ye, for thus saith the Lord, except ye repent I will visit this people in mine anger; yea, and I will not turn my fierce anger away.

The next day, with Amulek walking beside me, I returned to the square where I had suffered such indignities on my previous visit. Before I had come to preach; now I came to warn of the disasters which would come if the people didn't repent. A crowd quickly gathered as I began speaking. Amulek stood behind me on the steps of the temple. His presence gave me added comfort.

"People of Ammonihah," I cried. "The Lord has commanded me to come to your city to give you warning. He commands you to repent, and unless you repent, you cannot inherit His kingdom. But even more important, unless you repent He will utterly destroy you."

A man standing in front interrupted me. "Who are you who calls us to repent? Did you think we would believe your word that we should be destroyed? As well might we believe you if you said the earth would pass away!"

I was amazed that they were so ignorant of the Gospel that they didn't know the earth would pass away. Before I could speak, another man shouted:

"You expect us to listen to you? As well might you prophecy that this great city be destroyed in one day."

Another shouted, "Who is this God you speak of who would send only you to declare unto us these things of which you speak?"

The crowd was once again beginning to turn into a mob. I could feel the tension as some moved toward me.

With all my soul I prayed for God's Spirit to quiet the mob so I could speak. I felt a burning in my bosom. The Lord was indeed with me!

I proclaimed loudly, "Oh, you wicked and perverse generation, how you have forgotten the truths which your fathers taught. Yes, how soon you have forgotten the commandments of God.

"Don't you remember that our father, Lehi, was brought out of Jerusalem by the hand of God? Don't you remember how he was led by God through the wilderness?

"Have you forgotten how many times God delivered our fathers out of the hands of their enemies and preserved them from being destroyed?

"If it had not been for God's matchless power, and mercy, and long-suffering towards us, we should have been destroyed from the face of the earth long before now.

"As I said to you, God now commands you to repent." I then went into a discourse of how the Lamanites had not kept God's commandments and how they had been cut off from his presence.

"But," I said, "God will be more tolerant towards the Lamanites in the day of judgment than He will you, if you remain in your sins. They sin because of the traditions of their fathers but you have been taught correctly.

"If you persist in your wickedness the Lamanites shall be sent against you and will destroy you."

Many more things did I preach to the people of Ammonihah. I told them of God's workings with our forefathers, of angels He sent to speak with men, of spiritual gifts He had given His people. Then I spoke of the coming of the Son of God.

"And not many days in the future the Son of God shall come in His glory, which is the glory of the Only Begotten of the Father, full of grace, equity, and truth; full of patience, mercy, and long-suffering; quick to hear the cries of His people and to answer their prayers.

"Prepare yourselves now, that you might be ready when the Lord comes."

When I finished speaking, the people again surged forth, anger and hatred in their expressions. I was convinced they really intended to kill me.

Before they reached me, Amulek stepped forward, his hands stretched towards the people. The roar of the crowd died down as men recognized Amulek as one of their own.

"I am Amulek," he said. "I am the son of Giddonah and a descendant of Aminadi. Aminadi, whom you remember, was a direct descendant of Lehi who came out of the land of Jerusalem. I am a man of reputation among you. Many of you know me and know I do not speak falsely. Some of you are friends and relatives and know that I have become a wealthy man through my own industry.

"In my life to this time, I have never known much about the Lord and His ways. I had seen His power manifest but hardened my heart and rebelled against God. Then last week, as I was on my way to visit my cousin, an angel of God appeared to me and said, *Amulek, return to your house, for you shall feed a prophet of the Lord; yea, a holy man, who is a chosen man of God, for he has fasted for many days because of the sins of this people, and he is hungered, and you shall receive him into your house and feed him, and he shall bless you and your house, and the blessings of the Lord shall rest upon you and your house.*"

I felt tears of joy burning my eyes as Amulek spoke. What a choice man he was.

He continued. "I obeyed the voice of the angel. As I returned to my house, I found the man the angel had spoken of. It is this man," he rested his hand on my shoulder, "who has just spoken to you today concerning the things of God. I know he is a holy man because the angel told me so. I also know that the things he has told you today are true."

Amulek paused in his sermon and looked out over the crowd. Then he plead with them.

"Listen to him. This man has blessed my house, my wife, my children, even my father and relatives. The blessings he has given to us are of the Lord."

He stopped speaking and the crowd was silent.

Several men stepped forward. even without the brightly–colored robe and feather headdress I recognized the man who had called himself Zeezrom.

"You say an angel testified to you that this man was a holy man?" he asked.

Amulek must have perceived the lawyer's intent. he responded hotly. "Oh, you wicked and perverse lawyers. You serve the devil by laying traps and snares to catch the holy ones of God.

I could not have said it better, myself.

"You lay plans to pervert the ways of the righteous and to bring down the wrath of God upon your heads, even to the total destruction of this people."

I listened, surprised at Amulek's eloquence as he told what Mosiah had said concerning what would happen if this people should choose iniquity and fall into transgression.

"They will be ripe for destruction," he said. "The Lord sees your iniquity and cries to the people by the voice of angels, *Repent ye, repent, for the kingdom of heaven is at hand.*

"I tell you that if it were not for prayers of righteous men like Alma we would even now be visited with total destruction. Through the prayers of the righteous we are spared but if we cast the righteous from among us the Lord will no longer stay His hand. His fierce anger will come against us and we shall be smitten by famine, pestilence, and the sword. We must repent now!"

I watched as Amulek spoke these words. Few seemed to listen. People became angrier by the minute. When he finished speaking, one of the lawyers standing beside Zeezrom spoke:

"Because this man reviles our laws and our lawyers, he should be cast into prison along with this Alma." He motioned towards me.

A loud shout from the people acclaimed his words.

Amulek was incensed. "Oh, you wicked people," he cried. "Satan has such a hold on your hearts! Why will you listen to him and will not listen to the words Alma and I have spoken?

"Have I testified against your law? No. You say I have spoken against the law but I have not. I have spoken in favor of the law to your condemnation.

"The foundation of your destruction is being laid by the unrighteousness of your lawyers and judges."

Amulek had hardly finished speaking when an angry shout went up from the people. Zeezrom climbed the steps and motioned them quiet.

"Now we know that this man is a child of the devil," he cried."He has lied to us. He spoke against our law and now says he did not speak against it. Also, he has reviled our lawyers and judges."

He turned to Amulek, piercing him with his eyes, attempting to intimidate him. "Will you answer a few questions?"

"Yes," Amulek answered, "if they are in accordance with the Spirit of the Lord."

The lawyer held out his hand. In it I could see the flash of silver coins.

"Here are six onties of silver. All these I will give you if you will deny the existence of God."

I looked intently at Amulek. An onti of silver was more money than most Nephite artisans made in an entire year. Six onties were considered a fortune. I wondered how Amulek would handle this situation.

"You child of hell," Amulek retorted. "Why do you tempt me? Don't you know that the righteous don't yield to such temptations? You, yourself, know that there is a God, but you love money more.

"Besides, you have lied before God and me. You offered me six onties if I would deny the true and living God, hoping that by my denying His existence you could destroy me. You had no intention of giving me the money even if I had done so."

A sly look appeared in Zeezrom's eyes. "You say there is a true and living God?"

"I proclaimed it for all to hear. Did you not listen?"
"Answer the questions. It is you who is on trial here, not I."
"On trial?"
"Yes. You have reviled both the law and those who administer the law. I asked you a question. You say there is a true and living God?"
"Yes. there is a true and living God."
"Is there more than one God?" Zeezrom asked.
"No."
"How do you know these things?"
"An angel has made them known to me."
"Your friend, Alma," he motioned towards me, "has said that God shall come to the earth. Who is he that shall come? Is it the Son of God?"
"Yes."
Zeezrom then asked, "Shall he save his people in their sins?"
"He shall not! It is impossible for Him to deny His word," Amulek answered indignantly.
Zeezrom turned to the silent crowd. "Remember what this man has said. He has said there is but one God, and yet he said that the Son of God shall come. Then he said that this Son of God shall not save his people—as though he had authority to command God."
Amulek interrupted Zeezrom. "Once more you lie. You said that I spoke as though I had authority to command God because I said He would not save His people in their sins. The Lord said no unclean thing can inherit the kingdom of heaven. So, how can you be saved except you inherit the kingdom of heaven? Therefore, according to God's own word you cannot be saved in your sins."
Zeezrom asked another quick question. "Is the Son of God the Eternal Father?"
"Yes," Amulek answered. "He is the Eternal Father of heaven and earth and everything in them. He is the beginning and the end, the first and the last.
"And He shall come to the world to redeem His people. He shall take upon Him the transgressions of those who believe on his name. These are they who shall inherit eternal life. Salvation comes to no one else.
"Therefore, the wicked remain as if there had been no redemption except for loosing the bonds of death. Then the day will come when all shall rise from the dead and stand before God to be judged according to their works."
I listened as Amulek continued to exhort concepts of the atonement. The Lord had truly blessed him with understanding. He had learned well in the short time we spent together.
He was still speaking. "This restoration shall come to all: old and young, bond and free, male and female, wicked and righteous. There shall not be so much as a hair from their heads be lost. Everything shall be

restored to its proper frame and men shall be brought to stand before the bar of God to be judged according to their works, whether they be good or whether they be evil."

He spoke a few more words in summary, then stood watching Zeezrom and the now very silent crowd. The people appeared to have been astonished by what Amulek had spoken. Apparently they had never heard anyone so filled with the spirit of the Holy Ghost. Zeezrom, who had been so sure of himself when he began questioning Amulek, now stood perspiring and trembling before him. The time was right for me to finish what Amulek had begun. I stepped up beside Amulek and Zeezrom.

"Zeezrom," I said. "Seeing that you have been taken in your lying and craftiness, remember what I proclaim to you and to this people.

"Your lying was a subtle plan spawned by the devil himself to deceive this people. His greatest desire is to subject all of you to his will. He desires to enslave you with his chains, that he might bring you to everlasting destruction."

Zeezrom's whole body shook as I spoke. I knew he recognized the error of his ways and I almost felt sorry for him, but he had brought this predicament upon himself.

He fought to gain control of himself, then asked, "What does Amulek's statement mean, that all shall rise from the dead, both just and unjust, and be brought to stand before God to be judged according to their works?"

"It is given to man to know the mysteries of God," I said. "But they are commanded to impart these words only to those who give heed to them. If a man hardens his heart, he will receive a lesser portion of God's word. Those that open their hearts are given a greater portion of God's word until they know all the mysteries of God."

"What did you mean by the chains of hell?"

"Those who refuse to listen are taken captive by the devil and are led by his will to destruction."

"Amulek spoke of death, and how man will be raised from mortality to a state of immortality, and will be brought before God to be judged according to his works," Zeezrom continued.

I spoke with great patience. "If we have not listened and obeyed God's word, then we shall be condemned. Our own words and our works will condemn us. In this awful state we shall not dare to look upon God and would hope He would command the rocks and hills to fall upon us to hide us from His presence.

"But this could not be. We must come forth and stand before Him in His glory and acknowledge that His judgment is just. We must admit He is merciful unto the children of men; that He has the power to save every man that believes on His name and repents of his sins."

I paused and looked past Zeezrom at the silent crowd, praying they were listening and understanding what I was telling them.

Zeezrom asked another question. "What of the second death you spoke of?"

"This is a spiritual death and will bring on the torments of an everlasting destruction. Then it shall be for those people as if there had been no redemption made, for they cannot be redeemed by God's justice for they are now in captivity to Satan, having subjected themselves to his will."

Zeezrom seemed to be contemplating what I had said.

Another man stepped forward to stand beside us. He wore a feather headdress so I assumed he must be one of the leaders of Ammonihah.

"I am Antionah," he said. "I am chief ruler of this people."

I nodded to him in acknowledgment.

"Did you say that man will rise from the dead and be changed from mortal to immortal and that the soul shall never die?"

I nodded, expecting more lawyer subtleties.

"How does that agree with the statement from the scriptures which says that God placed Cherubim and the flaming sword on the east of the Garden of Eden so our first parents could not enter and take of the fruit of the tree of life and live forever."

He didn't allow time for an answer but looked triumphantly at me. "So you see, it is impossible for man to live forever."

"Thank you," I said. "That is just what I was going to explain. Adam did fall by partaking of the forbidden fruit, according to the word of God, and by his fall all mankind became a lost and fallen people. If Adam had partaken of the fruit of the tree of life at that time, there would have been no death, and the word of God would have been void, making Him a liar, for He had said, *If thou eat thou shalt surely die.*

"But we see that death did come for mankind, which Amulek spoke of as temporal death. However, there was time given for man to repent, making this life a probationary state, a time to prepare to meet God. This life is also a time to prepare for that endless state which I have told you about which comes after the resurrection of the dead.

"If it had not been for the plan of redemption, there could have been no resurrection of the dead, but that plan was laid from the foundation of the world."

I then went on to expound to Antionah and his people the concepts of temporal death, the judgment, and God's dealing with man.

"Thus, He gave men commandments and taught them the plan of redemption; that if they did evil and did not repent the penalty was the second death, which was an everlasting death.

"God called on men in the name of His Son, saying, *If ye will repent, and harden not your hearts, then will I have mercy upon you, through mine Only Begotten Son.*

"Therefore, whosoever repents shall have claim on mercy through mine Only Begotten Son unto a remission of his sins, and shall enter into my rest. And whosoever hardens his heart and continues in iniquity, I swear in My wrath that he shall not enter into My rest."

I again called upon the people to repent, saying "Let us repent and harden not our hearts, that we provoke not the Lord to pull down his wrath upon us, but instead, let us enter into the rest of God which is prepared according to His word."

I then rehearsed to the people the order of the holy priesthood, telling them of its history and power. I challenged them once again to repent and turn to their God and His priesthood leaders.

"Now, my brethren, I would that you should humble yourselves before God and repent. Behold, the scriptures are before you and if you ignore them it shall be to your own destruction."

When I said this I reached my hands towards the crowd. "Brothers and sisters," I entreated. "Now is the time to repent, for the day of salvation is near. The voice of God, by the mouth of angels, declares it to all nations. He has declared it to us. We declare it to you.

"Even angels are now declaring God's message to many throughout the land, preparing the hearts of the children of men to receive His word at the time of His coming. The time cometh, we don't know how soon. I wish it would be in my day, but whenever it is I will rejoice."

I gazed at the crowd, seeing that many were touched by my words. I concluded humbly.

"Now, my brethren, from the depths of my heart I desire you to listen to my words and cast off your sins and not procrastinate the day of your repentance. Humble yourselves before the Lord. Call on His holy name and watch and pray continually that you may not be tempted. Be led by the Holy Spirit, becoming meek, submissive, patient, full of love and long-suffering.

"Have faith in God with hope that you shall receive eternal life. Have the love of God in your hearts that you may be lifted up at the last day and enter into His rest.

"May God grant unto you repentance, that you may not bring down His wrath upon you; that you may not be bound down by the chains of hell; that you may not suffer the second death."

Chapter 14

Prison, Fire, and Repentance

When I finished speaking, I expected more angry shouts. People were strangely quiet. Shining eyes and tear-stained cheeks evidenced that the Spirit had touched some of those standing before us. Even Zeezrom's eyes showed comprehension and belief. I motioned to Amulek and walked down the steps and mingled with the crowd.

Dozens of people, repentance and contrition written on their faces, pressed forward to clasp our hands. We were surrounded by believers. I silently praised God for giving them witness in their hearts.

The anxious crowd pressed against us, forcing Amulek and me back to the steps. I climbed several risers so I could view all the people. The judge, Antionah, and his lawyers stood back from the press of the crowd, seemingly unsure of what to do. I ignored them.

"I believe in what you say. What do I do now?" one man cried.

His cry was echoed by many voices.

I held up my hand for silence.

"Trust in God. Seek Him in prayer. Read His word in the holy scriptures." All afternoon I taught and answered questions of those who believed.

Dusk settled on the square as the sun set behind the western hills before the crowd finally thinned. The lawyers, critical and still unbelieving, stood to one side. I noticed several scribes stood with them, busily writing as Antionah and his lawyers dictated. Excitement over those who believed filled my thoughts, and I thought no more about the scribes.

Amulek and I, arm in arm, returned to his home. Annadee and the children greeted us noisily. We ate a delicious supper of corn cakes and squash. After the children were asleep on their pallets, Amulek rehearsed to his wife all that transpired. I smiled at his excitement.

Our reverie was interrupted by a loud pounding on the door. Amulek looked at me, a question in his eyes, then went to the door.

Several warriors, armed with swords and spears, filled the doorway. Behind them, by light of the lamp, I recognized one of the lawyers who had stood with Zeezrom.

"What is it?" asked Amulek.

"You are to come with us," a warrior replied.

I heard Annadee gasp softly behind me.

"What reason do you have for taking us?" Amulek asked.

The lawyer spoke up. "You are to be tried for lying to the people and for reviling the law and the judges."

"In the middle of the night?" I asked. "That is against all law which Mosiah gave us."

"Stop your talking and come with us," the lawyer said.

Amulek looked at me. I shrugged helplessly. He stepped to Annadee and kissed her, then quietly went to where his children slept and tenderly tucked their coverings around them, giving each a kiss.

We stepped out into the dark night with the warriors and the lawyer. Before we could protest, our hands were tied behind us with stout cords and we were led back through the square to the judgment chamber.

Flickering light from many torches illuminated hate-filled faces. The room was crowded. I recognized many of them as those who had surrounded Antionah on the temple steps. Zeezrom and the other lawyers were there. Antionah himself sat on a raised platform at one end of the room. People stepped back forming a corridor through which Amulek and I were pushed until we stood before him.

The noise of the crowd hushed.

Antionah spoke. "You are accused of inciting riot by lying to the people and by reviling against our laws and our judges. What do you say to the charges?"

Amulek and I stood without speaking.

"Since you have no answer to the charges, is there anyone here who will witness against them?"

Clamoring in the room signified that many wished to be witnesses. One after another stepped forward and gave testimony. I shook my head as I listened. This was not a court of law but a travesty.

"He lied and said...."

"He defamed..."

"He reviled the law...."

"They testified that there was but one God and that He should send His Son among the people, but He should not save them."

"He said an angel appeared to him."

"They accused our entire people of being wicked."

The testimony went on, long into the night.

Amulek and I said nothing in our defense. What was the use. I knew from the moment I stepped into the room what the outcome would be. Our lives were now in the Lord's hands.

I was surprised when Zeezrom stepped forward. His eyes had a tortured look as he peered at us before facing the angry and hostile crowd.

"Men of Ammonihah," he cried. "These men are not guilty. It is I who am guilty."

"Zeezrom, are you also possessed of the devil?" Antionah interrupted.

Several who had stood by Zeezrom when he questioned Amulek during the day now turned on him. They spit on him and dragged him from the room.

As he went out, he shouted, "These men are spotless before God. Let them go."

Antionah waited for the tumult to die, then he spoke. "I find you guilty of stirring the people to rebellion, for speaking lies, and for reviling the laws of this land. For those crimes, you shall be cast into prison." He motioned to the warriors who stood by the door. "Take them away."

Light of morning silhouetted eastern mountains as the guards hustled Amulek and me through the door. We had been before the so-called court all night. The guards dragged us to the prison, our hands still tied tightly behind our backs. The prison keeper, blazing torch in hand led us down a dark, grimy corridor to a cell below ground. The guards opened the cell door and roughly shoved us inside.

The heavy door slammed with a bang, the sound echoing against thick stone walls. Though day was lighting the world outside, inside the windowless, dungeon-like prison it was dank and dark. The air was foul with odor of excrement and urine.

A foot at a time, I groped my way to the wall. I leaned against it, then slid to the floor, my back against the hard stone. I couldn't see Amulek and wondered what he was thinking. A sense of doom impregnated the place. Feeling stifled, I chided myself to remain calm.

We had not slept at all during the night but I was not sleepy. A weariness lay heavy on me, but it was the weariness of disappointment in mankind. Would people never learn to forget selfishness and trust in God?

As the day warmed outside, dim light outlined cracks around the door. Flies buzzed around piles of human offal. Smell of the place nauseated me. Though I couldn't see them, sounds of bugs scurrying across the dirt informed me that the prison was well-inhabited. Occasionally huge hairy cockroaches crawled on my legs. With hands still tied behind my back I couldn't even brush them off. I shivered with revulsion.

About mid-morning, Antionah himself came to the prison. The door creaked open and he faced us, torchlight revealing a look of self-satisfaction on his fierce face.

"Are you ready to recant the words you have spoken against our laws and our people?"

Neither Amulek nor I answered.

He smiled wickedly. "Those who believed in your words are no more."

I looked at him in astonishment and tried to sit up straighter.

He grinned again, relishing his own words. "This morning all men who believed your lies were cast from the city and stoned."

Now I remembered the scribes who had been writing yesterday afternoon. I finally understood what they were writing.

"The women and children?" Amulek gasped.

Antionah's lips curled in a smile, but his eyes remained hard and cruel.

"Today when the sun reaches its highest point you will see them."

Amulek and I sat without talking. I knew Amulek was worried about Annadee and the children. I, too, was concerned. The wickedness of Antionah and his followers knew no bounds. What did he plan to do? I uttered a silent prayer on behalf of the believers, praying that they could be released. A solemnity pervaded my thoughts and I knew that my prayers were not to be answered the way I had intended.

The guards came for us at what must have been noontime. My wrists were chafed raw by the stout ropes which bound my hands behind my back. We had not eaten since the previous night but I felt no hunger—only anger at the way we had been treated. Guards hauled us through the streets. Before we even reached the walls we could see smoke and flames rising high into the air. Outside the east gate a bonfire raged in a small depression.

Sitting with backs to the city wall were women and children. I noticed with dismay the ropes which bound them hand and foot. Annadee and her children sat in front, hair disheveled and clothing torn.

Amulek cried out and tried to go to them. The guard cracked him with the staff of his spear and held him back.

Dazed, Amulek looked at me, a question in his eyes. Then he looked back at those he loved.

Antionah, surrounded by his lawyers, walked through the gate and stood before us. He was dressed in full, colorful robe and feather headdress. His hand rested on a long staff. He looked grimly at the fire and at the prisoners. Then he turned back to us.

"Observe the results of your lies, Alma," he said. "You, and you alone, are to blame for what is about to happen."

He signalled with his staff.

The warriors who had been feeding the flames with large tree limbs, went to where the women and children sat.

Amulek cried, "No!" and attempted again to break away from the guards. One slapped him across the face and he slumped to his knees.

Warriors carried out their grim work of death. Dragging and carrying the screaming women and children, they tramped as close as they could to the raging fire, then cast their helpless burdens into its midst. The awful sight seared itself on my eyes; smell of roasting flesh and burning hair clogged my nostrils; screams of the dying burned my ears. I was sick inside. I pleaded silently to the Lord. Please stop this murder. A whispering from the Lord came to me.

Amulek, tears streaming down his cheeks, cried to me. "Alma, I can no longer bear to watch. Call down God's power and save them from the flames."

"I cannot," I whispered. "The Spirit has whispered to me to let it be."

"Let it be? But why?" cried Amulek. "Why would the Lord permit this to happen? Why should the righteous die while the wicked continue to live?"

I was almost as distraught as he. "Amulek, my heart hurts because of what I see before me. I know that what I say has no power at this moment to comfort you, but I do know that the Lord receives those who die unto himself. They shall be glorified. My friend, God permits this evil to happen so His judgment against the wicked shall be just. The blood of these innocents shall stand as a witness against their murderers."

Annadee, little Sarah, Mary, and baby Aaron were carried past. Cruelly, the guards brought them almost within arm's reach of Amulek. They were so close I could see the fear and pleading in Annadee's eyes. Amulek, hands still tied behind his back, struggled and fought to get to them. The guard knocked him to the earth as his family members were thrown into the fire. Great sobs racked his body. I gritted my teeth and turned away from the awful sight.

"Turn around and watch," Antionah shouted. The guard grabbed my hair and twisted me back until I again faced the fire.

On his knees, Amulek begged the guard, "Cast me into the fire also."

"No, Amulek," I whispered hoarsely, "That is not what the Lord wills. Our work is not yet finished."

He looked at me, eyes filled with horror. I could not face him but bowed my head and looked at the ground. Memory of what we had witnessed would never be forgotten.

After the women and children had been thrown into the fire, Antionah again spoke to us. "Now see what happens to your precious scriptures."

The warriors, arms filled with scrolls, ran to the fire. As they cast in the scriptures, I shook my head in dismay. The Ammonihahites had sealed their fates. God would destroy them as He had promised.

As the flames died, Antionah stepped in front of me. I looked sadly at him. He was a doomed man with all his people. He drew back his hand and slapped me hard, then backhanded me on the other cheek.

"After what you have seen," he cried, "will you preach again to this people? You spoke of being cast into a lake of fire and brimstone. Your prediction has already come true." He rubbed his hands together, apparently gloating over the evil he had just done.

I didn't answer him. I loathed the man and all he stood for.

"You didn't have power to save those cast into the fire; neither did God save them even though they were converted to your faith."

He hit me again, then slapped Amulek who stood dazed before him.

"What do you say for yourselves?" Antionah shouted.

Neither of us answered. Once more he struck Amulek. A gout of blood streamed from Amulek's nose.

"Take them away," Antionah commanded and turned from us.

* * *

Despondently, I sat in our cell. Darkness did not shield me from the vivid recurring sight of women and little children as they were thrown screaming into the flames. I sat with eyes shut, thinking of holding little Aaron and seeing the soldier toss him, like a sack of chaff, into the cauldron of fire. I thought of Annadee and her kindness to me and of my helplessness in preventing her death. The flames seared my brain and again and again I experienced the agony of the scene. I knew similar scenes haunted Amulek. He sat, his back against the wall, his head on his knees. We didn't speak at all to each other that day. Neither the putrid smell nor the whispering bugs penetrated our consciousness.

Next morning, guards brought a thin gruel of cornmeal and onions and untied our hands so we could eat. I massaged my hands to get circulation again, but left the food untouched. About mid-morning Amulek broke the silence.

"Why, Alma? Why did they have to die?"

I tried to answer him though I was also hurting inside. "Amulek, can you imagine what would have happened if they had died before their conversion? Without repentance? Annadee and the children are now in the bosom of the Lord. His judgments are just. He is merciful to His children and has power to bless everyone who believes on His name and comes to Him with repentant hearts."

"The children were so young, so innocent," he anguished.

"My friend," I consoled. "Their very youth and innocence guarantees them a place in God's kingdom. Do not mourn for them. Mourn rather for those who remain unrepentant upon the earth, for their reward shall be damnation."

Amulek was quiet, involved in his own thoughts.

Several times in the next two days I tried to get Amulek to talk with me, but he wouldn't respond. Neither of us had stomach to eat anything. Then I realized that we were weakening ourselves. We would need our strength to get through this nightmare.

On the third morning, I said, "Amulek, it is time we began looking to the future. There is nothing we can do now for Annadee and the children, or any of the others who perished. They are now with God and will receive their reward. We must gain strength so we can continue the mission which we have started."

Amulek looked at me, eyes empty and face haggard. He watched me eat my bowl of gruel, then ate from his own. I was so famished that even the watery cornmeal tasted good. More than three days had passed since we had eaten. A few moments after the guard retrieved our bowls, tramping of many sandals in the corridor brought me to my feet.

Antionah, followed by lawyers, priests, and teachers, trooped through the door. Antionah looked me over with his cold eyes.

"You were chief judge of the land of Zarahemla?" he said. It was more a statement than a question.

I didn't answer.

"While you were chief judge, you condemned a man, Nehor, to death?" Another statement phrased as a question.

Now I made the connection. I thought I had recognized some of the priests who followed Antionah. They were of the order of Nehor. Serpent worshippers! So that was why my words had little impact on them. I closed my lips firmly and refused to speak. Amulek, too, was silent.

"Why don't you answer me?" Antionah shouted angrily. "Don't you know I have power to have you burned? Answer my questions!"

I looked at him with pity. What did he know of power?

The door slammed behind them as they left. I shut my eyes and shook my head, desiring to rid myself of the sight and thought of such despicable men as Antionah and his followers. If I could have done so, I would have called down fire from heaven to destroy them. Why do such men even live? I asked myself. I spat on the ground to rid myself of the vile taste. Having done so, I sensed, rather than saw, Amulek's attention. I again leaned back against the wall, ashamed of myself for acting so childish. When the Lord was ready to destroy men such as Antionah, He would do so.

I spent another restless night. My nightmares alone would have kept me awake, but now we were also plagued with rats. One ran over my bare chest; another nipped me on the toe. I could hear Amulek's restless movements and knew he was also awake.

The next day repeated the previous day. Again we heard tramp of many feet. Antionah, in all his regalia, followed by his cohort, paraded into the cell.

Amulek and I sat this time, our backs to the wall. Torches of guards threw wavering shadows on the walls, illuminating the faces of those before us.

"Get up," Antionah commanded.

When I didn't move, one of the guards hauled me to my feet, twisting my arm high into my back. Antonium angrily slapped my face. I looked at him implacably.

Another priest slapped Amulek, then turned and hit me with the back of his hand. I seethed with indignation, but stood silently.

A lawyer, one who had stood with Zeezrom, stepped forward and hit me hard in the nose. My eyes watered and blood gushed forth.

"Will you again preach judgments against our people and our law?" he shouted. "If you have power to damn us," he sneered, "why don't you save yourselves?"

He spit in my face. My hands clenched in anger at my side.

A priest laughed, "How shall we look when we are damned?"

Others guffawed. After their little fun, they left. The darkness of our cell was welcome.

"How long must we endure this?" Amulek asked quietly.

I was pleased. These were the first words he had spoken in days. "Until the Lord releases us," I responded.

The door opened again. Two guards were framed in its light. They were almost apologetic as they put their torches in carved niches and entered our cell.

"Antionah has commanded us to take your clothing," one said as he stepped towards me.

I quietly stripped off the robe Annadee had made me. Embarrassed, the guard motioned towards my loincloth. I gritted my teeth, removed the loincloth and stood naked before him. Amulek was also stripped.

The guard produced a rope. "Now we must bind you," he said.

I turned by back to him and put my hands behind me. He quickly trussed them tightly, then left.

Amulek and I were now naked and bound.

No food or water was brought to the cell. For three days we lay there, bound, dirty, hungry, thirsty, wallowing in our own filth.

On the fourth day we heard familiar tramping.

Two guards, flickering torches held high, stepped into the cell followed by Antionah and his bunch of lawyers and priests. Antionah looked at us with distaste, then motioned to the guards. They stooped down and roughly dragged Amulek and me to our feet. I was so weak I could hardly stand, but I forced my quivering legs to hold me up. I would not appear weak before these children of the devil.

Antionah took delight in looking at my naked, miserable condition. I glared at him, my dislike mirrored in his own eyes.

He slapped me hard. Then slapped again. I flinched and fell to the floor.

Antionah smiled evilly down at me. "If you have the power of God, which you say you have, then free yourselves from the ropes that tie you. Then we will believe that God will destroy this people as you have said."

I stared at him silently. He moved over to Amulek and slapped him, repeating the words. A lawyer stood above me, leaned over and slapped me as Antionah had done, and repeated exactly the same words. Each of the group did the same. I thought grimly that they must have practiced what they were to say before ever entering our cell.

As each man stepped before me, slapping me and repeating the memorized challenge, I became more and more angry.

Then, as if given rebirth, I felt God's power surging through me. Apparently the Lord was through letting us be tried. I'd had enough, and apparently so had He. This debased people could not treat servants of God in this manner.

I struggled to my feet, no longer feeling weak. Out of the corner of my eye I saw Amulek rise.

"How long shall we suffer these afflictions, Lord?" I shouted. Antionah and his followers fell back, astonished. These were the first words they had heard us speak in more than a week.

"Oh, Lord, Give us strength according to our faith in Christ, even to deliverance." I cried.

I flexed my hands. The cords broke and fell from my wrists. Amulek looked at me with astonishment, then did the same.

Antionah, seeing what happened, turned and ran for the door, his followers trailing hurriedly after him. In their haste the guards dropped their torches which smoldered in the dirt at our feet.

I picked up a torch and stepped into the corridor. Judge, lawyers and priests had been in such a hurry to escape the prison that they had tripped over one another and now scrambled on hands and knees towards the outer door.

Rumbling shook the prison. Stone walls swayed back and forth. Amulek hurried to my side, a frightened look on his face. I put my hand on his shoulder to calm him. Walls shook again, then dust mushroomed up around us as walls and ceilings crumbled to the earth. Screaming erupted from the corridor, then all was silent. Through the dust I looked to where I had last seen Antionah. A heap of stones was jumbled in the corridor where he and his followers had been. All had been crushed beneath the falling walls.

Just outside the cell, in what had been the corridor, I found the bundle of clothing the guards had taken from us. I handed Amulek his loincloth and robe, and hurriedly put on my own. It felt good to be dressed again, even in clothes filthy with lice and grime. Amulek fumbled with his clothing, apparently still in a state of shock over what had happened.

When he was dressed, I led him from the remains of the prison. Dirty, bedraggled, but with power of God, we walked through the city. Hordes of people lined the streets, attracted by the noise of the prison's collapse. None dared try to stop us.

As we walked through the east gate, I stopped and shook the dust from my feet in final condemnation of this wicked city. We averted our eyes from the blackened hollow where so many innocent people had lost their lives, including Amulek's loved ones.

Once outside the gate, we made our way down river. Haze lolled in flat layers in the valley. I looked back at Ammonihah. Instead of haze, smoke layered itself above the doomed city. Three black specks rose clumsily into the sky. Vultures.

The river and hut I had built such a few short weeks before were welcome sights. We stepped into the cooling water, clothes and all. What blessed relief! I sat right down, letting healing water flow around me, washing dirt and dust and filth from me, soothing abrasions and sores. I stripped off my robe and pounded it on the rocks, cleaning some of the filth from it, then hung it on a branch to dry. Leaning upstream, I drank long, quenching my deep thirst.

Thoroughly refreshed, I stepped from the water, slapped my skin until I was dry, then waited for Amulek.

"Now we must find food," I said.

Without weapons we were unable to kill any game, so we gathered bananas and mangos from the forest along the river. Our feast, though simple, was kingly fare.

That night, clean, hunger satiated, thirst quenched, we knelt and thanked God for our deliverance. We slept soundly once again as free men.

* * *

Sorefooted, after walking barefoot for three days on rocky trails, we crossed the Sidon River and limped into Sidom. Passers-by looked at us curiously. Then someone recognized us. We heard shouts.

"It's Alma and Amulek!"

Several men ran towards us. Amulek cried out, "Joseph! Nimrah!"

The two men—I recognized them as converts from Ammonihah—ran forward and threw their arms around us, dancing around and around.

"We thought you were dead," they sobbed.

One grabbed each of us by the hand and pulled us forward. Soon we were surrounded by men who had fled Ammonihah. Sores and cuts on some still testified to the stoning.

"Tell us of our families," they begged.

They hushed as they saw the pained look on our faces. As gently as possible, I told them of the sacrifice of their wives and children. Amulek, showing strength beyond what I expected, then gently spoke to them.

"They have received their reward and their glory," he said. "No longer must they suffer here upon the earth, but are now in the very presence of God. Through His love, if we remain worthy, we will someday be with them again."

All afternoon we visited with them, understanding their anguish, attempting to heal their hurt. We told of Antionah's evil actions, and our deliverance from prison.

Before dinner, servants brought water to wash our feet. Amulek and I were given new robes and sandals. A banquet was set before us: roast monkey and peccary, fresh-baked bread, baked squash, beans, corn, and many varieties of fruit.

Before we finished eating, Joseph said, "Have you heard of Zeezrom?"

"No. The last we saw of Zeezrom he was being led from the judge's chambers in Ammonihah." I spoke thoughtfully. "I believe he was finally repentant for his part in leading the people astray."

Joseph nodded. "He is here in Sidom."

"Here?" Amulek asked.

"He is very ill," Nimrah said. "He believes his wickedness caused your deaths. That, in addition to his other sins, has been harrowing his mind until now he is consumed by fever and must soon die. When he heard you were here in Sidom he sent for you."

I put down the leg of monkey on which I had been chewing and turned to Amulek.

"We must go see him," I said.

"He has brought this illness upon himself," he commented.

I could feel his hurt and knew his feelings towards all that Zeezrom represented.

"Zeezrom feels remorse for what he has done. Should any of God's children be denied the opportunity to repent and renew themselves in Him?" I asked quietly.

He shook his head. "Forgive me. I must learn to be forgiving."

With Joseph as guide, we hurried to the house where Zeezrom lay ill. He looked weak and pale upon his bed. I placed a hand on his forehead. It was burning. He looked up at me with feverish eyes.

I took him by the hand. "Do you believe in the power of Christ unto salvation?"

"Yes," Zeezrom replied weakly. "I believe all the words you have spoken."

"If you believe in the redemption of Christ," I said, "you can be healed."

"Yes," he said, attempting to rise, "I believe according to your words."

I knelt beside his bed.

"O, Lord," I cried, "have mercy on this man and heal him according to his faith in Christ."

Even I was surprised as Zeezrom leaped to his feet. He walked to Amulek and hugged him, then turned to me and threw his arms around me, thanking me for healing him.

"It was not I who healed you," I said, "but the Lord through your own faith."

"I believe the words of God. What can I do to be saved," Zeezrom asked.

"The Lord's process has always been the same," I said. "Have faith in Him, repent, and be baptized unto eternal life."

"I desire to be baptized," Zeezrom said.

"And I," Amulek added.

I looked at my friend. Here he had been preaching right alongside me and I had forgotten that he had not been baptized.

"We will baptize tomorrow at the river," I said. "Pass the word to all those who left Ammonihah that any who desire baptism should meet at the Sidon at daybreak."

For the first time since staying at the home of Amulek and Annadee I slept indoors on a pallet. Our days in the prison and subsequent days hiking from Ammonihah to Sidom lacked all comfort. With full meal inside me and comfortable pallet underneath, I should have slept like a baby. But I was too excited.

Though I had been rebellious at the time, I remembered Father's excitement when Limhi and his people were baptized at Zarahemla. I remembered my own excitement as the peoples of Zarahemla, Gideon, and Melek had come forth to the waters of baptism during the past year. Now that transcendent experience was to be repeated.

Dawn was glorious. The sun, shining from a heaven devoid of clouds, filled the earth with warmth and beauty. The sky seemed bluer, and even the grass and trees seemed greener.

Removing my robe, I waded waist deep into the Sidon. Behind me the line of converts reached almost to the city gates.

Amulek was first to be baptized. "I baptize you in the name of the Father, and of the Son, and of the Holy Ghost."

He came out of the water radiant, his eyes shining with new life. He was happier than I had seen him since before Annadee's death. Zeezrom and each of the others came forward and was baptized.

That afternoon, I called for Amulek, Zeezrom, Joseph and Nimrah.

"My brothers," I began. "The Church has need of stalwart men, men who bear the priesthood and can lead people through adversity and trial."

I looked around at this little band of faithful men.

"I feel inspired to ordain each of you as a priest of God, to carry on His work in this area. Are there any objections to my doing so?"

Zeezrom stood humbly, his head hanging. "After all I have done to thwart the work of God," he said, "I don't know if I am worthy of the priesthood."

"Zeezrom," I said. "Your sins were washed to the sea this morning in the waters of Sidon. You stand clean before the Lord. Do you desire to be ordained to His priesthood?"

"Oh, yes," he cried, clasping his hands. "I do desire very much to hold the priesthood."

"And the rest of you?"

A chorus of "yes" greeted my question.

After ordaining the men priests, I said, "Each of you has the power given by God to baptize unto Him any who desire baptism. You are set apart to teach and counsel the people of His Church."

Pausing, I looked at them once more. "If there are any of your people who are worthy to be teachers, who will work under your direction in teaching the people, please recommend them to me."

Several names were suggested. The next day these were ordained.

That night I considered all I had done. I had organized the Church in Sidom and it was now in good hands. We could do nothing about the wicked who remained in Ammonihah. They had built their own shack of iniquity; now they would have to live in it.

I stayed in Sidom for a few more days, observing how the people had humbled themselves. A new Church building was already begun, and people worshipped God and prayed for deliverance. I could now go home. Many months had passed since I had seen Ruth and my boys.

I found Amulek working on the church building.

"Amulek," I said, "you have given up your home, your gold, silver, and all other precious things for the Church. You have even lost your wife and children by your decision to defend me and be part of the Church."

He nodded to me, tears filming his eyes as I reminded him of Annadee and the children.

"You can now remain here as a priest in Sidom, or come with me to Zarahemla."

"Which would you prefer me to do?" he asked in his humble way.

I smiled at him. "I value our friendship. We have suffered much together. I would hope you would come with me to my home and meet my wife, Ruth, and my children."

Amulek reached out and clasped my forearm.

"My brother," he said. "I desire that very much. Above all other things, I desire to work with you in the ministry."

Chapter 15

Anti-Nephi-Lehies

My brush moved rapidly capturing my thoughts on bark paper. I sat by the window where afternoon sun highlighted the figures. I stopped and read what I had written.

"I have preached and established churches in the cities of Zarahemla, Gideon, Melek, and Sidom. I failed at Ammonihah. That city still awaits God's judgment."

Ruth brought me a bowl of sweetened chocolate and sat beside me. We sipped in silence. What a peaceful feeling, to be home again with my family, my wife beside me, children playing quietly out back.

"Is your missionary work now finished?" Ruth asked, breaking the silence.

I put down the drink and smiled.

"Missionary work, like marriage, is never finished, my love. I still haven't visited the smaller cities. Perhaps, too, I will have to return to those where churches are established."

Ruth pouted a little, her face showing disappointment.

"Dear one," I laughed. "When and if I go, I promise you I won't stay away long."

She sighed. "The children and I miss you so much when you are gone. And Helaman...?"

I gently prodded her to finish her sentence. "What about Helaman?"

"He's almost twelve and really needs a father. I worry about him. He hunts often by himself and the forest is so dangerous."

Her words came in a torrent. I took her hand.

"And the other boys?"

"They all need you. Helaman teaches Shiblon and Corianton how to hunt with the bow, and they all help me in the garden, but they need you." She squeezed my hand. "I need you."

"Where are they now?"

She smiled. "Amulek is teaching them to make willow whistles."

Our quiet reverie was interrupted by a beating on the door. I sighed. "I knew it would too soon end." I squeezed Ruth's hand as I stood up. She followed me to the door.

A runner in military uniform stood outside.

"What is it?"

"General Zoram sends word that the Lamanites have attacked Ammonihah."

I could hear Ruth's sharp intake of breath.

The messenger continued, "The general has taken his army to drive them back to the wilderness."

"Have you notified Nephihah?"

"I've just come from the judgment hall. Nephihah asked me to inform you."

"Thank you." I shut the door and leaned against it. Ruth moved into my arms.

"Will it never end?" I whispered. "If we aren't fighting among ourselves we're fighting the Lamanites."

Ruth squeezed me. I buried my face in her fragrant hair.

"What does it mean?" she asked, a note of fear in her voice.

"I don't know. I hope it is just a small band which Zoram and his army can drive out. But...."

I left the rest unsaid. Six years had passed since our last big battle with the Lamanites. Surely they had gained fighting strength during that time. I knew we might be in for a major war, and our new churches were just now beginning to do so well.

Ruth was tense in my arms. I stroked her back but she didn't relax.

I held her at arm's length and looked at her. She ducked her head but I tilted her chin up. Tears welled in her dark eyes.

"What is it, my sweet?"

"I'm worried about our sons. Will they have to fight? I don't want them to go into the army."

***

As Amulek and I hurried to Nephihah's judgment hall, I thought of Ruth's words. Didn't all mothers in Zarahemla feel similarly? My own mother had never complained, but I remembered the hurt look in her eyes when I told her I was enlisting for warrior training. Was sending sons off to war something mothers would always face? Would men never live righteously enough lives that war and fighting would end?

Nephihah was speaking with several older men when we entered the judgment chambers. Amulek and I stood in the back until he had finished. He motioned us forward.

"What is your feeling about the Lamanite attack?" he asked.

"I don't have enough information. Do you have other word?" I answered.

"I expect other messengers momentarily." He looked at Amulek. Amulek shook his head.

"Amulek," Nephihah asked, "you were a citizen of Ammonihah. Why have the Lamanites attacked our land to the north? That is the long way around. In the past they have attacked by way of Manti and the valley of the Sidon."

Amulek shook his head. "The west wilderness and seacoasts have always been controlled by the Lamanites. Several times we tried to drive them out but it was no use."

"Then perhaps the Lamanites are just seeking a weaker part of the land in which to attack first," Nephihah mused.

I wondered if that were the reason, or whether God was using the Lamanites to fulfill his promise to destroy Ammonihah because of the wickedness of the people.

The next day a runner summoned Amulek and me once again to the judgment hall.

Nephihah was visible distressed.

"Ammonihah has been totally destroyed," he said, a pained look on his face. "When Zoram arrived with his armies the Lamanites had already departed into the wilderness."

"Were any other cities...?"

Nephihah interrupted me before I finished the question. "They attacked Noah and have carried off many prisoners."

I shook my head in sorrow. Oh, if only the people would have listened. They were warned that this would happen. I thought of the women and children thrown into the fire while Amulek and I were forced to watch. I looked at Amulek. I could tell he was also thinking of Annadee's and his children's look of pleading and fear before the flames consumed them. Frightened screams of the children had disturbed my sleep for months. Yes, the Lord is just.

"Zoram has sent word he needs your help." Nephihah's words snapped me out of my reverie.

"My help?"

"That's what he said."

"He is in the city?" I was surprised.

"Not yet," Nephihah said. "He sent word with the runner that he and his two sons come quickly to inquire of you concerning the route of the Lamanites."

* * *

Zoram, gray-haired, erect, scars of many battles on his face and chest, stood tall before us. He was years older than I, yet had the bearing of a young man. He had fought as a warrior for thirty years. After Nabob was killed in battle with the Amlicites, I appointed him chief captain over the armies. He stood now, flanked by his sons, Lehi and Aha, reporting to Nephihah. I felt pride in this older brother of mine and his stalwart sons. They were Nephite heroes.

Zoram told of walking through the now dead city of Ammonihah, of bodies heaped in piles, of black buzzards standing defiantly over their carrion, of carcasses torn and mangled. He told of the stink of dead bodies—people, dogs, chickens, large pigs—mingling with acrid smell of smoke from the burning city. Not one soul had survived; the only living things remaining in the city were some yapping dogs and the ever-present buzzards.

I shuddered involuntarily, thinking of the beauty of the city and the thousands of people who had lived there. I could not deny that the Lord's judgment was just. He had given the people every opportunity to repent, but the influence of Nehor and his priests was too strong. Besides, the people were too willing to accept idol worship.

Zoram was still talking. "We organized details and buried bodies in shallow graves."

Lehi interrupted, "But it was a waste of time. Before we were out of the city, dogs and wild animals dug them up."

"The stench of decaying flesh is so strong," Zoram said, "that many years will pass before that land will be again possessed."

He turned to me. "My brother," he said, "your help is needed."

"What do you want me to do?" I asked.

"God speaks to you as His prophet. Ask Him where the Lamanites and their prisoners are. We will meet them in battle and return the prisoners to their homes."

"Your faith in God will be rewarded," I said. "Amulek, please take Zoram and his sons to my home where they can rest while I inquire of the Lord." I winked at Zoram. "Ruth baked bread and cakes this morning."

Zoram and his sons saluted Nephihah then followed Amulek from the room. I smiled. Fresh bread was a powerful enticement to a field warrior. As I left the judgment hall and walked to the temple I thought of Zoram. His wife, Micael, had been dead almost ten years. His daughter Ma'Loni was married and lived with her husband and four children in Melek. Lehi and Aha, the two sons, had never married. Being general over the army was now Zoram's full life.

In my room at the temple I knelt and supplicated the Lord. The sun lay low over the western hills before I finally felt the sweetness of the Lord's voice.

Zoram was showing Corianton his sword when I entered my house. Ruth stood to one side, disapproval showing on her face as Corianton attempted to lift the heavy sword. I wasted no time.

"The Lord has spoken, my brother. Lamanites are journeying by way of the west seacoast to the south. They will cross the Sidon just beyond Manti. If you meet them there, on the east of the river, the Lord will deliver them and their captives into your hands."

Zoram and his sons stayed for dinner. Ruth had fixed roast young kid, sweet potatoes and beans from our garden, fresh bread, and a fruit drink. I enjoyed watching Zoram and his sons eat; I could imagine the kinds of meals they were used to in the army. Years had passed since I had visited with Zoram. We talked of his family while eating. Then over sweet cakes and fruit we talked of his present assignment. I could tell he was really concerned about the upcoming battle with the Lamanites.

"The Lord is on our side," I said, attempting to calm his fears.

"I know that," he smiled. "But even with the Lord on our side some of my men will be killed. These are good men; I hate to lose any of them."

When finished with dinner, Zoram clasped my arms, thanked Ruth and immediately left. I tried to get them to stay the night, but I knew Zoram's urgency to lead his warriors in pursuit of the Lamanites.

A week later a messenger reported the success of Zoram's army. They had crossed the Sidon and marched to the land of Manti. The Lamanites were where the Lord said they would be. Zoram's army scattered them and drove them back into the wilderness. Every Nephite prisoner was rescued and returned to his own land.

I knelt in praise and thanksgiving to the Lord.

* * *

Eleven years had passed since I had been appointed chief judge by Mosiah; more than two since I had given up the judgment seat. For the most part, we had dwelt in peace during those years. I prayed that we might have continued peace while people strengthened their faith. Then I smiled as I realized that people's faith was strengthened more during periods of adversity. But who wanted to pray for adversity?

With the Lamanite army scattered and Zoram's army alert throughout the land, I felt the Lord would bless us with peace.

I was torn in my own feelings. My main responsibility was to my family but as high priest I also needed to visit the people throughout the land. I determined the best way to accomplish both was to do as my father had done: visit a city, establish the Church, ordain worthy men to continue the work, then return home.

Amulek and I established a regular pattern in each city: preaching repentance, baptizing, and ordaining worthy men to the priesthood. As the Church was established and righteous men ordained, we returned to family. The priests we ordained went forth throughout the land, preaching against strife, malice, lies, and all other grievous sins.

Through priesthood leadership, the Church flourished. Not only the Church, but our people prospered just as the Lord promised we would when we kept His commandments. In answer to my prayers, the Lord granted us three years of peace. In that three years, as people turned to Him, He poured out His Spirit throughout the land, preparing people to receive His word. We lived in equality, with priests working beside their people. Nehor had taught class structure, with priests supported by the people, but we were living the Lord's plan.

Even when we were home, Amulek was restless. He desired to be out preaching. I decided we would make another tour of the southern cities. We preached in Gideon, strengthening the Church there, then headed southward towards Manti.

Few people were on the road. Amulek and I were in the midst of a discussion concerning the coming of the Savior when I noted a band of Nephites coming towards us from Manti. Robbers were always a problem in these isolated places so I cautioned Amulek to be very careful. Yet, there was something familiar in the way they walked.

A hundred paces away I recognized the man in lead. Ammon! Dearest friend of my youth in Zarahemla! I ran forward, threw my arms around him and we embraced. Fourteen years! Long years! So many changes, and yet Ammon and his brethren had not changed significantly. All were gray-haired; several had gray beards; Himni, who was somewhat plump when he left was lean and sinewy. But the light of the Gospel still shone strongly in every eye.

As I turned to embrace Aaron, Ammon slumped to the ground at my feet. He had fainted. Aaron and I carried him to the bank of a nearby stream. I sponged his face with the cool water and he quickly revived. He sat up, somewhat embarrassed.

"My joy at seeing you was so great I was overcome," he whispered.

In my excitement I had forgotten to introduce Amulek. I called him over and introduced him to Ammon, Aaron, Himni and Omner. As I looked around at the smiling faces I recognized once again that we were all truly brothers. Without even asking, by light of their faces, I knew that these, my brothers, had remained true to their covenants. I knew that in the past fourteen years they had waxed strong in knowledge of the truth, that they had searched the scriptures diligently and had fasted and prayed for increased testimony.

Through the letters I had received from Ammon, I also knew they had the spirit of prophecy and revelation and that they taught with power and authority of God. I yearned to have them tell us the story of their mission.

"Where do you go?" I asked.
"We return to Zarahemla," Ammon replied.
"Is your mission then completed?"
"No," he said. "Let me tell you of it."

I looked at Amulek. Would he be disappointed if we didn't go to Manti?

"I will return to Zarahemla with you. Amulek?"

He smiled easily. "I, too. I would not miss the report of such a mission."

As we walked towards Zarahemla, Ammon and his brothers filled us in on their mission. They rehearsed much of what I had read in their letters, then continued with their story.

"Thousands were brought to the knowledge of the Lord," Aaron said.

"All were brought to believe the traditions of the Nephites," Omner interjected. "We taught them all the prophecies which have been handed down to us."

"The amazing thing," Ammon said quietly, "is that none have fallen away through apostasy. They are a righteous people, have laid down their weapons, and will never more fight against God or their brethren."

"In one of your letters you said they called themselves Anti-Nephi-Lehies," I said.

"Yes," Himni said. "They no longer want to be known as Lamanites."

Omner added, "If only we had been as successful with the Amalekites."

"Those who rebelled against the Nephites?" Amulek asked.

"Yes. They are still light-skinned and live with the Lamanites in the land of Jerusalem," Ammon said. "What Omner is saying is that in our fourteen years there, we only converted one Amalekite"

"In your letter you also mentioned the Amulonites," I said.

"They are descendants of the wicked priests of King Noah and their Lamanite wives. They are as stiff-necked as the Amalekites. Most of them live in the land of Amulon and the land of Helam which your father and his people settled. We have had no success in those lands. And because of Amalekites and Amulonites, the Lamanites who live in those areas won't listen to the truth."

"Are you saying that the Lamanites are now a divided people?"

"That's the big problem," Aaron said. "The Anti-Nephi-Lehies are converted to the Gospel and refuse to use any weapons of war. The other Lamanites, Amalekites and Amulonites are rebellious and warlike."

"It's really the fault of the Amalekites," Ammon said. "Without their leadership the Lamanites would not be troublesome."

"That's true," continued Aaron, "but because of trouble-making Amalekites and Amulonites, the Lamanites have grown to hate those who are converted. They have taken up arms and fully intend to destroy them."

"I thought the king of the Lamanites was one of your converts," I said.

"He is, and a valiant one, too," Ammon said. "But because of the hatred of the Lamanites against the Anti–Nephi–Lehies, they rebelled against the king and took up arms against the converted people."

"Thank goodness the king wasn't aware of the rebellion," Aaron said. "He died in the faith that very year."

"But what of the kingship?" Amulek asked.

"He conferred it upon his son who was also a righteous man," Omner said. He smiled. "In fact, he was so righteous that he changed his name to Anti–Nephi–Lehi."

"When we saw the Lamanites preparing for war, we met in the land of Ishmael and counseled with King Lamoni and his brother, Anti–Nephi–Lehi," Himni said.

"That's when I asked them what they would do to defend themselves against their wicked brethren," Ammon said.

"I was amazed, yet pleased, with their answer," Aaron said. "The king replied, 'We will not take up arms and we will not make preparations for war.'"

"Then to reinforce that decision," Ammon added, "the king actually commanded the people that they should not arm themselves."

Himni pulled a scroll from his pack. "I wrote down his words. Would you like to hear them?"

"Of course," I said. Amulek nodded. "Let's stop and get a drink while Himni reads."

Himni read the king's words: "I thank my God, my beloved people, that our great God has in goodness sent these our brethren, the Nephites, unto us to preach to us, and to convince us of the traditions of our wicked fathers.

"I thank God that He has given us His Spirit to soften our hearts, and to convince us of our sins. I am most grateful that He has granted us that we might repent and be forgiven and the guilt removed from our hearts.

"Since God has taken away our stains, let us not stain our swords again with the blood of our brethren, for if we stain them again, they might not be washed bright again through the blood of the Son of our great God, which shall be shed for the atonement of our sins.

"God has had mercy on us and has showed that He loves us by showing us the plan of salvation so that we might not perish. Oh, how merciful is our God! And because He is merciful, I feel we should hide our swords that they may be kept bright, as a testimony to our God when we shall be judged before Him, that we have not stained our swords in the blood of our brethren since he gave us His word and forgave our sins.

"If our brethren destroy us, our swords will be buried deep in the earth, and we shall go to God and shall be saved."

My head bowed as I listened to what the king had said. What a powerful testimony! How many of our Nephite people could be so strong?

Ammon said quietly. "That very day the people gathered together and buried their weapons of war. This was their testimony to God that they would never again use their weapons for shedding man's blood."

"They entered into a covenant," Aaron added, "that they would rather give up their own lives than shed the blood of anyone else. They also said they would no longer be idle but would labor from that time forth with their hands in serving others."

Tears were in Ammon's eyes as he continued. "When the Lamanites came against them in battle, our people went out and prostrated themselves on the ground before the army. They knelt there defenseless, calling on the Lord in prayer. The Lamanites angrily came upon them, slaying them by the hundreds."

"That's when another miracle happened," Himni said. "When the Lamanites saw that our people would not flee and would not fight, but simply knelt before them and sang praises to God as they were killed, many felt sorrow for what they had done."

"Many Lamanite warriors threw down their swords and repented of their murders, joining the people of Anti– Nephi–Lehi," Aaron finished.

"Over a thousand of our people were slain," Ammon said, "but more than that number of Lamanites joined with our people."

"Since those who were slain were righteous," I said, "their reward will be great."

"There was not a wicked person among them," Ammon said. "And because of their deaths, over a thousand more were brought to the truth."

Amulek nodded. "Yes, the Lord works in many ways to save His people."

I knew he was thinking of those righteous people, including his entire family, who had been slain in Ammonihah.

"An interesting thing about the situation," Ammon said, "is that not one Amalekite, Amulonite, or follower of Nehor joined the people of Anti–Nephi–Lehi. Every convert was a literal descendant of Laman or Lemuel."

I shook my head. "After a people have once been enlightened by the Spirit of God, and then fall away, they become hardened and are worse than those who have never been converted."

After our rest by the stream, we continued our journey towards Zarahemla. I could feel the urgency in Ammon and his brothers, but I wanted to hear more of their story.

"Please continue. What happened after that first battle?"

Ammon didn't slow down his walk, but told of the converted people.

"The Lamanites did not continue killing our people, but swore vengeance upon us and the rest of the Nephites. They organized their armies and went into the west wilderness, planning to attack the Nephites."

"When they returned," Aaron added, "they were scattered." He shook his head. "The Nephites must have really given them a beating."

"How long has that been?" Amulek asked.

"Just about a year ago," Himni volunteered.

Amulek nodded.

"That's when the Lamanites completely destroyed the city of Ammonihah," I told them. "Not only that, but they captured many Nephites as prisoners and were heading back to their lands with them. Zoram, my brother who is chief captain of the Nephite armies, headed them by Manti and recaptured the prisoners."

"So that is why they were so disgruntled," mused Aaron. "Especially the Amulonites."

I looked at him and was about to question him about what he meant, when he continued.

"When the Lamanite army returned, most of the Amulonites were destroyed. The remainder fled into the east wilderness where they persecuted the Lamanites who had believed on our words."

"More Lamanites now believed?" I asked.

"Yes, after suffering such defeats at the hands of the Nephites, many remembered our words and started disbelieving the traditions of their fathers. They turned to the Lord because He had given such great power to the Nephites. Many were converted."

"But the wicked descendants of Noah's priests put those who believed to death," Ammon continued. "The Lamanites became so angry that they searched out all the descendants of Amulon and his fellow priests and killed them."

I was curious. "How did they die?" I asked.

Ammon looked at me. "It's interesting that you would ask. In almost all cases the Lamanites burned them to death."

I nodded. "That's what I suspected."

"Suspected?" Ammon asked.

"Yes. You remember my father's writing about Abinadi whom the priests of Noah burned at the stake?"

"Uh huh."

"Abinadi's prophecy concerning the seed of the priests who put him to death has now come to pass. He told them, 'You shall die in the same manner as you kill me.'"

"And that, too, served God's purposes," Aaron said. "Many of the Lamanites were converted and came to dwell with the people of Anti-Nephi-Lehi. They buried their weapons of war and became a righteous people."

"And that just about brings us up to the present," Ammon said. "The Amalekites were upset that so many Lamanites became converted and laid down their arms. They again came against our people." He shook his head sorrowfully. "I can't describe in words the slaughter," he said.

"The Anti-Nephi-Lehies were people we loved; people we had taught and worked with. They treated us as angels sent from God to save them from everlasting destruction, and here we were, unable to help save their very lives."

"Ammon went to King Anti-Nephi-Lehi," Aaron said quietly, "and asked him to gather the people together and bring them down to Zarahemla where they would be protected from their enemies."

"The king was afraid," Ammon said.

"Why?" I asked.

"He felt that because of their previous battles against the Nephites, the people of Zarahemla would destroy them. That's when I decided to ask the Lord for His direction," Ammon said. "The king agreed that if the Lord told them to go they would go, even if they had to be slaves of the Nephites."

"Of course Ammon told him that it was against our laws to have slaves," Himni said. "But the king was still reluctant to go."

"He wouldn't even consider bringing his people to Zarahemla unless the Lord told him to do so," Ammon said.

"Apparently the Lord did speak," I said.

"Yes, he did," Ammon replied. "These were His words, *Get this people out of this land that they perish not, for Satan has great hold on the hearts of the Amalekites who do stir up the Lamanites in anger against their brethren to slay them. Therefore get thee out of this land. Blessed are this people for I will preserve them.*"

We walked quietly for awhile, thinking of God's goodness.

I spoke first. "I am guessing that the reason you are here is to prepare the way for your people?"

"Yes," Ammon said. "When I took the Lord's words to King Anti-Nephi-Lehi, he immediately organized his people to gather their flocks and herds and what possessions they could carry. They wait in the wilderness south of Manti while we go to the chief judge."

Again we walked in silence.

"I have a story for you," Ammon said.

"A story?" I replied.

Ammon smiled. "You are always telling us of the importance of one man."

I laughed. "You mean like the influence Abinadi had on my father, and through him an entire people were saved?"

"That's right," Ammon said. "In my letters I already told you about Abish, who made it possible to convert the people of King Lamoni."

"Yes, and I have felt great pain for the way I treated her and her parents when they were invited by my father to his house in the land of Helam."

"We found another individual who influenced his people for good."

I waited, knowing Ammon would tell how that related to me. I thought he was enjoying keeping me in suspense.

"He had been a Lamanite warrior, and though an old man when we met him, was one of our earliest converts," Ammon said. "His name, Taymon, would not mean anything to you. In a battle many years ago, when Limhi and his people were still in the land of Nephi, a tall, very blond, Nephite warrior led his people in battle against the Lamanites."

"That would have been Gideon," I interjected.

"That's right." Ammon paused. "This Gideon, in the heat of battle, had the chance to slay Taymon, but instead spared his life. It was Taymon who prepared the way for us among the Lamanite people in the city of Shimnilom."

"I guess it is always one," I said. "Through man's history from Adam to us, God has always worked with individuals. Then through individuals civilizations are saved. Thank goodness for individuals like Lehi and Nephi."

"And Abinadi and your father, Alma," Ammon added.

"And thank God for Alma and Ammon and his brothers," said Amulek, who had been listening.

Ammon changed the subject as he looked at me. "You spoke of Abish a moment ago."

"Whatever happened to her?" I asked.

"She is with the Anti-Nephi-Lehies," Ammon replied.

I wondered if I were mistaken, but it seemed to me that Ammon blushed. I looked at him intently.

He cleared his throat. "I hope to make Abish my wife when she reaches Zarahemla," he said self-consciously.

"Wonderful," I shouted.

Aaron, Himni and Omner hurried to catch up.

"What is it?" Aaron asked.

"Ammon just told me about him and Abish. I'm excited for them," I said.

For the rest of the journey to Zarahemla the six of us chattered almost like when I and the sons of Mosiah were together in the school of the scribes. By the time we arrived at Zarahemla, we had Ammon's wedding all planned.

Chapter 16

That I Were An Angel

The study was almost dark. Outside, the sun had slipped below the west mountains, bathing the sky in dulcet tones of orange and pink. The only sound was the scratching of my stylus on the soft plates. I leaned back, looking through a window at wisps of clouds colored by sunset.

Preaching the gospel of repentance throughout the width and breadth of Zarahemla had consumed my time for many years. Much had been accomplished but there was so much still to do. I held the plate up to the window and read what I had just inscribed.

"O, that I were an angel, and could have the wish of my heart, that I might go forth and speak with the trump of God, with a voice to shake the earth, and cry repentance unto every people!"

The angel, appearing to me so dramatically, changed my life and gave me new direction and purpose. Now I wished I had the same power to change other's lives.

"Yes, I would declare unto every soul, as with the voice of thunder, repentance and the plan of redemption, that they should repent and come unto our God, that there might not be more sorrow upon all the face of the earth."

I sighed. Why should I have such desires? I should be content to be me. The Lord has blessed me with a noble heritage, a beautiful family, and the opportunity of baptizing thousands into the Church. Yet, I thought, God places desires in man as ripened seeds ready to burst forth into fruit. A man who believes strongly enough in what he desires will almost always accomplish those desires, if he doggedly strives for them. I smiled. My desires, to a great extent, had all been granted.

Some people accomplish little because they desire little, I thought, twiddling my stylus between my thumb and forefinger. Others have larger desires but are unwilling to work or sacrifice to achieve those desires.

I thought of Lehi's counsel to his son, Jacob, that each of us is free to choose between good and evil; liberty and eternal life; captivity or death. Wasn't that choice also based on our desires? I know, I said to myself, that through our desires, every man is free to determine his spiritual goals—whether salvation or damnation. Ammon and his brothers came to mind. Could an angel have done more than they? I thought not. They had a burning desire to convert the Lamanites. Through their work thousands had given up their evil ways and accepted conversion.

I felt that inherently, it is usually man's destiny to carve his own future, to fill his own desires, to achieve his own goals. I pulled over a piece of bark paper and brushed on my thoughts.

Most people, I wrote, if they knew the consequences, would always choose righteous goals.

I tried to analyze my thinking. Since I knew these things, why should I desire more than to perform the work to which I had been called? Why should I desire that I were an angel, or that I could speak to all the earth?

Troubled, I sighed again. I knew what the Lord had commanded me to do. I gloried in my calling and knew great joy with each soul brought to repentance. I thought again of my missions to Zarahemla, Gideon, Melek, and Sidom, and of all the souls who were now truly penitent—people who accepted the word of God in their lives. My soul swelled with joy. I thrilled again at the accomplishments of Ammon and his brothers in the land of Nephi. They had brought forth much fruit and great should be their reward.

Much had transpired since their return from the lands of the Lamanites. Ammon had married Abish and was now high priest over the people of Ammon—the new name given to the Anti-Nephi-Lehies—in the land of Jershon. The people of Zarahemla gave that land to the people of Ammon with promise that the Nephites would protect them against the Lamanites who sought to destroy them.

What a wonderful people they were. Oh, that all people could be so zealous in their worship of God; so perfectly honest and upright in all their dealings with others.

The Nephite army had already fought one fierce battle to protect the people of Ammon from the huge army of Amalekites and Lamanites which had followed them from the wilderness. As thought of my brother, Zoram, came to mind, my heart filled with sadness. In the battle with Amalekites and Lamanites, thousands of both Nephites and Lamanites were killed. Among the Nephite dead were Zoram and his son, Aha. I mourned their loss. Zoram was a fine brother and a great warrior. Zarahemla and I would miss his loyal service.

Though Moroni, who had been my aide in the battle against the Amlicites, was still young in years, I had recommended to Nephihah that he be appointed chief captain over the Nephite armies to replace Zoram. Nephihah had agreed. Moroni chose my nephew, Lehi, as his assistant.

I put away my writing materials and thought again of what I had just written. In my remaining days I could have the effect of an angel. There was still much teaching to be done if this people were to be ready when Christ came.

I walked home. Helaman, sixteen and almost a man, waved at me from the step. Shiblon, a diligent youth of almost fifteen, was working in the vegetable garden. He dropped his hoe and ran to greet me. Corianton charged from the house, a large hare hanging from his hand.

"Father, look what I shot today," he cried.

I put my arms around his and Shiblon's shoulders and walked to the door. What a beautiful feeling the love and faithfulness of my children gave to me. But even after all these years a twinge of guilt went through me as I thought of how, as a youth, I had failed to give my father that feeling.

"How was the school of the scribes today?" I asked Helaman as I approached.

He smiled. "I am still having difficulty in memorizing reformed-Egyptian characters."

I nodded, remembering my own difficulty in learning the Egyptian characters.

Ruth waited inside the door. Each day I looked forward to this moment, when once again I could greet the ones I love. I let go of the boys and hugged her to me. What joy filled my heart. I could ask for no more than this: wife and children who love me, a Father in Heaven who has given me a holy calling, and a people whom I could serve.

Since the great battle with the Lamanites in which Zoram was killed, our nation had lived in peace. Zarahemla had continued to grow in numbers and buildings even though many people had moved northward into the land Bountiful where they settled new villages and cities. For sixteen years judges had ruled the land and the cities, and for the most part their rule was just.

The Church prospered as never before. The Nephites kept God's commandments and were strict in observing the ordinances of God according to the law of Moses. The people of Ammon were a great model for our people to follow. To think that just a few short years before they had been a wicked and idolatrous people.

"Alma! Alma!" The shouting of Muloki, one of my priests, disturbed my reverie.

He stepped panting inside the door.

"What is it?"

"A man is in the square before the temple. He preaches against the prophecies of Christ. He says we as priests only serve in order to get gain. Can I have him arrested?"

"Arrested? No, there is no law against a man preaching." Thank God, I thought, that King Mosiah was wise enough to establish laws which did not punish a man for his beliefs. Aloud, I spoke to Muloki. "The law permits people to have beliefs and to teach them, even if they are contrary to our own. But tell me more about this Anti-Christ."

"His name is Korihor," Muloki said. "He preaches against everything we teach."

"Is he in the square now?"

"Yes. A large crowd listens to him."

"I think I shall hear what he has to say."

Korihor, a small, dark-haired man in brown, flowing robes, stood on the steps before the temple. I walked into the crowd of curious onlookers, greeting those people I recognized. As I listened, I grudgingly admired the man's eloquence and presence before the people. He shouted his message.

"You people are bound with a foolish and vain hope. Why do you look for a Christ? No man can know of future things. These things which you call prophecies are only foolish traditions of your fathers. How do you know of their surety? You cannot know of things you cannot see."

Someone shouted from the audience. "We look forward to having a remission of our sins."

Korihor was quick with his answer. "Such ideas are products of sick minds. No atonement can be made for your sins. Every man prospers according to his own genius, conquers according to his own strength, and will fare according to his own management of this life. Therefore, whatever you do is no crime. Why look forward to an atonement for things which are not sins? When you are dead, you are dead. So why not enjoy life to the fullest?"

I shook my head as I listened. Such foolishness. Korihor's blatant, self-seeking tripe was the same message Nehor had preached years before. Would people never learn to accept truth and quit flirting with the fiction of satanic falsehoods? Some of our weaker people would accept Korihor's logic, but we could not protect people from ideas. Men had to be strong enough to make correct choices. If not...I left the thought dangling. Perhaps such opposition was good. The flock would be pruned and thus strengthened. Those strong in their faith would always survive. It was the Lord's way.

Korihor had little success in Zarahemla. He moved on to Gideon and then to the land of Jershon, hoping to have success with the ex-Lamanite people of Ammon.

I received a letter from Ammon, high priest of Jershon, informing me that Korihor had been taken prisoner by the people of Ammon and escorted out of the land.

Good for them, I thought.

After being forced to leave Jershon, Korihor returned to Gideon to preach. Giddonah, high priest and chief judge of Gideon, brought him back to Zarahemla.

Giddonah fumed, "When this man Korihor began preaching his lies to the people, they bound him and brought him before me. I asked him, 'Why do you go about perverting the ways of the Lord? Why do you teach this people that there shall be no Christ? Why do you speak against all the prophecies of the holy prophets?'"

"How did Korihor answer you," I asked quietly.

Giddonah shook his head ruefully, "I must say that Korihor is bright. He spoke eloquently in answer to my questions. 'You say this people is a free people. I say they are in bondage. You say your ancient prophecies are true. I say that you do not know that they are true. You say that this people is a guilty and fallen people because of the transgression of a parent. I say that a child is not guilty because of his parents. You say that Christ shall come and be slain for the sins of the world. I say that you do not know that there shall be a Christ.'"

After receiving Giddonah's testimony concerning Korihor I sent for Nephihah. This was as much a civil matter as a religious one. It wouldn't hurt to have the chief judge present.

When all were assembled, I had Korihor brought in. "What is it you preach to the people? What words would you say to me and the chief judge?" I asked him.

Korihor looked at me with scorn. "You priests hold the people in bondage, glutting yourselves through their labors. You have oppressed them and led them away after foolish traditions of your fathers. You keep them down so you can enrich yourselves through their labors. You priests yoke them according to your desires, teaching them if they misbehave they will offend some unknown mysterious being who you say is God—a being who never has been seen or known; who never was and never will be."

I was shocked by his blasphemous words and reviling of the priests. Forcing myself to stay calm, I said,

"Korihor, you know that we do not glut ourselves upon the labors of this people. I have labored even from the commencement of the reign of the judges until now with my own hands to support myself and my family. Even as much traveling as I have done to teach God's word, I have not drawn from the people but have depended upon my own resources.

"Notwithstanding the many labors I have performed in the Church, I have not received even one senine for my time and efforts. Neither have my fellow priests, unless they also serve as judges. Even then we have only received what Mosiah stipulated in the law.

"Now if we do not receive anything for our labors, what does it profit us to work in the Church unless it is to declare truth that we may rejoice in the joy of our people? Why do you lie and say we preach to get gain, when you know we don't get gain? Do you really believe we deceive this people?"

Korihor looked at me sullenly, answering with one word. "Yes."

I could see I was getting nowhere. I changed my line of questioning.

"Do you believe there is a God?"

"No," he replied.

I struggled to control my feelings. "Do you deny there is a God? And do you also deny the Christ?"

He nodded.

My testimony burned within me. I said quietly, "I know there is a God and also that Christ shall come. What evidence have you that there is no God? Or that Christ comes not? You have nothing as proof but your own word.

"But I have many witnesses that these things are true. I believe you also know they are true but a lying spirit has possessed you which causes you to deny these things. I believe the devil has you in his power and is using you in an attempt to destroy the children of God."

Korihor looked at the floor as if confused. Without looking at me he said.

"Show me a sign. Then I may be convinced there is a God and He has power. Then I'll be convinced of the truth of your words."

Contempt burned within me for this man who tore down without having anything to build with. "You have seen signs enough. Will you tempt God? Can you honestly say, 'Show me a sign' when you have the testimony of all of these priests plus the prophets in the holy scriptures? The scriptures are laid before you. Have you read them? All things tell us there is a God: the very earth we live on, all things on the face of the earth, the revolution of the earth around the sun, the planets which move in their regular orbits. All these things testify of a Supreme Creator. Yet you go about attempting to lead away the hearts of this people, testifying to them there is no God!"

I swept my arms wide, encompassing all of those in my chambers.

"Do you still deny God's existence, in front of all these witnesses?"

Stubbornly he answered, his eyes still on the floor. "Yes, I still deny unless you show me a sign."

"I am grieved," I said. "Because of the hardness of your heart you still resist truth." I shrugged helplessly, "But it is better that your soul be lost than that you should be the means of bringing many souls down to destruction by your lies and flattering words.

"Therefore, if you deny God once more, God shall make so you shall never again open your mouth to deceive this people."

Korihor glanced up, a wild look in his eyes. "I do not deny the existence of God, but I do not believe there is a God. I don't think that you know there is a God, and unless you show me a sign, I will not believe."

I sighed resignedly. "All right, this will I give you for a sign. God shall strike you dumb according to my words." I pointed my finger at him.

"In the name of Almighty God I command that from this time forth you shall neither hear nor speak."

Korihor grabbed his throat, then put both hands on his ears. An incredulous look passed over his face. He fell on his knees before me, a pleading look in his eyes.

When Nephihah saw this he wrote on a piece of bark paper and handed it to Korihor. "Are you convinced now of the power of God?"

Korihor looked at Nephihah, then signed for writing materials. He wrote, "I can't speak. Nothing but God's power could bring this upon me. I always knew there was a God, but the devil deceived me. He appeared unto me in form of an angel and said that people had been led astray after an unknown God. Then he said to me, 'There is no God.' Then he taught me the words I should say. I have taught them because they were pleasing to the carnal mind. For that reason I have resisted the truth. Now this great curse is brought upon me."

He looked imploringly at me, then wrote, "Pray to God that this curse can be taken from me."

I shook my head, then wrote. "No, Korihor. If God took this curse from you, in a few months you would again be leading away the hearts of this people. The curse shall stand."

Korihor was taken from my chambers and turned loose on the street.

We sat in silence after his departure. Finally Nephihah spoke.

"Today's happenings need to be published. I will see that a proclamation is sent to each city informing them of Korihor's words and what has happened to him."

I nodded. "Yes. Those who believed in his words must be given opportunity to repent so similar judgments won't come upon them."

Reports during the next months indicated Korihor was begging from house to house, from city to city. Then a courier from Antionum brought word that Korihor had been killed by the Zoramites. No one mourned his death, but I was saddened to think that anyone would follow the fickle preachings of such a man, turning aside the testimonies of prophets and scriptures. I knew that this would always happen. Some people will always look for the easy thing—that which doesn't require faith or work.

The messenger who brought word of Korihor's death also informed me of the wayward teachings of the Zoramites in Antionum. I shook my head in wonder. Would people never cease from leaving truth for error?

"Who is Zoram," I asked.

The messenger shrugged. "He is the leader in Antionum and teaches people to bow down to dumb idols."

I walked from the temple to Nephihah's hall of judgment. He received me gladly.

"Another problem has arisen," I said. I then rehearsed to him what the messenger had told me.

Nephihah looked thoughtful. "Antionum borders Jershon and wilderness controlled by the Lamanites. If Zoram rebels he might enter into an agreement with the Lamanites. Such an agreement would have serious consequences for our people."

"What do you propose?"

"Perhaps we could send Moroni and the army to put down any rebellion before it starts."

"My friend," I said, "the word of God has more effect on people than the sword. I think it best to send missionaries to Antionum."

Nephihah looked doubtful. "Do that, but have your missionaries keep their eyes open. If rebellion is present, I will send in the army."

I didn't tell Nephihah that I would be the missionary. I also hated to tell Ruth my plans. Antionum was a week's journey, and I had no idea how long I would be gone. As I walked toward my home a strong impression hit me. *"Do not go alone to Antionum. There will be strength in numbers."*

"Thy will be done, Lord," I whispered.

* * *

Years had passed since Ammon and his brothers had served as missionaries with me. Why not take them? And Amulek?

Rather than go straight home, I went to the temple. The more I planned, the more enthusiastic I became. This would be the greatest missionary force ever!

By messenger, I sent word to Jershon telling Ammon of my plans and asking him to join me. Messages also went to Aaron, Omner and Himni, asking them to meet me in the temple a week hence. Then I wrote a short note to Amulek and Zeezrom, both of whom were ministering to the Church in Melek. After sending the messages, I made my way home. I needed to tell my plans to Ruth.

Complicating the telling of my plans was Ruth's health. Several months had passed since she had really felt well. She was still pale from her bout with the fever. I sat beside her on the window seat. Together we looked at her flower garden. Before I got around to telling her about the journey to Antionum, she spoke.

"You are going away again."

I squeezed her hand and smiled. "You know my every thought, don't you?"

Her eyes, normally filled with sparkle, seemed lifeless. "Where are you going?"

I told her about the Zoramites in the land of Antionum. Enthusiastically I reviewed for her my impression to take many missionaries with me. I turned so I faced her.

"I even want to take my sons. The mission will be a growing experience for them."

"I would be alone?"

"No," I would leave Helaman here to watch over you. He is the best hunter and can keep you supplied with meat and can also help you in the garden. I also want him to continue his training in the school of the scribes."

"Isn't Corianton young to be serving as a missionary?"

"He's sixteen, and he's as tall as I am. I feel he needs this kind of experience to strengthen his testimony. I have been very concerned with his lack of sincere belief."

Ruth, always supportive, gave no arguments.

* * *

In seven days Aaron, Omner, Himni, Amulek, Zeezrom, my three sons and I all met in the temple. I looked proudly over these men who meant so much to me. Five were tested and tried missionaries. I missed seeing Ammon, but he would meet us at the river crossing east of Gideon.

A major concern was for someone to remain in Zarahemla to serve the Church and care for Ruth. The Zoramites were wicked; we could all be killed—a chance we had to take. I had already decided to leave Helaman to care for Ruth. I prayed to determine who else should be left behind.

The impression came that Himni should remain in Zarahemla.

"Please let me go," he said.

"No, Himni. The word of the Lord was clear."

Helaman was also anxious to go with us. "Let Corianton stay and care for mother."

I was almost tempted. Helaman would certainly be a more mature missionary. "No, son. Corianton needs the growing-up experience and I feel that only you are mature enough to stay home and take care of your mother."

"I will stay, Father," he said reluctantly.

Now that was settled, I hoped Shiblon and Corianton would contribute—or at least get some good missionary training.

A week's journey brought us to the land of Siron, south of Antionum. We had traveled from Zarahemla to Gideon, then cut through the mountains on a well-beaten trail. A day's walk beyond Gideon

Ammon joined us. What a joyful reunion! Missionary companions once again after all these years!

The land of Siron was on the seacoast, forming a neutral buffer between Antionum and the east wilderness of the Lamanites. I had never been to the East Sea. The dazzle of white, sandy beaches facing the limitless expanse of blue water was breathtaking. People of all cultures mingled here together. Siron was really a resort area with many inns. We spent one day sight-seeing before turning north to Antionum.

On our journey I had instructed my sons about proper decorum among the Zoramites.

"These are Nephite dissenters," I said. "They have been taught the word of God but now have rebelled against it. Our task is to lead them back to God's word."

I looked at Corianton. He didn't appear to be listening. I was disappointed. Perhaps I had made a mistake in bringing him.

We were astonished when we entered Antionum. Beautiful stone synagogues, sitting atop stepped-up pyramids dotted the city. Even in Zarahemla we had no finer buildings. The day we arrived was apparently their day of worship.

Many people, elegantly dressed in multi-colored robes of fine-twined linen, climbed the pyramids to the synagogues. Feather headdresses waved freely, adding additional color to the scene. Most of the people, both men and women, were adorned with ringlets, bracelets and other ornaments of gold and silver.

I felt somewhat ill at ease. Amid all the opulence, we were still dressed in traveling clothes. People looked at us with disdain, but I ignored them, intending to learn as much as I could of their religious ritual. I even stopped one well-dressed man and asked him what was happening. He informed me that this was the "day of the Lord." The one day of the week on which they called on the Lord.

A man, not one of the priests, climbed up a steep stairway in the center of the synagogue. Standing on a high platform, he stretched his arms towards heaven and cried out in a loud voice.

"Holy, holy God! We believe that thou art God, and we believe that thou art holy, and that thou wast a spirit, and that thou art a spirit now, and that thou wilt be a spirit forever."

Mentally, I shook my head at such a concept. Never in my life had I beheld such worship. The man continued.

"Holy God, we believe that thou hast separated us from our brethren because we do not believe in their traditions which were handed down to them by the childishness of their fathers. We believe that thou hast chosen us to be thy holy children and has made it known to us that there shall be no Christ."

I looked at Ammon and the rest of the missionaries. They seemed as astonished as I. Shiblon looked back at me, a question in this eyes. Corianton seemed preoccupied. I shrugged and turned back to the speaker.

"God, thou art the same yesterday, today, and forever. Thou has elected us that we shall be saved while all those around us are elected to be cast down to hell. We thank thee that thou hast elected us, that we may not be led away after the foolish traditions of our brethren which binds them down to a belief in Christ and which leads their hearts to wander from thee, O God."

I wondered how much longer this could go on. Was the man demented? Could anyone actually believe that they were chosen by God to be saved and everyone else was to be consigned to hell?

He finished, "And again, we thank thee, O God, that we are a chosen and holy people. Amen."

When he was through speaking, he climbed down the steps and another took his place. I was interested to see what this man would say. Was I surprised! He repeated verbatim what the first man had said. Then followed over a dozen more who one after another repeated the same words. When the last man had finished reciting the prayer, the people started climbing down the pyramid to go home. I stopped the same man I had questioned when we arrived. The rest of the missionaries crowded around.

"How often do you worship?" I asked.

"Once a week," he replied.

"Are your worship services all the same?"

He looked at me sharply, then nodded.

"Do you pray at home or any other place?" Ammon interjected.

He shook his head. "No," he said, "we are commanded only to pray when on Rameumptom."

"Rameumptom?" Aaron asked.

The man pointed at the place for standing which was empty now, then hurried down the pyramid, apparently anxious to get away from such questioners.

As a group we walked silently down the pyramid. We found an inn where we could stay the night. The inn was run down, but the beds were clean and the food tolerable.

During our dinner of fresh-caught fish we discussed the Zoramites. I had been grieved at what I had seen—a wicked and perverse people with hearts set on gold and silver—a people lifted up in boasting and pride.

After dinner we retired to the forest for prayer. Each of the brethren took turns praying. Lastly, I lifted my voice to God, praying for the Zoramites, asking for strength and patience. Calling upon the Lord to give us success in converting the Zoramites.

"O Lord," I cried, "give unto me success, and also my fellow laborers: Ammon, Aaron, Omner, Amulek, Zeezrom, and my two sons. Comfort all of these. Give them strength that they bear their afflictions which shall come upon them because of the iniquities of this people. O, Lord, grant unto us that we may have success in bringing them again unto Thee in Christ.

"Behold, O Lord, their souls are precious; many are our brethren. Therefore, give unto us power and wisdom that we may bring these our brethren again unto Thee."

After our prayer, I laid my hands on each of the missionaries to bless them and set them apart for the work. I blessed them that the Holy Spirit would guide them in their mission.

The next morning we separated into pairs of missionaries, each pair going to a different area of the city. Amulek went with me. I felt it best that my sons go with strong missionaries other than myself so I assigned Shiblon to Aaron and Corianton to Ammon. We preached on street corners, visited people in their homes, conversed wherever we found people to listen. Each night we met back at the inn to compare success.

Our prayers were being answered. We were filled with the Holy Spirit, bearing testimony of the Savior to all we met. Our success began with the poor, those who were not allowed to worship in the synagogues because of their poverty. The rich cast them out and would not listen. Only the poor in worldly goods seemed teachable.

At the northwest edge of the city a grass-covered hill rose several hundred feet into the air. Locally, it was known as the hill Onidah. Here I taught the curious and the humble who came to listen. A large group had assembled on the third day of my mission. Some were there to listen, others to heckle.

A small group came up the hill behind me. One cried out, interrupting my discussion of Gospel principles. "Is what you say for us, or only for the rich who despise us because of our poverty?"

I turned from those I had been teaching and looked at this man. He was about my age, gray-haired, barefoot and naked except for a tattered brown skirt, his skeleton precisely articulated.

"The message of Christ is for all people, rich and poor," I said.

"In Antionum we are unable to worship," he said. "Because of our poverty, the priests throw us out of the synagogues which we have built."

I rejoiced in this man's teachableness. He and those with him seemed humbled and ready to hear God's word. I stepped towards them, my arms outstretched.

"I see that you are lowly in heart. Blessed are you."

Many of those I had previously been teaching made their way around the hill.

I pointed to the one who had spoken. "This brother has said, 'What shall we do for we are cast out of our synagogues and cannot worship God?'

"Do you suppose that the only place you can worship God is in your synagogues?

"Do you suppose that you must worship God only once each week?

"It is well that you are cast out of your synagogues. Because you have humbled yourselves you now listen to me and some have even become repentant. You are blessed because you have been compelled to be humble, but more blessed is he who is humble without being compelled. Blessed is he who believes in the word of God and is baptized of his own will, without being compelled."

I nodded towards those who had previously been heckling me.

"Many of you have said, 'Show me a sign from heaven and then we will believe.' I ask, is this faith? No! If a man knows a thing he has no cause to believe, because he knows it.

"Cursed is he that knows the will of God and doesn't do it."

I spoke of faith, telling people that "faith is not to have a perfect knowledge of things." I said "if you have faith you hope for things which are not seen which are true."

I said to them, "If you will awake and arouse your faculties, even to experiment upon my words, and exercise a particle of faith, even if you have no more than just a desire to believe, let this desire work in you until you can believe some of what I tell you."

I then compared faith with a seed which would swell and grow and eventually, if nourished, become a tree. "Then," I said, "you shall reap the rewards of your faith, diligence, patience and long-suffering, waiting for the tree to bring forth fruit unto you."

Much more did I say concerning faith. I quoted the prophets Zenos and Zenock. I finished the sermon with these words.

"Now, my brethren, I desire that you shall plant this word in your hearts. As it begins to swell, nourish it with your faith. It will become a tree, springing up in you unto everlasting life. Then may God grant unto you that your burdens may be light, through the joy of His Son."

The Spirit had taught me what to say. Now it was Amulek's turn. I motioned him to his feet. He looked upon the group before him. I could see the Spirit burning in his eyes. He began speaking.

"My brethren, I think it is impossible that you should be ignorant of the things which Alma has spoken to you concerning the coming of Christ. I know that these things were taught you bountifully before your dissension from among us.

"You have asked Alma what you should do because of your afflictions. He has told you to prepare your minds and has exhorted you to have faith—even so much faith as to plant the word in your hearts that you may try the experiment of its goodness."

Much more did he speak unto them concerning having faith in Christ. He told them of His great and last sacrifice.

"For it shall not be a human sacrifice, but an infinite and eternal sacrifice. Behold, this is the whole meaning of the law, every whit pointing to that great and last sacrifice, which sacrifice will be the Son of God, yea, infinite and eternal."

He expounded to them the necessity of prayer, telling them to call upon God wherever they were: in their houses, in their fields, wherever. The important thing was that they pray often, for their own needs and the needs of those around them.

"But behold, my beloved brethren," he said, "do not suppose that this is all. After you have done all these things, if you turn away the needy, and the naked, and visit not the sick and afflicted, and impart of your substance, if you have, to those who stand in need—I say unto you, if you do not do any of these things, behold, your prayer is vain, and availeth you nothing, and you are as hypocrites who do deny the faith. If you do not remember to be charitable, you are as dross, which the refiners will cast out because it has no worth."

Words seemed to come to Amulek faster than he could speak them. "Now is the time and the day of your salvation. If you will repent and harden not your hearts the great plan of redemption shall be brought about for you.

"For behold, this life is the time for men to prepare to meet God. Yea, behold the day of this life is the day for men to perform their labors."

My brush flowed over the paper recording Amulek's words. He ended by telling the people to have patience in their afflictions and not to revile those who had cast them out of their synagogues

As he finished speaking, a stone hit me on the back of my neck. I turned. An angry mob surged up the backside of the hill. Rocks landed all around us. I grabbed my papers, leaving brushes and paints, and together Amulek and I ran.

Chapter 17

A Blessing for Helaman

"Amulek," I called.

He came quickly. He had been working in the archive room, copying scriptures for his personal library.

"I'm sorry to disturb you," I said, "but I need your help."

"My help?"

I looked him in the eyes. "Yes. I think there is something you haven't told me about what happened in Antionum or Jershon."

Amulek looked at me quizzically.

"Since our return," I continued, "I have felt as if Corianton is drawing away."

Amulek dropped his eyes. "I have noticed his glum looks and sour temper," he offered.

"That's part of it. What's more, he refuses even to talk to me." I looked at Amulek. "What is bothering him? What happened in Antionum?"

"I have heard rumors."

"Like what?"

Amulek seemed reluctant to tell me.

I prodded him. "My friend, Corianton is precious to me—too precious to lose. And unless we get to the root of his problem, I may lose a son. Help me."

Amulek sighed. "You remember the day we were forced to leave Antionum and flee to Jershon?"

I nodded.

"Several days later we were joined in Jershon by Shiblon, Zeezrom, and Ammon and his brothers."

"I remember."

"You wondered at the time where Corianton was...."

I interrupted him. "Yes, I was very concerned when he didn't arrive with his brother or Zeezrom."

Amulek cleared his throat. "Zeezrom didn't want to hurt your feelings so he didn't tell you that Corianton had returned to Siron."

"To Siron? Why would he return there?" Then I remembered. When we arrived at Siron on our way to Antionum, Corianton had been infatuated with a trollop who served at the inn.

"Not that...?" I couldn't even think of her name.

Amulek nodded. "Isabel."

I frowned. We were driven from Antionum so quickly we had no time to gather our missionaries together. Not only had we been driven from Antionum, but all who believed our words were also driven from the land by the priests. We were kept busy finding homes for them and taking care of their other needs. The people of Ammon had been marvelous, opening their homes in Jershon, preparing meals, giving them clothing.

Almost a week passed before Corianton joined us. I had worried about him but the week had been so hectic I could not even search for him.

Then reports came from Antionum that the Zoramites had joined with the Lamanites for war against the people of Ammon and the converted Zoramites. I sent word to Nephihah and within the week an army had come from Zarahemla to maintain order in the land. With our help the people of Ammon gave their lands to the convert Zoramites and moved from Jershon to the land of Melek so the army and the convert Zoramites would have room to fight. By that time Corianton had rejoined us, so we returned to Zarahemla.

I realized now that I had never pressed Corianton as to why he was so late in returning.

Amulek was silent, waiting for my response. I looked at him. He fidgeted nervously under my gaze.

"What happened in Siron?" I asked him, but in my heart I already knew.

He shrugged helplessly. "The report I received from some of our converts was that he..." Amulek swallowed, struggling to say what he knew would hurt me, "...he committed fornication with Isabel."

I turned and sat down. Since Amulek began talking I had suspected what he would tell me, but I was still shocked.

Without looking at Amulek, I asked quietly, "What do you suggest I do now?"

His voice was troubled. "The process of repentance is for all. Won't he have to go through that process like you and any other sinner must?"

I nodded, remembering the pain of my own repentance.

"How many know of his sin?"

"Many of our converts knew. It was a common topic of conversation."

"Why didn't someone tell me?"

I could feel his anxiety. "I suppose we were afraid of hurting your feelings."

Almost angrily, I turned to face him.

"In trying to spare my feelings, this delay in telling me could lose me my son!"

Amulek looked at me with pain in his eyes.

More gently I added, "If I had only known sooner I perhaps could have helped him more. Now...," I spread my hands helplessly.

Amulek started to say something. I shook my head and waved him away. I needed time to myself to think this through. Through God's goodness and the process of repentance there was still hope. But from my own experience with sin I knew the helplessness which Corianton must be feeling. Satan had a way of using sin to alienate one from family and God. Sin led to sin, not that the sinner desired to continue sinning, but often because there seemed no hope of overcoming sin.

After a restless night, I felt I had the answer. For some time I had wanted to bless my sons. As a father such an ordinance was not only a right, but an obligation. By giving each a blessing, Corianton would not feel singled out. In talking with him, hopefully he would confess his sin which would start him on the road to repentance.

I called again for Amulek. He looked sheepish as he came in the door. I put my arm around him.

"Please forgive me for my sharpness yesterday," I said. "Hearing of Corianton's sin was a burden for me."

Amulek wiped a tear from his eyes. "Please forgive me for not understanding my responsibility to come to you sooner," he said.

"All that is past," I said. "Right now we must do what we can to bring about repentance and forgiveness."

"What do you propose?"

"I will give each son a blessing. As part of the blessing I intend to tell my own story so Corianton will understand the repentance process. Then I will bless him individually and help him overcome his guilt."

"What do you want me to do?" Amulek asked.

"Please be my scribe. I desire to record my blessings for future posterity."

* * *

I knew the importance of what I was doing. A person's soul might rest on a word or a phrase. Amulek brought all three sons together to my room in the temple. I looked around at them. These were men, though Helaman was barely twenty and Corianton only seventeen.

"My sons," I said, "I am getting old and desire to give each of you a blessing. Lehi set the pattern when he blessed his children and grandchildren before he died. But even before that, Abraham, Isaac, and Jacob each blessed their sons." From the corner of my eyes I saw Corianton's scowl but I ignored it.

I motioned to Helaman. "Helaman, as oldest son, you be first." Shiblon and Corianton started to rise. I motioned them to sit. "I would like you both to stay. Much of the story I tell Helaman may be of interest to you."

I laid my hands on his head. "My son, give ear to my words. I swear unto you that as you keep the Lord's commandments He will prosper you in the land. Remember your heritage. Remember the lessons learned by me and your grandfather. You are still young and can learn from me. I know that whoever puts his trust in God shall be supported in all trials, troubles and afflictions, and shall be lifted up at the last day."

I then recounted the events leading up to the visit of the angel, including his words to me.

"I did not hear all his words," I said, "for when he said *if thou wilt be destroyed of thyself, seek no more to destroy the Church of God,* I was struck with such fear that I fainted. I was racked with eternal torment, my soul harrowed because of the sins I had committed.

"At that moment I remembered all my sins and was tortured with the pains of hell. I saw that I had rebelled against God and had not kept his holy commandments. Even worse, I had led many of His children from the Church and into sinful ways. Thus I felt like a murderer. The very thought of being in the presence of God filled me with inexpressible horror."

Though I was blessing Helaman, my words were also for Corianton's ears. I hoped he was listening.

"Oh, I thought, if I could just become extinct and disappear so I wouldn't have to stand before God and be judged of my sins.

"For three days and nights I was racked with intense pain—tormented by thoughts of what I had done.

"It was at that time I remembered hearing Father's sermon concerning the coming of Jesus Christ, a Son of God, who would atone for the sins of the world. With all my being I cried, 'O, Jesus, thou Son of God, have mercy on me who am in the gall of bitterness and circled about by the everlasting chains of death.

"He heard my prayers. My pains disappeared; I felt them no more. What joy I felt! My son, my soul was filled now with as much joy as it had been previously with my pain. Nothing could have been more excruciating than my pains. On the other hand, nothing could have been sweeter to me than my joy.

"I then saw a vision similar to what our forefather, Lehi, saw. There was God, sitting on his throne, surrounded by concourses of angels singing and praising Him. My son, my soul longed to be there.

"My son, it was then I regained consciousness. I was in the temple in Zarahemla, surrounded by teachers and priests. Next to me kneeled my father, praying loudly for my deliverance.

"From that time until now, my son, I have labored without ceasing that I might bring souls to repentance; that I might bring them to taste the exceeding joy which I tasted; that they might be born of God and be filled with the Holy Ghost."

I glanced at Corianton. He was bowed over, his head in his hands, but he appeared to be listening.

"The Lord has given me great joy in the work I have done. Many have been converted to the Gospel, have tasted as I tasted, and have seen eye to eye as I have seen. Their testimonies have been powerful.

"I have been supported under trials and troubles of every kind. God has delivered me from prison, from bonds, and from death. With my trust in Him, He will still deliver me. I know also that He will raise me up at the last day to dwell with Him in glory. I will praise Him forever."

I rehearsed once more the travels of our fathers in Jerusalem and in our own land. I closed with a promise and a warning, intended as much for Corianton as for Helaman.

"My son, inasmuch as you keep the commandments of God you shall prosper in the land. But inasmuch as you do not keep the commandments of God you shall be cut off from his presence."

I removed my hands from Helaman's head and grasped his shoulders.

"For the rest of your blessing, I desire you to come with me to the archives."

I motioned for Amulek to follow as Helaman and I walked to the room where all records were stored.

As we entered the room, I detected the same reverent wonder in Helaman's face as I had felt when Father and King Mosiah brought me to the vault in the palace where the records had been housed.

"Helaman, my son, these are the records of our people. From this time forth they will be your responsibility. I command you to take the records which have been entrusted with me; keep a record of this people on the plates of Nephi as I have done."

I then instructed him in all the records which were before him.

"These plates of brass contain the genealogy of our fathers from the beginning. They are the writings of Joseph and his descendants. They are to be preserved and handed down from one generation to another until they shall go forth to every nation, kindred, tongue, and people."

I told him the purposes of the records, that by small things such as keeping the records, whole nations would be convinced of errors and brought back to a knowledge of God. Many more things did I tell him concerning the holy records.

"Remember, my son, that God has entrusted you with these things which are sacred, which he has kept sacred, and which he will keep and preserve for a wise purpose for showing forth his power unto future generations. If you transgress the commandments of God, these things which are sacred shall be taken away from you and you shall be delivered up unto Satan, that he may sift you as chaff before the wind.

"But if you keep God's commandments and care for these things as you are commanded, no power of earth or hell can take them from you, for God is powerful in fulfilling all his words."

I showed him the twenty-four gold plates which contained much more than Father's and King Mosiah's translation. I told him of the mysteries and works of darkness on the plates, and that he should not give to the people their secret oaths and covenants and secret combinations, but only tell the people of the murders and abominations and wickedness which the plates contained.

"My son, remember the words which I have spoken unto you. Trust not those secret plans to this people, but teach them an everlasting hatred against sin and iniquity. Preach unto them repentance, and faith on the Lord Jesus Christ. Teach them to humble themselves and to be meek and lowly in heart. Teach them to withstand every temptation of the devil with faith in the Lord, Jesus Christ.

"Teach them to never be weary of good works, but to be meek and lowly in heart for such shall find rest to their souls."

I took both of his hands in mine, and by the flickering light of torches looked deep into his eyes.

"O, remember, my son, and learn wisdom in your youth. Learn in your youth to keep the commandments of God. Yes, my son, cry unto God for all your support. Counsel with the Lord in all your doings and He will direct you for good."

I then showed him the interpreters, the other plates, and finally, the Liahona. I told him how the Liahona had guided our forefathers from Jerusalem to this land, but only as they kept the commandments. I drew the comparison between the compass which brought them to this land and the words of Christ, which would continue to give guidance to each of us as we kept the commandments.

"For just as surely as this director did bring our fathers, by following its course, to the promised land, so shall the words of Christ, if we follow their course, carry us beyond this vale of sorrow into a far better land of promise. My son, do not be slothful. See that you take care of these sacred things. See that you look to God and live. Go unto the people of this land, declare the word, and be sober.

Helaman had not spoken while we were in the record room. As we walked back to where his brothers were waiting, he put his arm around my waist and whispered to me.

"Father, thank you for trusting me with such a calling. I will not let you or God down."

Chapter 18

Blessings for Shiblon and Corianton

Helaman sat next to Corianton in the waiting room. I turned my attention to Shiblon, my middle son.

"My son, give heed to my words. I say to you the same as I said to Helaman, that if you keep God's commandments you shall prosper in the land. But if you don't keep the commandments you shall be cut off from God's presence.

"Shiblon, I have experienced great joy through the faithfulness you have shown. I was especially pleased when you were so diligent and faithful on our mission to the Zoramites. I know you were tied and stoned for the Lord's sake. Yet you bore it all with patience.

"Now, Shiblon, just endure to the end. There is no other way whereby man can be saved except through Christ. He is the light and life of the world. He is the word of truth and righteousness.

"Your mission is to continue to teach the people. Continue to be diligent and temperate in all things. Do not be lifted up in pride, boasting of your own wisdom and strength. Use boldness but not overbearance. Bridle your passions that you may be filled with love. Refrain from idleness.

"Pray not as the Zoramites, but ask the Lord for forgiveness for your unworthiness.

"May the Lord bless you, Shiblon, that He may receive you into his kingdom. Now, go my son. Teach this people. Be sober. My son, farewell."

* * *

"Corianton!" I called.

He answered sullenly. He knew I wanted to talk to him about his behavior. I sadly shook my head. He is so like me when I was his age. I hope I can help him overcome his problems so he doesn't have to go through the hell on earth that I have.

Corianton came in and slouched to the floor, leaning back in a defiant position. I waited, watching as he became more nervous under my gaze.

"Can I go now?"
"Stay with me."
"Why?"
"It's your turn for a blessing."

He turned his face away. I wanted to use just the right words. This was no time to offend.

"You remind me of me."

"What has that to do with keeping me here. I have things to do," he replied sullenly.

I quietly answered, "I was trying to think of a way to tell you about my life and about my father."

Corianton appeared to listen. He had never known his grandfather. "Well, tell me," he said, less sullenly.

I began, quietly at first, watching Corianton's reaction.

"Your grandfather was a mighty man of God. I watched as he helped our people. He won them to the Church, not by his eloquence, but by his sincere conviction. I watched and listened and was deeply impressed. I learned even before my teens that his sermons did not come from mental discipline or even by his wide reading of the sacred records—however essential these may be—but from life.

"Father loved me and wanted me to be a part of his life. His life was so wrapped up in the Church, though, that I tried desperately to escape, rather than being happy about his devotion. I had a hang-up about freedom. I didn't want to be restricted in any way. I didn't want to be fenced in like the goats I cared for. I didn't want to be inhibited but wanted to make my own rules."

Pausing, I noticed that Corianton's eyes showed interest. I continued. "As the high priest's son, I knew I was being watched by everyone, and I didn't like being watched."

The look of resentment had left Corianton's face. He now appeared to be listening intently. Perhaps he felt some of the same feelings.

"Always gnawing away at my mind was the faint suggestion that someday, I, too, would be called to the ministry. I tried to stifle such thoughts. No matter how good my home background was, no matter how insistent the call of God to my young heart, I determined to silence that inner voice and discover life for myself."

"What did you do?" Corianton asked.

Continuing was difficult. "I decided to make sure I wouldn't be called to the priesthood by preparing instead to be a warrior. I wasn't really anxious to be a warrior. It was just a way of avoiding the calling as a priest. All this time, however, I had a lurking suspicion that the thing I was fighting was the thing I really wanted. I was all mixed up and unwilling to admit it—to myself or anyone else."

Corianton leaned forward in his chair, intent upon my every word.

"I am so thankful to be where I am, realizing how narrow was my escape."

"Was it easy for you to repent?" Corianton's question was quiet but serious. It was the same question my father had asked me prior to his death.

I paused for a short time, pleased that we had come so soon to a teaching moment. Then I told Corianton of my repentance, that because of the depth of my sins I knew exactly where I stood with God.

"I knew my need for God. I was lost to the Church." I paused, as I thought of how lost I really had been. I related again some of the things I had told my father, about listening to his sermons and agonizing because I wasn't following his words.

"But I seemed helpless when I tried to tackle my own weakness." I breathed deeply to control my emotions, then continued. "I felt being religious was a sign of weakness. My experience with religion convinced me that the religious life was one of time and work with few rewards. I determined that I would rather work where I could earn more money and prestige. So I took up with every symbol of rebellion."

I knew Corianton could see the pain in my eyes as I talked. "But God did not leave me alone, even though I wanted to be left alone. I often remembered Father's sermons."

Corianton's head nodded subtly.

"While I walked between cities, I attempted stubbornly to put out of my mind the things I had heard him speak. But God was always right there. I was very uncomfortable. I didn't want Him to be that close. I felt as if the war between Lamanites and Nephites was going on inside me."

Corianton smiled understandingly. "What did you do?"

I told him the words I had told father, about going back to Zarahemla to hear Father speak once again. Though I wouldn't admit it, he was my ideal of a man.

"He was speaking to the congregation but every word cut through me like a knife. I finally walked away from the meeting and moved restlessly through the streets. I shall never forget those moments. In that still summer evening, with only the sounds of small insects and animals around me, looking up past the trees in God's own sky, I actually shook my fist at the heavens and cried aloud, 'God, leave me alone!'"

I heard Corianton's sharp intake of breath.

"I was shocked by my own defiant words. But I couldn't call them back. I felt cold inside. God's spirit had left me."

Then what happened?" Corianton asked.

"Even though God had seemingly left my life, I was not alone. I still had my conscience. I struggled. I had a deep sense of guilt that wouldn't go away. My guilt haunted me night and day. It persisted in making me miserable, and the only way I could fight back against it was in trying harder to fight against the Church and my father."

Corianton smiled. "Did that help?"

I smiled in return. "No, it demanded attention. My conscience refused to be still. Like a small pebble in a sandal, it just irritated and cut."

Corianton nodded. "I understand. You are telling me that the only way to rid yourself of the irritating pebble was to take off the old shoe of rebellion?"

I nodded happily. Thank goodness my son had maturity enough to understand what I was trying to tell him.

"Yes, my son. That is the only way to rid oneself of the irritation of sin and unworthiness before God."

There was a look of indecision on Corianton's face.

"My son, before giving your blessing, I wanted to chat with you, to let you know my feelings."

He ducked his head, looking at the floor.

I waited.

Finally, without looking up, he spoke. "Father, you know that I didn't return from Antionum with Ammon and the other missionaries."

Again I waited without speaking.

He looked at me. I knew the pain that was in his heart, but I knew also that he had to purge it himself.

"Father, I went back to Siron." Now words fairly tumbled from his lips. "When we were there on our way to Antionum, I met a girl."

He stopped, embarrassed. When I didn't speak he continued.

"Her name was Isabel." He groaned audibly, his face a mask of sorrow. "Father, I sinned." He put his head in his hands and sobbed.

I put my arm around his shoulders, comforting him, feeling his sobs shaking him.

"My son, many fall. Praise God that His son, when He comes, will take upon Himself all our sins."

"How does He do that?"

I shook my head. "I don't know. It is one of God's mysteries, but I know he will perform an atonement for all of our sins. But his atonement depends upon our own repentance."

"Tell me about repentance."

I stood and pulled Corianton to his feet. I feel that I can best do that as part of your blessing. Are you ready, now?"

Corianton faced me squarely, his eyes on mine. "I feel I am ready now, father."

"Please go get Amulek. He will be scribe for the blessing." Moments later he and Amulek were back.

When Amulek was seated, paper in hand, I laid my hands on Corianton's head.

"My son," I began. "What you have done is grievous in the sight of God. On your mission you failed to listen to my counsel and went about boasting of your own strength and wisdom. But most grievous of all, my son, was when you left the ministry and sought out the harlot Isabel in Siron.

"She stole many hearts with her beauty, but that does not excuse your behavior. You should have tended to the ministry to which you were entrusted. Fornication is an abomination in the sight of the Lord, and is one of the most damning sins of all. Only shedding of innocent blood or blasphemy against the Holy Ghost is worse. If you had denied the Holy Ghost, that would be unpardonable. And if you had murdered someone it would be difficult to obtain forgiveness.

"I wish to God you were not guilty of so great a sin. As you know, you cannot hide your sins from God and unless you repent your sins will stand as a testimony against you at the last day.

"Repent and forsake your sins, my son. Go no more after the lust of your eyes. Corianton, you are still but a youth. I command you to take counsel from your older brothers. Do not let yourself be led away by vain or foolish things. Do not let the devil lead you again after wicked harlots.

"Realize, that not only did you harm yourself with your sin but you set back the missionary work with the Zoramites. When they saw your conduct they wouldn't believe my words."

I continued his blessing, commanding him to refrain from evil, then I told him about the coming of Christ.

"I say unto you it is He that shall come to take away the sins of the world and to declare glad tidings of salvation to his people. This is the mission to which you are called, to bear these glad tidings unto our people, to prepare their minds that they may teach their children of the coming of the Lord."

I knew that Corianton was concerned about God's purpose in letting us know far in advance of the coming of His Son. I told him that the souls of our people are as precious to God as those who will be here at the time of His coming, and that we needed to know the plan of redemption so we could prepare.

Corianton had also expressed concern about the resurrection. I tried to explain.

"There is no resurrection until after the coming of Christ," I said. "He brings to pass the resurrection of the dead. There is a time appointed unto men that they shall rise from the dead and there is a space between death and resurrection. I inquired of the Lord concerning what happens in this space of time and an angel told me that the spirits of all men, as soon as they are departed from this mortal body, are taken home to that God who gave them life.

"The spirits of those who are righteous are received into a state of happiness, which is called paradise, a state of rest, a state of peace, where they shall rest from all their troubles and from all care and sorrow.

"The spirits of the wicked, those who are evil and have no part of the Spirit of the Lord, shall be cast out into outer darkness. There, they will weep and wail and gnash their teeth because of their iniquity. The righteous will remain in paradise and the wicked will remain in darkness until the time of their resurrection."

As I continued my blessing, I told him many more things concerning the spirit world and resurrection, when the dead would come forth and be reunited, soul and body, and be brought to stand before God to be judged.

"The soul shall be restored to the body and the body to the soul. Every limb and joint shall be restored to its body. Even a hair of the head shall not be lost but all things shall be restored to their proper and perfect frame. Then shall the righteous shine forth in the kingdom of God. But an awful death shall come upon the wicked, for they die as to things pertaining to righteousness, for they are unclean and no unclean thing can inherit the kingdom of God. They are cast out."

Words flowed through my lips as I blessed my youngest son. The only two sounds in the room were my voice and the soft swish of the brush as Amulek recorded my words.

"Therefore, my son, see that you are merciful to your brothers; deal justly, judge righteously and do good continually. If you do all these things then you shall receive your reward. You shall have mercy, justice, righteous judgment, and good restored to you."

I then spoke on punishment of the sinner and the justice and mercy of God in carrying out His plan of redemption. I told Corianton of God's mercy in allowing men to repent, and His justice in giving just laws and fixing punishment for the breaking of those laws.

"Thus God brings about His great and eternal purposes which were prepared from the foundation of the world. Thus comes salvation and redemption of man, and also their destruction and misery. Therefore, my son, whoever desires may come and partake freely of the waters of life but no one is compelled to come.

"Now my son, Let your sins trouble you enough to bring you to repentance. Do not endeavor to excuse your sins by denying the justice of God but let the justice of God and his mercy and long-suffering have full sway in your heart to make you humble. When this is done, my son, I desire that you should let these things trouble you no more."

After the blessing Corianton turned to me, pain filling his eyes.

"Father, you speak of justice and mercy of God. What does it mean?"

"The plan of restoration is requisite with the justice of God," I replied. "It is requisite that all things should be restored to their proper order. Thus the soul of man shall be restored to its body, and every part of the body should be restored to itself.

"It is also requisite with the justice of God that men should be judged according to their works. If their works are good in this life, and the desires of their hearts are good, then at the last day they shall be restored unto that which is good. And if their works are evil, then they shall be restored unto them for evil. Therefore, all things shall be restored to their proper order, everything to its natural frame, either raised to endless happiness to inherit the kingdom of God, or to endless misery to inherit the kingdom of the devil. It has to be one or the other."

I continued speaking about the restoration, but I could see that Corianton was still troubled.

"My son, do not risk one more offense against God. Do not suppose, as I have spoken about the restoration, that any can be restored from sin to happiness."

I looked at him tenderly, "My son, I can feel your unhappiness. I feel you have already learned the lesson that wickedness never was happiness."

He nodded, his dark eyes still wet with tears.

"Then live a righteous life, deal justly with your fellow men, judge righteously and do good continually."

"But father..."

"What is it, Corianton?"

"I am still concerned about God's justice in punishing the sinner."

"Do you think it is injustice that the sinner should be consigned to a state of misery?"

He shook his head.

I attempted to explain this principle to him. "After the Lord sent our first parents forth from the garden of Eden, he placed a cherubim and a flaming sword at the east end of the garden of Eden that Adam should not partake of the fruit of the tree of life. You see, Adam had become as God, knowing good and evil. If he should put forth his hand and take of the fruit of the tree of life he would have lived forever.

"So we see, man was given a time to repent, a probationary time where he could repent and serve God. If he had taken of the tree of life, he would have lived forever with no time for repentance. That would have made the word of God void and the great plan of salvation would have been frustrated.

"By this you see that our first parents were cut off both temporally and spiritually from the presence of the Lord and became subjects to follow after their own will. As the soul could never die and the fall had brought upon mankind a spiritual death—being cut off from the presence of the Lord—as well as a temporal death, a way had to be prepared for man to be reclaimed from spiritual death."

"How did that happen?" he asked.

"The plan of mercy could not be brought about except an atonement should be made. Therefore, God himself atones for the sins of the world to bring about the plan of mercy, to appease the demands of justice, that God might be a perfect, just God and a merciful God also.

"According to the justice of God, repentance could not come except there were an eternal punishment—a punishment opposite but equal to the plan of happiness.

"Now, how could a man repent unless he sinned? How could he sin if there were no law? How could there be a law unless there was a punishment?

"There is a law given and a punishment affixed, and a repentance granted."

"How does mercy fit it?" Corianton asked seriously.

"Mercy comes because of the atonement and the atonement brings to pass the resurrection of the dead, and the resurrection of the dead brings men back into the presence of God. Thus they are restored to His presence to be judged according to their works.

"Justice exercises all his demands. Mercy claims all her own. Thus, none but the truly penitent are saved.

"Do you suppose that mercy can rob justice? No, not one whit. If so, God would cease to be God. Thus God brings about his great and eternal purposes which were prepared from before the foundation of the world. Thus comes about the salvation and the redemption of men as well as their destruction and misery."

I could see Corianton's shoulders trembling. He silently wept. Tears were in my own eyes. A lump rose in my throat and I had difficulty speaking. I stood and replaced my hands on his head in order to finish the blessing.

"My son, as soon as you feel a oneness with the Lord again, you are called of God to preach the word to this people. Declare the word with truth and soberness, that you may bring souls unto repentance, that the great plan of mercy may have claim upon them. May God grant unto you even according to my words. Amen."

I removed my hands from Corianton's head. He stood and threw his arms around me, his tears blending with my own.

Chapter 19

My Last Days

The letter said, "Father, I had two converts this week."

I carried Corianton's letter to the bedroom where Ruth was resting. She smiled wanly at me.

"I am so proud," she whispered. Her voice was hollow, lacking strength.

Joy over Corianton's success was tempered by sadness caused by Ruth's lingering illness. I sat by her bed once again until she slept. Carefully I walked from the room.

I placed Corianton's letter with others from my sons. They all reported great success on their missions. Helaman was steady as a rock, always faithful, never faltering. Shiblon, to my knowledge, had never strayed from the truth. But I was proudest of my youngest son, Corianton. I knew the struggle he had gone through, his repentance, and now his steadfastness in the Gospel. I shook my head in wonderment—he was so like me.

Ruth coughed. I hurried to her side. She wanted a drink. I dipped a cotton cloth in water and placed it on her forehead. She was so hot. I fetched her water, then sat by the pallet holding her limp hand. The signs weren't good. I had seen too many people die of fever. As much as I hated to admit it, Ruth was fading rapidly.

She slept. I stayed by her bed, applying cool cloths to her fevered forehead, heart sad as I listened to her moaning and calling my name in her sleep.

Morning light filtered through the window, rousing me from my stupor. I must have dozed. I reached over to feel Ruth's forehead. It was cool to my touch. Panicking, I grabbed her hand. It, too, was cool and beginning to stiffen. My head dropped to my chest, tears wringing from my eyes. My wife of twenty years was dead. Mid-morning came before I felt I could leave her side. In my study I wrote Helaman, Corianton and Shiblon to come home.

Messengers were sent to Melek where Zeezrom and Himni were serving missions; to Ammon who was also there, high priest over the people of Ammon who had moved there from Jershon; to Cumeni for Amulek and Corianton. This was a time I wanted to be surrounded by friends. I arranged for Ruth's funeral with help from Aaron and Omner.

I had preached about the spirit world for so long that I did not mourn for Ruth. I mourned for me and my loss. Where she was going she would be happy. My only desire was to join her there as quickly as possible.

Light rain fell unnoticed on bare heads. The dreary day reflected my feeling. As Ruth was buried I stood dry-eyed, flanked by sons and friends. I thought of this woman who had been my loyal and loving wife. Other than my mother, she was the most faithful woman I had ever known. Never had she doubted; always had she supported me in my callings and responsibilities. Even when I had to be away from home for long periods she had never complained.

My house was so empty without her. I couldn't stand it. Corianton and Amulek lingered for several days in Zarahemla. When they left to return to Cumeni I went with them. I didn't care how long I lived, but I wanted to spend the rest of my life in missionary work.

Word came to us of continued fighting in the land of Jershon. Apparently the Zoramites, Amalekites and Lamanites were still fighting our Zoramite converts and Nephihah's army. I felt confidence in the army. My young friend, Moroni, was chief captain and no finer soldier lived.

Corianton and I returned to Zarahemla, to care for the church there. Sadly, we learned of more dissension within the Nephites. Nephihah, the chief judge called me to his office. We embraced, then I held him at arm's length. He had aged, as I had aged. It was the nature of life.

"What troubles you, my friend?" I asked.

He sat down heavily in the chair. "Amalakiah is what troubles me," he answered, a frown on his face.

"Amalakiah?"

Nephihah grimaced. "A young judge who is stirring up problems among the people. He is proud and ambitious and I have heard that he is encouraging people to overturn Mosiah's laws, raising him up as king over all the land."

I shook my head in sorrow. Why? Why couldn't people learn to live together and be obedient to God's laws and the laws of the land?

"What are you doing about him?"

"What can I do? He has not broken the law."

"His supporters?"

"Both in and out of the Church. There are many in the land of Zarahemla who would like to return to the kingship. What do you think I should do?"

I smiled sadly and quipped, "You had better make sure that Moroni's army remains strong."

I was praying in the temple at Zarahemla when I was disturbed by several warriors. They were in full battle armor, their feather headdresses brilliant even in the dim light of the temple.

"Why do you seek me?" I asked.

"Our commander, Captain Moroni, desires that you inquire of the Lord where his armies should go to defend themselves against the Lamanite army."

"Where is his army now?"

"Scattered along the borders of Jershon."

"When last did you see the Lamanite armies?"

"They came just beyond an arrow shot of our army, then turned and moved back into the wilderness."

The other messenger added, "Captain Moroni feels they will attack somewhere else in the land of Zarahemla."

I smiled. "And he wants me to find out where?"

They both nodded.

"Go refresh yourselves and eat," I said. "I will inquire of the Lord. Return here when the sun is at midpoint in the afternoon."

When the warriors returned, I told them what the Lord had said. "The Lamanite army is marching through the wilderness and will come out near Manti, on the east bank of the Sidon." I handed them the letter I had prepared for Moroni. "Give this to your commander. The details of the spot which the Spirit had whispered to me are all there."

The warriors looked puzzled, seeming to wonder where I had found such an answer, but shrugged and left to take the message to Moroni. He would know where the information came from.

Moroni himself came to tell me of the battle. The Amalekites and Zoramites led Lamanites against Moroni's army under their commander, Zarahemnah. Thousands were killed in fierce fighting. Moroni told of the Lamanites fighting like dragons.

I praised God that the Nephites were fighting for a better cause. Whereas the Amalekites, Zoramites and Lamanites fought for monarchy, revenge and power, our men were fighting for their homes and liberties, their wives and children, and their right to worship.

They fought for duty to God for the Lord had said to them, *Inasmuch as you are not guilty of the first offense, neither the second, you shall not be slain by the hands of your enemies.* He had also told us to defend our families even unto bloodshed if necessary.

I remembered what Moroni had once said on eve of battle. "There is no victory without a battle, and there is no battle without a cause." Therefore, our warrior's cause for fighting was greater than that of the Lamanites and their Nephite dissenter allies.

When I finished writing of this battle in the Nephite records, I put my stylus down. I felt I had written my last word.

* * *

I had a stirring within me that I could not understand. It was a restlessness—a feeling of being needed somewhere else. The feeling was similar to that I felt when I was called to preach in Ammonihah and the land of Antionum. Nervously, I put away the plates on which I was working, then decided to take a walk.

My steps led me to my home. I felt an urgency to talk with Helaman.

The coolness of morning hung over patio and garden. I chose a sunny place and motioned Helaman to sit with me.

"My son, are you still committed to keeping the records?"

"Yes, father, I know the importance of keeping the records and accept full responsibility."

"Do you still believe in Jesus Christ and that He will come to earth?"

I could tell Helaman didn't understand why I was questioning him. He acted a little hurt that I would ask him such a question.

He answered, "Yes, father, I believe all the words you have spoken to me."

I put my hands on his shoulders, looking him steadily in the eyes.

"One more question, son. Will you keep the Lord's commandments?"

Helaman looked at me without blinking, "Father, I promise you that I will keep all the commandments. With all my heart I am committed to do so."

I leaned back, relief permeating my being.

"My son, blessed are you," I said. "The Lord will prosper you in this land because of your faithfulness.

"Son, I get old. I am not sure how much time the Lord will let me remain on the earth to govern His church, but He has whispered to me that you are to be High Priest. Therefore, today I desire to ordain you.

Helaman started to protest, but I held up my hand.

"Listen to me. I have some prophecies to tell you, but these are not to be made known to the people. Write them so they become part of the records. Then, after the prophecies are fulfilled, they will be made known."

"Wait while I get my writing materials," Helaman said.

I leaned back against the cool stone wall, still not understanding the urgency of what the Lord wanted me to tell Helaman. I shrugged. I had learned long ago to trust the Lord. His will be done!

Helaman returned with bark paper, brushes, and paint. When he was seated, I dictated.

"These are the words: *Behold, I have seen that the Nephite people, according to the spirit of revelation which is in me, in four hundred years from the time that Jesus Christ shall manifest himself unto them, shall dwindle in unbelief. Wars and pestilences, famines and bloodshed, shall be upon them until the Nephite people shall become extinct."*

Helaman interrupted, a look of anxiety on his face. "But, father..."

I shook my head. "It saddens me, also, my son, but such has the Lord told me will come to pass."

"But why, Father? Why should our people die out?"

"The Lord has shown me that they will dwindle in unbelief and will fall into works of darkness. They will become a lascivious people, doing all manner of iniquities."

"But Lamanites are all of those things right now."

"I know, son, but the Lamanites know no better. Once a people has knowledge of right and wrong their sins are much greater than when they are ignorant of the law. The Nephites will sin against the light and knowledge they have, therefore from that day, even the fourth generation shall not all pass away before this great iniquity shall come."

"But will all our descendants have to be destroyed? Won't there be any righteous people?"

I shook my head. "I don't know, son. All I know is that the Lord has told me that those who are presently numbered as the people of Nephi shall be no more. All who remain at that day, and are not destroyed, will become like Lamanites and will be numbered among them. A few of the Lord's disciples will remain but they will be hunted down by the Lamanites until they, too, are destroyed."

Helaman finished writing. The awesomeness of what I had told him was apparently as difficult for him to comprehend as it had been for me. I sat silently, waiting for him to respond.

He looked at me, sorrow mirrored in his dark eyes.

"Why have children," he asked, "if you know that your descendants will be destroyed?"

Gently I reminded him. "Remember, even Nephi, our forefather, saw that the people would be destroyed. Yet he carried on and built a great civilization. What would have happened to you and me if he had become discouraged because of the future, and had not had any descendants?"

Helaman smiled. "That is true. Even though calamities shall come, we can live and enjoy life. Our attitude is our own decision."

"True, my son."

Helaman, Shiblon, Corianton and Amulek were all at dinner that evening. After our simple meal of fruit and nuts I gave each of them a blessing. Then I blessed the earth, the land of our inheritance.

"The Lord has told me, *Cursed shall be this land unto every nation or people which does wickedly. As I have said so shall it be; for this is the cursing and blessing of God upon the land, for the Lord cannot look upon sin with the least degree of allowance."*

"Bless the Church that it may prosper, and the people in the Church that they may stand fast in the faith from this time forward."

Next morning I said good-bye to my sons and Amulek.

"I go to Melek. Good-bye, my family. Good-bye, Amulek."

"Let me go with you," Amulek pleaded.

"No, this is one time the Lord has instructed me to go alone," I replied.

I hugged each one.

"Whatever else you do," I said as last words, "keep the faith. Keep the faith."

Hot tears obscured my vision as I walked out the door.

EPILOGUE

For almost twenty years Alma had been chief high priest and leader of the church; nine of those years he also served as chief judge. Now he was gone. At sixty-one, he was still in good health. He had started out for Melek, ostensibly to visit Leesa's family, and had disappeared. His sons and their families did not know what happened to him.

Helaman worried about what had happened to his father. He prayed for answers.

In a dream, he found himself in a heavenly city; a city as white and shining as the snow sometimes seen on the tallest of the west mountains. He saw his father, who beckoned to him, then disappeared. Helaman hurried toward where he had seen his father. A stranger—a beautiful white-haired stranger—stopped him.

"You seek your father?" the stranger asked, his mellifluous voice penetrating deeply into Helaman's being.

"Yes, I seek him. Where did he go?" asked Helaman.

"Your father was a righteous man. He is no longer upon the earth but has been taken up, even as Moses."

Helaman opened his mouth to ask the stranger another question when his dream faded from him. He awakened, a feeling of peace and calmness permeating his being. He now knew what had happened to his father. The Lord had taken Alma to himself.

Robert H. Moss

Robert Moss was born in the little Swiss community of Santa Clara, Utah. He graduated from Dixie College in St. George, Utah, where he studied under several talented authors and through them he developed a love for history and a desire to write.

Following college he entered the US Army, and served on several bases in the United States and Germany. After his discharge he finished his studies at the College of Southern Utah and Brigham Young University. He taught elementary school for five years, was an elementary school principal, and became a superintendent of schools. Upon completion of his doctorate in educational administration at BYU, he became a college professor, teaching at the University of Northern Colorado and Southern Utah State College.

His church service has included callings as bishop, bishop's counselor, Young Men's president, stake missionary, Seventy's Quorum president, Sunday School teacher, and temple ordinance worker.

He is an active person and enjoys parachuting, backpacking, rappelling, survival training, and other outdoor activities. Robert and his wife Roberta, have five sons and several grandchildren. They reside in Salt Lake City, Utah.

His previous books include *I, Nephi...A Novel of the Sons of Lehi, Valiant Witness: A Novel of Moroni, The Covenant Coat, The Waters of Mormon, A Novel of Alma the Younger,* and *Celestial Child.*